His HIDDEN JEWEL

BOOK ONE OF OUR HIDDEN VALUES

SARAH DA SILVA

Cover by Estheticah

Formatted by True North Design

ISBN - Paperback: 3979-8-218-76656-6

Praise for Sarah Da Silva

"An enchanting story where One Night with The King meets Beauty and the Beast" - Jessica Spruill (author of Bound By Wishes)

"Sarah's writing is rooted in faith and redemption, bringing stories to life with a depth that lingers long after the final page. In one year, she released two powerful debut novels—a romantasy inspired by Esther and a heartfelt cowboy romance —showcasing both her range in writing and her purpose. Her characters feel achingly real, shaped by struggle, grace, and the quiet strength of belief. Her heroines could be your best friends, her heroes the kind you'd trust with your heart, but it's the spiritual journey woven through every chapter that truly sets her stories apart. Sarah doesn't just craft fiction—she writes with eternal truth in mind." - Elizabeth (Instagram: @teaandinkwithelizabeth)

This book is dedicated to the people that feel like there is no more hope for them. That they are filled with darkness and fear and simply want to give up because of it.
Jesus isn't finished writing your story.
Wait a little longer because it will be worth the wait.

This book is dedicated to those who feel like they don't have a purpose or don't know what to do.
What if... what if you were born for such a time as this?

"In the world you will have tribulation. But take heart; I have overcome the world."
John 16:33

I am the voice of the one who shouts in the wilderness.

Trigger Warnings

His Hidden Jewel includes elements that might not be suitable for all readers. The death of loved ones, murder, blood, violence, dark powers, war, alcohol addiction are mentioned in this novel. Readers please take note and be advised.

Cliff Hanger Warning

The following chapters may cause severe emotional distress due to plot twists and characters making bad choices. Warning: You will want to slap the daylights out of some characters. Proceed with caution, sit in a comfortable seat so if you have the urge to throw your book or reading device, it will not break. Proceed with caution...the ending is not for the faint of heart.

THE LAND OF THE DEAD

Apiritah

LAND OF THE
RGOTTEN

His HIDDEN JEWEL

Prologue

A hundred years ago, no living person realized that darkness ruled the land. Hope was as rare as gold in the kingdom of Aales. Surviving the plagues and famine was what one could only dream of. Clean drinking water was scarce. People would kill just for a drink, desperation in their eyes transpired into their actions.

Amid those people, a family brought hope. They led with love, joy, and brought back faith in the unseen. In order for the people of this land to rule over themselves, they chose a particular family. The land supplied them with endless riches and nutrients.

In every fairy tale, there is always one who rebels, one whose pride overrules them. In the darkness of the woods, a man lingered amid the trees. Day and night, he planned to assassinate, steal, and overrule. No one expected it of him; no one expected an enemy out of a friend. Trickery was his game, befriending all so that nobody would suspect him. So, no man would stop his plan.

He wanted all the praise and glory claimed for himself, not

the royal family. As each day went by, his ego grew and his heart hardened. All he desired was to be adored and worshiped by all. He had convinced himself he succeeded any soul on earth.

One day, after they discovered a gold mine in a new land, everyone celebrated with songs of praise. Everyone laughed with joy at having conquered a new land and discovered a mine full of gold.

Everyone was out of their minds, drunk on wine and joy. During all that, he concluded it was the perfect night to get rid of them once and for all. He poisoned all the royals' drinks while they were occupied with the townsfolk. He wanted them gone without a trace. When he was satisfied with how much poison was in the cups, he went to their castle. He looked around with the darkest smirk and set fire to it all. In all their history, all their gains, everything they owned, shriveled up in the fire.

When he returned, a twisted smile spread across his face as he watched the family's every step with depravity. One by one, they drank. The color drained from their faces as life slowly slipped away.

In the blink of an eye, they lay on the floor, lifeless. People wept in despair, crying that the gods were angry and punishment was coming. Yet he wasn't satisfied. Even in their deaths, his hunger for cruelty was never satisfied.

The man stepped into the thick crowd, feigning sorrow; fake tears rolled down his face. He played a game where no one around was wise enough to see the lies hidden behind the curtain of malignant darkness. He comforted each one of them, only lies left his wicked mouth.

Let me reign with the same passion, love, and hope they once did, a dark lie he spoke over the people.

Everyone fell into his snare; his plan was completed. The worship and adoration flowed to him; they filled his soul with pride and grew his ego. He thought he was king. A god in their eyes, a savior.

Years passed, and the kingdom didn't grow. Instead, life slowly drained away. Riches were taken, food robbed, and faith absent. Not a single soul comprehended how they were back where they had once started.

The king laughed as he ate stolen food. He clothed himself in gold and the earth's most precious gems. Women danced constantly, throwing themselves at his feet. He regretted nothing he had done. He thought his life was paradise, no words to describe the pride within his rotten heart. Some compared him to Satan himself. Few escaped his dark reign.

One thing he never prepared himself for was that no matter how rich or powerful he became, riches don't last forever.

Soraya

Chapter 1

Belts and sashes around my waist left me gasping for air. My body swayed side to side like a boat at sea. Fabric swallowed me entirely; my body a mere figure to hold it upright.

I can't believe that this is actually happening.

Months flew by as if it were nothing. I missed the fields of Uosulia so much that it hurt. The land that I grew up in felt like a distant memory. It felt like a knife had been placed inside my heart, it dug deeper as the time passed. Nevertheless, I knew why I was here. I needed to sacrifice my will to save the people from death.

The day I dreaded for so long had finally arrived. This was my only hope, a hope I was bound to. This marriage could be my only saving grace despite how tortuous it might be.

The person in the mirror looked like a stranger. Jewels clinked against one another as I moved my arms, the gold shimmered in the sunlight. Exotic oils and lotions were rubbed onto my arms. My hair was braided with flowers intertwined, adorned with gold, diamonds, and countless jeweled pins.

A small huff left my lips, unsure of how to feel. The amount of attention I received felt overwhelming. I was seen constantly yet no one knew me. I wanted to fade into the background, into the unknown but I was about to do the opposite of that.

The ladies rushed back and forth. They chattered amongst themselves, leaving me completely out of the conversation. Each servant on an automatic mode, my presence and feelings were set aside.

"I can't believe the king is actually going to marry someone." One of the ladies whispered.

"I don't think it's going to last." Someone responded.

I looked like a chandelier.

After all this time, I learned you can't complain about anything. There couldn't be a single detail that was imperfect. People took care of me as if I was incapable of doing it myself. Feelings and ideas irrelevant to the king. Anything besides what he thought and wanted was a waste of his time.

The grueling process of the bridal selection taught me more than I thought. Barely seeing the king during that time made candidates not stop talking about him. And the brief moments I saw him, were nothing to how he truly was now.

I have been stuck in Ephraim's haunted palace for 1 year, 6 months, and 2 days, but who's counting?

Once everyone was done with the final touches, they looked me up and down several times. Not a single compliment came out of their lips. The glare in their eyes already gave me the answer I needed. They were only doing their obligations, my feelings irrelevant.

Finally, after hours of being handled and decorated, I needed a moment. A second to breathe, to realise what was about to happen. The wedding was a few moments away and I couldn't bring myself around to that. I was marrying a man I didn't love, something I never thought would happen in my lifetime.

Deep breaths, Soraya. Keep yourself sane for a few moments.

A cutting jagged breath tore deep into my lungs. A reminder who I was doing this for. It wasn't for money or power but for safety and freedom. Five minutes passed like a blink of an eye before someone came calling me, "Soraya, we are ready for you."

My trembling fingers brushed over the gem covered pink dress. Each direction I turned, another blinding light would shine everywhere.

Suffocated in a dress that dug deep into my rib cage. It was tied so tight that the ribbon dug into my skin.

That's going to leave a painful mark.

This color didn't suit me but I never voiced that complaint. Everything was chosen for me, predestined before I even arrived at this palace.

Even though I couldn't see myself in the midst of this all, the ladies did an outstanding job. They turned nothing into something. A broken woman into a queen.

Little bells sounded when the earrings shook side to side. The rings on my hands to the gems on my feet, made me feel hidden.

This wasn't the real me, even if I was still trying to find out who I was.

When the brass doors creaked open, the king's royal advisor awaited me. His gaze swept over me, leaving me flustered, my cheeks hot and body tense with embarrassment.

It was hard to get used to attention, get used to the feeling of always needing someone's approval. Impression and looks mattered above all else. Feelings weren't going to be important and I didn't need anyone to tell me that. I didn't need anyone to tell me that my voice wasn't going to matter in this palace.

"You look beautiful, Princess. Please allow me to escort you." His arm extended, waiting for me to take it.

My heart thumped erratically in my chest, I couldn't move. My muscles frozen stiff as my mind scrambled faster. I didn't think I would freeze until now, I didn't know I would be so nervous but I was. I was petrified at the thought of marrying this man. From everything that I had heard about him, my stomach felt like a bottomless pit.

"Princess?" the advisor's voice was filled with concern.

I looked up at him and his eyebrows scrunched together. I knew that I was cutting it close and everyone was waiting on my arrival.

Maybe it wasn't too late to escape and go back to my precious life?

I could find another way to save my people and I prayed that I wouldn't have to do this. To be bound to a stranger who knew nothing about me.

"Oh yes, thank you." I slipped my hand onto his arm as we began to walk down the staircase. The servants, the maids and guards stopped themselves in their tracks bending down in reverence as I passed. I wanted to stop them and say it wasn't needed but I bit my tongue back before I said anything that could humiliate me.

The palace was decorated beyond what I expected. Every type of exotic flower lined the staircase. Scarlet carpet rolled in the center of the aisle, leading to where the ceremony would take place. The palace before was beautiful, but this is beyond what I ever dreamed of.

The air was infused with frankincense, myrrh and hints of cinnamon. The scents seemed to give me a type of peace, like I still had a piece of home with me. With each breath I took, I could smell another note like sandalwood and agarwood. They were only using the best and a part of me felt like it was only to display riches and the fame of the kingdom.

When we reached the wooden doors, I finally let go of the advisor's arm. I couldn't stop the constant tremble in my hands, squeezing the flowers tighter.

My gaze fell to the bouquet of flowers in my hands, fiddling with the ribbon around the stems of the flowers. It was beyond beautiful. The color of the lilies complemented the jasmine and the saffron flowers.

I didn't even get to pick the flowers for my wedding. My dreams smashed into pieces, the years of dreaming were worth nothing.

I should have expected all this. I should have expected this, nothing should have been a surprise.

I drew myself back to reality, the guards slowly opened the colossal doors. Gasps and *awws* erupted when eyes laid on me. Everyone looked at me with admiration and love. All the faces were strangers, not a single person to comfort me. The knife in my heart pushed deeper.

I looked up, and into the eyes of each guest. Smiling at each person despite the raging turmoil inside of me. An urgent feeling slowly boiled inside me. My mind told me it was the right thing to do but my stomach warned me otherwise.

I had finally made it halfway down the aisle. I avoided glancing at his eyes, refusing to meet his gaze unless I was forced to. My body trembled in his presence. This marriage was the bare minimum of what was expected of me. I had to make an agonizing choice, a sacrifice for the greater good.

When I finally reached the front of the altar, my fingers gripped the stems of the flowers even tighter. My gaze focused on the floor, my dress, anything except him. My breathing rapid, I became lightheaded from the lack of oxygen. I needed to control my emotions, or I was going to kill myself slowly.

Then, I finally looked into his dark eyes. Just by a glance, there wasn't an ounce of love or care in those pools of darkness. The hatred and death swirled in those dangerous eyes. We didn't care about each other: which was the only thing we agreed on. How could I care about a person who was trying to kill me without knowing it was me he was trying to kill?

Every thread which covered his towering body was black, matching his soulless irises. He was the embodiment of darkness, and it showed in his appearance.

I trembled, not from fear but rage for this man. The epitome of evil, whose plans I despised. He seemed to only have one thing in his mind; death.

The minister's voice slowly faded as I tried to bring myself back to reality. I tried to compose my thoughts. Anxiety rapidly flooded my mind, thinking of the possibilities of what could happen. I forced myself to think positively in spite of everything this man had already made me go through. The moments where we met, he didn't even know who I was. My face was constantly covered but now he treated me differently. Some days he was possessed mind, body, and soul. Other days he would think like a sane person.

"Princess?" The minister's voice cut through my thoughts. I blinked the thoughts away.

Don't lose it Soraya.

"I do" I replied, gritting those painful words through clenched teeth.

"Do you take Princess Soraya as your wedded wife, King Ephraim?" The minister turned towards Ephraim and looked deep into his eyes, awaiting a response.

If I took a long time to answer, he took an eternity. If I hated this idea, he despised it.

Marriage, the last thing on our minds. For reasons the other didn't know.

We were binding ourselves to each other for the rest of our lives, until death.

His jaw clenched tight, hating the words that he needed to speak forcefully, "I do." His bitter deep voice thundered.

You have a purpose, a mission, I constantly reminded myself.

The minister finally looked back at the people, a huge smile on his face. Slowly, the words I dreaded the whole engagement were spoken. The words that I wished were revocable and not permanent.

"I present to you King Ephraim and Queen Soraya. You may now kiss your bride," he declared.

I stayed in place, afraid for him to lay a finger on me. Despite the roaring feelings, I needed to keep up appearances. He wrapped his strong arms around me, gripping my waist tightly, pulling my chest against his.

His lips brushed against my ears, leaving me unsettled as he sneered, "I hope you know what you have signed yourself up for."

With that, he pressed a hard kiss against my cheek.

No Passion. No Love. Nothing.

The people jumped and exclaimed, celebrating the union. They were overjoyed that a new queen was now seated on the throne, with a hope that I might bring change to the kingdom.

All of them were in denial. This wasn't a celebration. Far from it, war had begun. I bound myself to a man that might be the very end of me.

Soraya

Chapter 2

The celebration turned into a night of suffering. Guests constantly congratulated us. And with each passing second, Ephraim's fingers dug deeper into my exposed waist. I wanted to yelp from the pain but bit it back. Both of us needed to keep up appearances.

"Let me go," I hissed, slowly pushing myself out of his embrace.

Out of spite, he gripped me tighter. Then, for the first time, he looked deeply into my eyes. His eyes haunted; they seeped into my soul. The moment his grip lessened, I pulled myself forcefully away.

As another guest came to us, we plastered fake smiles, generous gifts being laid at our feet. Everyone gave their best. People did the opposite of everything that I thought was true. I wanted to tell them to keep it, but I would be humiliated instantly. I couldn't stand another second being close to that infuriating man. A sensation of fire flickered in my bones as I clenched my fists. My emotions riled up the longer I stood beside him.

A servant walked past me and offered me wine, his eyes focused on the ground below him. I extended my hand to take a glass, and before I could thank him, he rushed away.

I hated what this man did to his people. He oppressed and tortured them. In the months of living at the palace, servants were treated as dogs. The nickname street rats would be a compliment. Each person who dared to look Ephraim in the eyes was instantly killed. Treated and beaten like slaves, not people. Every time I looked at how they were treated, it made me hate Ephraim even more. I hated this kingdom and the evil way it ran itself.

I took a small glance at Ephraim; my body tensed at the sight of him. Multiple women laid around him as he drank wine and was fed grapes. One moment he wanted a pristine appearance, and later he allowed women to throw themselves at his feet.

He can't even make up his own mind.

From the distance, our furious gazes focused on each other. A brooding glance always shot in my direction.

Burning my throat, I swiftly drank the rest of the wine, replying, "Please excuse me." I couldn't recall half of what he said; I really didn't need this right now.

Politics were in my lungs all day, and for once I needed to forget about duty and life. How to rule a kingdom was the father that made me grow. Duty, the mother who taught me to be strong. Families filled me with compassion.

As I stomped to my new chambers, I ripped the tight jeweled heels off my feet. Finally, I was barefoot. A small part of me could finally breathe. My eyes looked up, instantly over-whelmed by the number of ladies in the room. No one had noticed me at first, but as soon as I cleared my throat, every eye fell on me.

They prepared the bedding, leaving the ambiance romantic. Essence infused the air, and the bedding had been changed into ruby red satin.

My stomach revolted at the thought and sight of this. "You may excuse yourselves, ladies." My finger pointed to the door, ready to be left alone.

They fumbled a hundred reasons why they couldn't leave. With very little authority left in me, I demanded it. It wasn't an option, but a need for my sanity. All reason silenced, they bowed their heads and sped out of the room. When the door locked behind them, an agonized breath escaped my lips.

As I unlaced the ribbon, the liberty to breathe filled my lungs. I threw it across the room and put on the silk royal robe. All I really wanted was to escape this oppressive palace. Where there wasn't a king that controlled my every move. A place where there weren't ears to listen to my every word.

But I must do what I came for.

This bedroom was the most pristine room that I have ever been in. It just showed how many riches King Ephraim loved to spend on himself. He spent all this on himself, yet he wouldn't help the poor, who didn't know when their next meal would be. Immense walls covered with solid gold, hundreds of diamonds and gems placed pristinely. I surveyed the bed; it seemed to be worth thousands on its own.

The room was big and spacious, with a balcony that overlooked the garden. I stood there for a moment, inhaling the cold air. A type of peace came over me, something that wasn't found within these walls. Everything inside the palace felt different in a way. Something within these walls kept me from using my powers freely.

Puny.

The air tickled my skin; it made me feel alive. I closed my sore, heavy eyes, soaking in the moment of silence. The calmness of the wind, the smell of the fresh flowers from below were my medicine.

The peace was broken in a flash. I could feel a looming presence walking towards me.

He was coming, and this silence and peace had vanished because of him. My feet glued in place, repeating the same words in my head.

Keep yourself calm. Keep yourself calm. Don't allow him to control your emotions.

With that came an aggressive sound. The doors slammed shut behind him. He said nothing, his paces quick and even. When he was close enough, his hands gripped my forearm and forced me to spin around.

He was much taller than I; his body towered over me. I had to look up to see his fiery eyes. Ephraim looked at me with a menacing gaze.

"You don't leave until I tell you to," he grumbled to me. His hand tightened, "I am your king."

My jaw tightened at the mention of him saying he was my king. He constantly prided himself on being better and bigger. I gave him the benefit of the doubt because he knew nothing. He was a fool who claimed to know everything.

Ignore him.

I wiggled myself out of his grip and walked away, putting distance between us. My knee brushed against the edge of the bed before I spun my head around. "No, you are not my king. I am not one of your servants to command what to do and when to do it." I scolded those words at him. He looked stunned for several moments.

His gaze fixed on me, his hands turned into fists, "Hold your tongue, or you will regret it."

We could burn down this place just by the looks we shot one another. "Or what?" I hissed back.

You really are wishing for a death sentence, a small voice spoke in the back of my mind.

I pushed that thought away, swept into the tension-filled moment. My choleric body already lost control of my temper. To my surprise, he didn't respond. He stomped away, his lips in a tight line. He grumbled under his breath when he slammed the door behind him.

You're not a good ruler if you lose your temper.

As I slipped into the cooling sheets, Ephraim walked back into the room and stood beside the bed. His gaze was hard, not a single detectable emotion. His arms crossed over his muscular, tattooed bare chest.

How can a despicable man like him have a stunning chest? I can't believe I just thought that.

He looked between me and the empty space on the bed. Silently questioning whether he was going to lie beside me. This bed was enormous, enough for 5 people, so the chances that our bodies would touch were slim.

"Why don't I just sleep in my room, since we are appalled by one another?" I quietly questioned.

"Because they expect us to have '*that*' tonight. And it's in the blasted law." His body froze in place.

"Then sneak into another room. Maybe another woman will throw herself at your feet and shower your pride with endless compliments. Glad to get a fraction of your attention." I mumbled.

He annoyingly stood there for several moments, not a single solution could solve his dilemma. A luminous moon replaced the glorious sun. Its light flowed into the room and illuminated the space. The light framed Ephraim's tall frame.

"No," he responded sternly.

The entire palace thought that we were in love, but we

weren't. Our marriage was merely a political benefit to both of us.

"This bed is big enough for both of us without me having to touch you." he barked, his feet slowly strolling to the other side of the bed.

He pulled back the comforter on the bed. The bed shifted underneath his weight when he rested on it. His muscular back was turned towards me. He was infuriating, but at least he forced nothing tonight. Probably because he focused more on himself than anyone else.

Today was the worst yet best day of my life. The worst part, I had bound myself to a dark evil king, who made choices that were fit in his eyes. And it was the best, because I had a chance to save my people. If he thought someone's life was worthless, he would put a swift end to it in the blink of an eye. Ephraim wasn't scared of killing someone; he and death had become one. The world was at his fingertips. With a snap of a finger, he could have anything that he wanted and kill anything he desired.

My goal was not to die. My job was to find this man's darkest haunting secrets and use them for the good.

If I could describe King Ephraim in one word, it would be: darkness. Wherever he went, darkness had a tendency to follow; death were his footsteps.

Soraya

Chapter 3

The eastern sun shone through the windows, waking me up from my deep slumber. After a long silent night, the kingdom of Aales was alive. The birds in the air chirped along with the melody of the wind. From a great distance, you could hear the chatter in the town.

A small hum escaped my lips as I stretched my arms. There were only a few moments left before the servants would rush to get me ready. That was a damper on my spirits. Heaviness fell on my shoulder, it had only been a few days since I had been married.

Ephraim wouldn't look me in the face or speak a proper introduction. When we were in front of other people, he gripped me closer to him. Ephraim only endured me because of views and opinions.

I mumbled a quick prayer, thankful for another day despite anything that could happen. I needed to be thankful because there was still air in my lungs and a heart beating in my chest.

You can do this. You have the strength to overcome any chal-

lenge. If you have made it until here, you can survive another day.

I encouraged myself when a light knock sounded at the door. My eyes instantly fluttered open, "Come in."

The door flung open, women rushing in. Each carried different supplies—one with beauty products, another with a dress, and some with jeweled pins for my hair. An older lady hung a dazzling gold dress with gems placed sporadically all over. Something over the top for an entire day of sitting and doing nothing.

After much convincing, I slipped into the bath alone. The door was the only thing that separated us. A moment not to lose my sanity.

This didn't exist in my country.

Women weren't treated as prized possessions; slaves weren't beaten until killed. They served because they wanted to, never obligated or forced. Women were treated like humans; each had a voice and value. No one belittled their worth. Each had an ability, a potential to improve our kingdom. My thoughts wandered and dreamt of everything that I missed. The food, my friends, and the children.

The food was similar in some aspects, but nothing beat homemade dinner from the elders. My heart gripped onto those memories, memories that formed me into the woman I now was.

I need to slip out of here for a bit and go back home.

The thought quickly dispersed when a gentle knock hit the bathroom doors.

"Your Highness, we must get you ready." Her voice was gentle and sweet, like the comforting whisper of a harp.

I exhaled deeply, knowing consequences would come if I didn't arrive on time. "I am coming."

The cool cotton robe against my freshly clean skin was a

sensation I never got over. I stood in front of a long golden mirror, admiring their hands as they worked rapidly.

The ladies tightened the ribbons which left very little room to breathe. The fabric was soft as a dove, hugging me gently. Hundreds of feet of fabric flowed in all directions. Gems dangled from the fabric; jingle sounds erupted when they bumped against one another.

Precious carnelian decorated my wrists and feet. It took much insisting to convince the ladies to give me dresses that barely covered my feet. Shoes were too restrictive. Feeling the cool stone underneath my feet made me feel grounded.

I remembered the times my mom smiled when I ran barefoot in the garden. She said it revealed the simplicity that lived within me. She was constantly proud that I hadn't let the power get to my head.

I wish she were still here.

A young girl brushed a soft brush against my cheeks, a beautiful rosy color on the bristles. There were droopy, dark circles underneath her beautiful doe eyes. My nostrils instantly flared at the thought of him. My lungs might burst at any moment.

He worked all men, women, and children endlessly. Servants were lucky to have a day off; Ephraim constantly forced them to be one step ahead.

She took a small step back, her gaze drifting all over me. She surveyed my face, and when everything was perfect in her eyes, she scurried away.

Who was that stranger in the mirror?

There were several types of jewels that covered me from head to toe. A crown dug deeply into my scalp. My head throbbed, begging to be set free from the small prison.

Maybe I needed all this because I wasn't pretty enough. Maybe I wasn't enough.

"You can do this." I sniffled at a lie I desperately tried to convince myself of.

The finish line seemed like a dream. *My life is a nightmare, a nightmare I am forced to live.* The truth and lies inside my mind blurred together; everything was gray.

If I have made it this far with no one by my side, then I can make it to the end. If I made it to the end with one last breath in my lungs, it would be enough.

The ladies showered me with praise and compliments; their eyes shimmered with admiration. It was fake. They admired what was on the outside, but my heart still felt lonely and unseen.

The only thing that raced through each of their minds was to finish quickly and leave. No one wanted to be with me, and my heart hurt with that truth. In unison, the servants marched out of view, leaving me in utter solitude.

"My queen, it is time for you to come. The king has requested your presence." Mavros announced near the front brass doors.

I strolled over, his thin arm ready for me. Mavros was always punctual and respectable. He never said anything wrong and never showed any emotions. Every step planned and calculated to perfection. And despite everyone's empty feelings towards me, Mavros gave me a sense of normality.

Every day Mavros was beside Ephraim. The both of them chatted constantly; the world faded around them. *If the king trusts no one but him, then that means something good, right?*

"What must I do today?" I prepared myself for a day of strolling around the palace and smiling at the walls.

Despite what I had already determined in my mind, Mavros rattled about an endless list that needed to be done. His mouth didn't stop moving as we walked. My body already ached from hearing the endless tasks. We finally reached the double silver doors. They were thick and reached all the way to the ceiling, frozen guards on either side. In synchrony, they turned to each other and reached for the golden handles.

The door cracked open, revealing a table full of high-ranking men. Each of them raised their heads higher when I entered. Everybody bowed down before me, except one, whose eyes burned with a deadly fire.

In the center of the room was a large rectangular table. It extended from one wall to the other. Decorated with freshly picked flowers and every type of food imaginable.

My stomach rumbled at the sight of everything; I haven't eaten all day. At the same time my stomach hungered for food, it was appalling. Sick to think that there were people dying of hunger when we weren't able to eat a fraction of this food.

Ephraim sat at the farthest end of the table, his eyes glued to my every move. Advisers and princes from all the provinces sat on either side. A single pillow awaited me; my lungs could finally breathe when I realized the distance between us.

The guard stood beside the pillow. He shuffled back when I got too close.

"Thank you." I smiled brightly at him. *Don't let a good deed slide under the rug.* From a distance, I heard my mother's sweet voice whisper in my heart.

His body was paralyzed, affected by those simple words. His gloved hands froze, and when he finally regained his composure, he dashed away.

"You aren't to talk to that peasant. He is doing his job, so you're wasting your breath saying such worthless words." Ephraim hissed from the other side of the table. His monotone voice bounced off the walls. His eyes focused on the guard, death forcefully swirling in them.

"He is just as much of a human as you or I." My hands

against my hips. He peeved me, his voice sour in my ears. His voice was far worse than any nightmare.

Our eyes spoke deadly things. Fiery gazes that burned with hate. For a moment, something flickered in his eyes. Something I had never seen before, but as swiftly as it came, it went away.

A general cleared his throat. Ephraim instantly broke contact. "We must finish eating so we may talk about important matters." His hands waved in the air to further prove his point.

"You don't tell me what to do. We eat when I want to." Ephraim barked back at the general, his eyes instantly drawn back to me.

"The guard isn't worth anything to me." Ephraim scolded. His voice was cold and emotionless.

"Well, then if he isn't worth anything to you, then what am I? Am I simply a trophy on your stand to show to all the people of the country?"

I wasn't supposed to say that.

All the noise and chatter instantly died. Every eye fell to the floor, scared of how Ephraim would react. He had a dour expression, his lips pressed hard against one another. His jaw hardened, not a single emotion displayed.

A storm swirled within his eyes. Terror overtook the faces of the guards and servants in the room.

No one had the bravery to talk to the king this way.

This will not end well. She should simply shut her mouth before he does something worse than death, were the unspoken words I could hear from miles away.

The longer Ephraim's snarky gaze looked at me, the more I wanted to run away. Every second, his eyes pierced deeper into me. An evil smirk formed on his lips when I broke the contact.

His hands extended to the nearest fork and knife, waiting for the cover to be lifted off his plate.

Dark linen clothing covered his tall frame. Freshly washed curls framed his face. Light stubble framed his square jaw. His appearance made him look like a perfect man. His face, hair, and body belonged to an angel. Appearances were deceitful, Ephraim simply another example of that truth.

His black shirt hugged every muscle, my eyes fascinated by the view. Ephraim: a sight to behold, but a deadly curse.

"You may eat," he broke the tension-filled room and devoured the food before him.

Different colors and flavors covered our dinner plates. The lavash bread freshly baked, boiled egg sliced on the side and endless of fruits. Roasted dates drizzled with wildflower honey. Turmeric and saffron seasoned rice releasing automatic steam.

I ripped a piece of bread, dipping it into the apricot jam. Time seemed to slow when the bread touched my tongue. My eyes rolled to the back of my head from the bold flavors and the amazing texture.

The flavors danced in my mouth, leaving me completely in awe. Uosuila didn't have any of this. We ate simple food, and we were happy. Our simple ways never failed us, and they never would. Why change something if it wasn't broken?

The man across from me tried to take everything we had. Riches, plantation, food, and even the luxury of having new fabrics for clothes. While my people were praying for a miracle, I still could have those things. My heart cried for the people who didn't, who had to settle for nothing. People in my kingdom depended on me for food, and I wasn't there to help them. The power of life that ran through my veins was my secret advantage.

The servants rapidly took away our plates so space would be made for paper, books, and hundreds of maps. I quietly thanked the old lady who picked my plate. Her eyes shone with happiness at the mention of a thank you.

Small gestures mattered.

"We have to start a war with them if we want to succeed once and for all." A deep voice spoke above all the chatter.

Another talked over him, "Yes, I agree. They can become too powerful and can overpower us. We can lose what we have worked so hard to gain."

Ephraim slammed his hand onto the table, glass clattering at the impact. He sent a threatening glance at each one, "No one is more powerful than me. No one who has ever crossed my path and challenged me, is still alive."

He turned his head towards Mavros. Mavros had an arm leaning against the top of Ephraim's chair, his hair in pristine condition.

"What do you think, Mavros?" Ephraim forced him to voice his opinion.

Why am I here?

"Well, my king, killing their resources off completely can be our first test. If they refuse or fight back, we kill them. I believe their end is in sight." He shrugged his shoulders as if killing off hundreds of people wasn't a problem. Death was the least of their concerns.

"That plan, we will follow. Cut off the rest of their resources. My victory is in sight," Ephriam replied.

An old man jotted down all the exchanged words. His back arched; there was not a single pillow underneath him to bring a level of comfort.

The men nodded in agreement and hummed about the new law. There wasn't a single soul who dared to disagree with him; they preferred the safety of their own lives.

"And if I may ask," my voice startled all of them.

Ephraim's eyes narrowed, "What is it? Why are you still here?"

I stood up quickly. The world instantly spun. "Well, why keep me here if my opinion is not welcomed?"

He rose from his seat as well. *How could a man possibly be that tall?*

Ephraim slightly leaned his body towards the table, his fingers gripped the ends of the table. "I don't want you here. I simply forgot to send you away. You may go to your quarters and leave this for the men to handle."

Ephraim

Chapter 4

———◆———

The look on her face was a mixture of confusion and anger. I didn't know why it would bother her the way it clearly did, but I cared little for her opinion. She was just bothering me and seemed to be another fly in my ear.

"What have they ever done wrong to you?" she hissed at me

I crossed my arms, "I owe you no explanation to you."

She huffed and, with a deep glance into my eyes, she picked up the hem of her dress and dashed away. That woman got on my last nerve, but any man could admit that she was beautiful. Of all the women that I have had the pleasure of meeting or knowing, she surpassed them all.

In all my life, I killed off any man who dared to question my motives, but for some reason, I couldn't control her tongue. I couldn't control her, yet I couldn't bring myself to do something to fix her attitude.

I sat back in my chair as I signaled for the servant to pour me more wine. I didn't care how many cups I had; I needed something to calm and soothe me even more. The servant took a small sip to make sure it was clean before handing it to me.

"What are you going to do with her, sir?" Mavros questioned, his eyes focused on the door that Soraya walked out of.

"I don't know, but she has a surprising ability to get on my last nerve." I huffed because, for once, someone had left me speechless, and that irritated me in ways I couldn't explain.

My brain pounded from the amount of talking I had to do. I had to repeat myself what felt like hundreds of times. From all the laws I had to sign, my hand trembled. When I finally couldn't take any more of it, I yelled at all the men to leave before they regretted it. Each of them scurried to collect their things before their lives vanished in the blink of an eye. I rubbed my sore temples, trying to soothe the raging ache away.

Every part of me screamed in agony. The very little patience that I had was being stretched to the maximum as I tried not to kill every single man who was standing in front of me and looking at me, waiting for me to tell him to do something.

As I walked to my office—where no one would be there to bother me—I saw something move in a passing window. I took a few steps back and leaned against the balcony to see what it was. I squinted my eyes to see, instantly knowing who it was.

Even from a distance, I could see that it was Soraya walking through the gardens. I had lost count of how many times she stayed outside. She seemed to find more comfort and peace outside than inside. I didn't care much about what she did or didn't do, but as king I needed to know everything. Most of the time, her wellbeing and interests were the least of my concerns.

I stood there for a moment, watching her walk among the flowers. Picking a few and holding them in her hand. She looked at the flowers as if they were worth something, like they were precious.

They are just flowers. Please don't tell me she finds worth in such a small thing.

Then she stopped for a second and turned around to look at something. Her eyes were pinned on something in the distance. I leaned against the edge to look closer. She waved at a little child, signaling for the child to come. She bent to look eye level, talking to her and making a big smile appear on the child's face before putting the flower into the little girl's hair.

That's stupid, I thought to myself

I rolled my eyes as I continued to walk away, *Soraya held herself to be of little worth.*

Maybe her beauty played a grand part in why I chose her, but I didn't know what I saw. Maybe I had been so desperate to get the wedding over with that I chose the first person who seemed decent.

As I approached my room, I noticed the door was open. Noise was coming from the inside, signaling that someone had entered and was messing with my stuff.

Who entered here without my permission?

I slammed open the door and saw a young man rushing to organize and clean as fast as he could. He stopped and turned around slowly, bowing in my presence, "Hello, my King."

I walked closer to him, looking down at his short stature, "What are you doing here?"

He fumbled over his words as he tried to explain himself. He kept repeating that he had done nothing other than cleaning the glass and dusting the shelves.

I didn't care what he did or failed to do, this space wasn't for anyone to enter. If someone had to come in here, it had to be someone under my supervision.

I wrapped my hand around his neck and forced him to look at me. I had very little restraint with anyone, and if I

33

wanted to, I would kill this man here and now. I didn't care if he was doing what he was supposed to; I wanted no one here.

"I want you out of this room. I don't want to ever see your face again, and if I do," I tightened my grip, his face turning red and different shades of purple, "I won't be so merciful."

With that, I released him as his small body scurried off to leave. His coughs and gasps for air slowly faded away as he ran from me. When he closed the door behind him, I released the yell that had been clawing at my throat.

Blast this cursed curse!

I ripped the crown off my head and threw it across the room. I tried to unbutton the buttons near my neck, letting me go from its grasp. With a cup of spirit in hand, I strolled around the room, contemplating which book to grab and study. In moments of stress, books were my first escort. Books of war, death, and history brought me comfort and understanding.

This study room was the first thing that I had built in this castle when I first started to rule. This place was my haven from the darkness that followed me. It felt like a small taste of freedom from the constant oppression. Freedom from people who drained my energy.

I poured more spirit into my cup as I flipped through a book that felt all too well in my hands. My eyes skimmed over ancient history that I knew by heart. I had read all these books countless times; they were imprinted on my heart.

Every war, past and present, had become my medication.

Every type of magic or power had become my nightmare.

Everyone who wasn't subject to me was my enemy.

Death was the reward for anyone who gave me a headache.

I hated it all, and nothing would stop me from ending it all. Nothing and no one would stop me from ending every single headache that I had.

I didn't know how many hours had passed since I had been in my office, and I didn't care. Time was irrelevant whenever I was in here; I could go days and days without interacting with the world. I was deep in my studies until Mavros came knocking at my door and insisted that I go to bed. His only reason was that it was past midnight and the next day we had important things to resolve. He was among the very few people I tolerated. There were days I wanted to kill him but held myself back because I needed him.

I walked into my chambers, slightly surprised that Soraya was already there. She stood in front of the mirror as she brushed her long brown hair. Soraya had her eyes closed as she hummed a tune that I didn't recognize. It slightly angered me that she was so peaceful, and I was tormented day and night.

When her eyes fluttered open, she froze when she saw me in the reflection. She glanced down and went back to ignoring me. She didn't bow or say any type of greeting; I was like a ghost to her. Her grip on the brush tightened, her body tense and upright.

At least I know that we both don't like each other; that is one thing that I am certain of.

I didn't want her here; Soraya was the last thing on my mind. Yet I couldn't let anyone suspect I disliked her. That I despise the woman I insisted on marrying. Then I reminded myself I never wanted to marry. I wanted to be alone, but it was the constant talk of the elders day and night.

I began to unbutton my shirt to avoid eye contact with her, "Aren't those women supposed to do your hair?"

Annoyed that she insisted on doing some things on her own. These people were meant to work, and I didn't like that she treated them as if we were equal. We weren't; in my mind there was always supposed to be someone superior. I wouldn't give up anything I had or treat myself like I was no one.

She turned around and took a step back, with her brush in her hand, giving me a moment to see her face filled with anger. Her eyebrows were furrowed together like she couldn't believe the words that came out of my mouth. She took several breaths in and out trying to calm herself down. She whispered something to herself before raising her voice, "Well then, there would be no reason to have hands."

She's trouble, Ephraim. Why did you pick her?

With very little willpower inside of me, I responded in a deadly tone, "Well then there is no reason to keep them alive if they don't do what they are commanded to. "

She stood shocked for a moment before stomping to the bathroom and closing the door behind her. I didn't want to have to deal with her snarky attitude tonight; I didn't want to have to deal with anyone. I would have found a companion to keep me company, but I had no energy for that either.

In a way it was a refreshing change, since all the women threw themselves at my feet. She was the only woman who would kill me if she could. I didn't know whether I enjoyed it or if it simply angered me even more. My emotions were a mess around her.

I slipped between the bedsheets and sighed at the soft silk against my aching skin. My arms were tired, and my back seemed to creak like an iron door. As I lay there, I looked at myself. On my right shoulder down to my right pec, there was a tattoo that had appeared over time. It never really bothered me, but I also didn't really want it. It seemed to be a mark of sorts that grew bigger as time went on.

Soraya slowly walked back into the room, not bothering a glance at me as she slipped onto the bed, putting as much space as she could between the both of us.

What is wrong with this woman?

Usually, I am worshiped and adored, but this woman

despises me. She had a snarky response when something angered her. Her loud and vibrant spirit silenced when she noticed something unjust.

It has been a week and a few days since we married, yet we have barely exchanged any words. We pretended to have a normal marriage in front of as many people as possible, but when we were alone; we were between knives and guns. Most people in the palace discovered that we weren't as in love as they originally thought, but they kept that to themselves.

I turned over and laid my head against my arm. Admiring the night sky that was filled with stars and a crescent moon. I had very few pleasures in this life; most have been taken away from me, but the sky was the one thing that had transcending peace. Peace never lasted long, but when I had it, I held onto it with everything that I had.

Ephraim

Chapter 5

B efore the sun had even risen, I was already awake. King duties never ended, so I never had time for myself. You never had time to breathe or just be alone, constantly surrounded by people and things to do. As if just to prove my point, Mavros walked into my training room.

"My king" he bowed deeply, his face almost connecting with his kneecaps.

I snorted in response, "What do you want?"

I responded, continuing to throw fists at the man in front of me. He was cushioned and covered from head to toe; you could barely see his eyes. He was worried that I would kill him in the process of destressing, which had a significant possibility.

"We have things to resolve, my king," he responded, his eyes focused on something in his hands.

"What is it now, Mavros?" I was already annoyed, not an ounce of patience for whatever he wanted to talk about.

"They are resisting," he said, and with that I released the strongest punch, leaving the boy on the floor from the impact.

Usually Mavros would be my human punching bag, and when he saw the boy was on the floor, he took several steps back.

I ignored the boy who was gasping for air and struggling to get up. I cursed under my breath because once again I couldn't have a moment to myself.

Another problem, great.

"Why can't those disturbing people give up?" I mumbled as I threw cold water on my face and damp hair.

The blazing sun burned my skin; my shirt long forgotten. The weather seemed to be hundreds of degrees. I waved to a servant to bring my food and wine as Mavros and I sat underneath a fig tree.

"I thought it would work. I thought that taking everything from them would make them weak, but I was wrong. It seems to make them even stronger."

I whipped my head in his direction, trying my best not to kill him with my bare hands, "You're supposed to bring me good news. You're supposed to help me eliminate these people. They are supposed to die, so what do you mean they aren't giving in to my oppression?"

I could feel my nails digging into my skin as he continued to talk, his voice making me more and more aggravated, "I understand, but this is beyond comprehension. I don't understand this. They were supposed to break, but they have something or someone keeping them together."

I lashed out in anger, not containing it anymore, "Get away from me before I kill you. Don't come back until you have found a resolution to this problem." I yelled at him.

He scrambled up from his seat, apologizing like a fool and running away with his tail between his legs.

"Fools. Fools. Why is everyone such a fool?" I said to myself and went back to losing myself in the anger.

I walked inside the palace, and everyone swarmed around me. They told me everything over again as if I didn't already know. Elders who reminded me that people were rebelling and complaining about every single thing I did. Nothing satisfied them, and it was pulling my last string. Problems just kept multiplying, and there was nothing that could resolve them.

I needed a new plan. I needed to approach this from a different perspective.

"My king, we must get this settled before another war begins." One of the oldest counselors whispered quietly. He sounded like a bee in my ear, just leaving me vexed.

"I think I might have found a resolution," someone else spoke behind me as I headed toward my quarters.

I spun around to look at him. He was very young, maybe in his early twenties. He was trembling, his eyes squeezed shut, afraid of what might happen next.

"Do you know if it will work?" I questioned because I wouldn't waste my time on something that didn't even have a good chance of fixing all of this.

He mumbled, trying to get his words in order, "Speak, you fool. I don't have all day." I yelled at him to move on.

He took a deep breath and finally spoke, "No, I am uncertain, but there is a chance it might work."

I huffed, *great*, the same response I have been hearing from everyone. No one can give me a solid answer, and therefore I don't trust anyone.

I turned back around and continued walking to take a bath. My footsteps had become heavier, dragging my body to move. The sound of my footsteps echoed off the dark walls.

All my men kept circling me, and when I reached the

doors, I turned around once again, "Meet me in the throne room in one hour. We will discuss all your awful plans then."

They rushed their small bodies out of the room, leaving me in complete silence and solitude. These were the moments that I loved and longed for. No nagging soul haunting me. Me and my darkness all alone.

The throne room was invaded with men chattering and speaking over one another. Maids rushed in all directions, and guards positioned themselves at each entrance. I don't know how long I have been here, but the conclusion I came to was that we got nowhere. Someone would say one idea, and another would automatically turn it down.

As they kept arguing and discussing amongst themselves, forgetting I was here, one of my guards came to me and whispered in my ear, "There is a man here for you."

"Tell him to come back some other time; I am quite busy dealing with these insane men." I hissed back at him.

He chuckled at the response but still kept his voice low, "Yes, my king."

I looked at him, satisfied that he didn't push it, but out of the blue, a rugged old man came in, running from two guards who were chasing him.

All the men silenced their arguments and went still. Everyone forgot the task at hand and focused on the man who had invaded my presence without my approval.

The guard beside me took a step down, blocking the man from coming any closer to me. One already had a hand on his spear, waiting for the word to end his life.

"You are the worst king that Aales has ever had. You reject

your own people the basic things to live." He continued yelling at me, my eyes glued to him.

His end has been determined, and I knew I was going to do it myself. I was going to end his life with determination and pleasure.

I stood up from the throne and stood in front of this man. His clothes covered in grime, *a servant of the streets.* At least I gave him a job that kept him alive. Yet people like him needed someone to remind him where his place was.

My hand whipped across his face, before I hissed into his ears, "You do know what happens when you come before the king unannounced."

He looked at me, standing even taller. Not minding the blood running down his nose, "Yes, I know, but I don't care."

Another slap across the face but harder. I wanted the rings on my fingers to leave marks on his skin, "You would risk your life to tell me what I do and don't do right?"

A humorous laugh left my lips, "You really are a fool, aren't you."

His lips were in a tight line, "I would risk my life to stand up against this dark kingdom. I would risk my life to say what people are petrified to say out loud. You are a wretched man, I wouldn't be surprised if you were friends with the devil. May the gods take the most precious thing from you, so you can feel it in your skin to lose something you love."

I gripped his neck even harder, "You wretch! May this day be the last day that words ever escape your lips."

I nodded to the guards who were holding him by his arms, "Hang him or feed him to the lions. I don't care, just kill the man."

As the guards dragged the man out, the man yelled, "Justice shall prevail and you shall die."

A yell erupted out of me, darkness instantly rushing out

my body and headed in his direction. A dullness settled over the room, hisses and grumbles filled the quiet space. The black smoke grabbed him by his neck, not letting go until all color from his face faded.

"Feed him to the lions."

With that, the business of the throne room continued and everyone disregarded what had just happened because it wasn't new. It wasn't the first time and it wouldn't be the last time. So they have grown used to it, knowing their end could be worse.

The servant already had a cup of wine ready for me to drink, letting it burn down my throat, *give me an effect*. I looked at every single man that was in this room. Everyone required something from me which felt like a constant reminder of my failures. Some even had the courage to tell me it in black and white words.

"My king, we must go back to the task at hand." a distant voice pulled me from my thoughts.

I surveyed his face; blank and emotionless. He knew I hadn't forgotten what we were here to do, so there was no reason to remind me. His mouth opened for several seconds, shutting them closed from just the words our gaze gave.

I stood there for a few more moments in silence. My head pounded furiously, my eyes were being burned alive. Even with all the surrounding noise, I could hear another petal fall. I could feel a heaviness fall over me; my heart anguished at the invisible pressure.

Your chances are counted, a voice grumbled in my mind.

Ephraim

Chapter 6
Flashback

It was a dark night. Dark black swirling clouds covered the sun. The entire kingdom was consumed in darkness. The kingdom plummeted into complete darkness and void.

My twelfth birthday appeared to be worthless even to my own parents. Not a single person congratulated me on another year of my life or for surviving everything my father has put me through.

All the guards spread out, preparing for the storm to come. The head guard barked constant orders. The counsel rushed to get everything sorted; *for them not to be prepared, it had to be abnormal.* I was lost in the middle of that mess, unseen by all. I could run anywhere and hide in the darkest part of the palace and not a single soul would notice.

Darkness settled over the empire of Aales in the blink of an eye, and no one had a clue where it came from. The scholars couldn't come to a single conclusion. The people of the kingdom panicked; no words brought peace to their feared hearts. Many thought it was the Apiritath Empire, but there were no signs of attacks. Confusion flooded the kingdom. There were no signs of controlled weather or a war, *What could it be?*

I ran into the throne room, desperate to find my parents, but they were nowhere to be found. Yells and chatters filled the endless hallways, voices coming from all directions.

When I found them, they were in the middle of the throne room talking to a woman I had never met. She was old and dressed in clothing that wasn't from here. Her face seemed familiar in a strange way. Maybe she had one of those faces where you think you have seen them before but in reality you never have.

I walked closer and stood beside my mother, who had a distressed expression on her face. She placed a hand on my back but didn't glance at me. Even my own mother didn't remember my birthday. I wouldn't be surprised if she forgot I was her son.

"You have avoided the ways of righteousness, the path of truth and honor. The God who rules over this world, the one who reigns perfectly, has judged your cause. You are no longer under the protection he once had over you."

The lady took a step back, her eyes instantly locking with mine. She had sadness written all over her face, sorrowful at what was happening. Her body language and words held authority. The only thing I knew for sure is that she wasn't a queen or king but she had something far greater than that. I would know because I have studied each and every single ruler that has existed.

"Because of your trespass, your son will pay the consequences. The curses that you have bestowed on this land will fall upon him. The curses that torment you day and night will fall upon him sevenfold."

Her finger pointed directly to me, her eyes pierced into my father's gaze. I looked between them, not understanding a word being spoken with their eyes. Judgment burned in her silver eyes and pride burned in his.

"Your son will be cursed for your act of disobedience. There is no saving grace; there is nothing you can do to change it."

When she turned to me, her eyes instantly filled with compassion. All thoughts faded away when she spoke to me. Her attention and focus solely on me.

I don't think I ever got this level of attention from someone.

"You will have a chance if you want it. When you see nowhere you can go, nowhere to escape and no more purpose in your life. When darkness has completely overtaken you and you want to end it all, that is when your saving grace will come. Nevertheless, if you reject it, that will be the end. You have one chance to make this right; don't waste it. Don't *kill* it."

She knelt before me, her eyes at my level. I couldn't comprehend why she had a comforting gaze despite her harsh words. The old lady gave me a sad smile, "A red rose shall appear to be a guide. It won't give you answers but a vague sense of the direction you should go if you want to change your life."

She placed her hand on my cheek before she whispered, "You will have one chance to change and make it right. Everything you ever do in your life, will forever be in your memory," Her voice thick with emotion. "You shall remember every single thing. You will be forgiven if you change your path but you won't forget what you did. It shall be a reminder for you not to follow the steps of the ones before you."

She stood up. All her emotions instantly locked away. "Because of your trespass, you shall not live much longer." Her gaze focused on both of my parents. My mother's eyes were filled with fury. My father looked paralyzed and emotionless.

"Because of your trespass, your son will suffer all the consequences starting the moment I leave these doors."

With that, she walked away. Never taking another glance back, never saying another word. That woman disappeared as if she had never existed. My body shook from fear and anxiety. My mind couldn't process the words that had just been spoken. Something inside me shifted the moment she stepped foot outside. My mother shook me on the shoulder, "Ignore her, she is simply just trying to get you rattled. She is a madwoman, she should be hanged for that."

If she was a madwoman, her words wouldn't affect me as much, right?

When I lifted my gaze to look at my father, he was paralyzed. Not a single word of comfort came from his lips. He didn't look at me; his eyes glued to the doors. He seemed to have been paralyzed mind and body, no emotion played on his face. Guards rushed in and out, people around him asking a million questions per hour. Yet he didn't respond, he stayed quiet as he looked at those doors.

Not even my mother could get him to move. And for a moment, we wondered if he was alive. When everyone gave up trying to get him to talk, he took his crown off, left it on the floor and walked out of the throne room alone.

Not even an hour had passed but the sky cleared up yet the darkness had fallen over me. There was no more peace, no more joy, no more life inside my bones.

Was I really going to be fine? Was this all really a dream? What is happening to me?

I asked myself those questions repeatedly but couldn't seem to find a comforting answer.

Soraya

Chapter 7

The grass tickled my toes; the peace flowed through my bones. This is what I needed. I needed to feel free again. It felt good to be home, even if it was for a few hours. It felt wonderful to feel the sand between my toes, the salt water in my lungs, and the sound of the leaves swaying in the wind.

I had to go back before anyone noticed I wasn't in the kingdom. Everyone thought I was simply taking a stroll in the kingdom or finding the next precious jewel for my collection. Without anyone knowing, I escaped on a boat that was ready for me miles away from the palace. I couldn't let anyone find out where I truly was.

Last night when I was heading to bed, a servant came in with a letter solely for my eyes. The curves of the letters belonged to only one man. *Come home for a few hours. I miss you.*

I didn't know how I would make it there unnoticed, but someone reminded me that the king didn't want to be bothered for the rest of the week. Somehow all the puzzle pieces fit into place, allowing me to slip away.

A nauseous feeling came over me from the boat rocking side to side. My dress slightly soaked from the splashing waters. The ocean breeze blew against my skin, leaving my skin tingling in the ocean breeze. With deep breaths, I centered myself and calmed the uneasiness.

When we reached land, kids played on the sand of the beach. Splashing each other with the frigid ocean water. They were so young and filled with life that when they noticed me; they dashed to wrap me with their small arms. To them it might have been only a year and a few months but to me it was an eternity.

"Soraya, we missed you," they all expressed in unison

Finally, no formalities. No one is waiting on me or doing everything for me. I feel free.

"Hello little ones, how are you?" I knelt onto the sand and looked them in the eyes. There were no worries that someone would scowl at me for getting grime onto my dress.

I admired their different colored eyes. The way they lit up at seeing me once again. It warmed my heart that they hadn't forgotten about me yet. I felt honored to be remembered in their beautiful minds.

"We are good." They smiled as they talked over one another.

Their innocence was the most beautiful thing I had ever seen.

A little girl hid in the distance. Her small frame hidden in the crowd. I stood up and strolled closer to her. I haven't seen her before, she must have been rescued but she had the most beautiful silver eyes. Her sun kissed hair cascaded down her small frame. She looked heaven kissed and her beauty was memorizing.

"Hello my love, what is your name?" I asked softly.

She looked like she would jump out of her skin if a leaf fell. I held her tiny hands in my own and I could sense her fear. The way her body trembled without even saying a word. The way her eyes were big and round at the sight of me.

I wouldn't doubt that she didn't know who I was but I still had patience with her. Having patience even though I could see the trauma in her eyes.

"My name is Lahja" she spoke quietly, barely even a whisper

Beautiful.

When one person arrived here or they were rescued from the middle of a war, that person would be loved by all. The mothers acted like they had another child, children would act like they had another sibling, and fathers acted like they had another person to protect.

"Well Lahja, my name is Soraya. Lovely to meet you" I smiled warmly at her, hoping her shell would crack slightly.

I looked deeply into her eyes, seeing a mix of boiling emotions.

Fear, anxiety, and no hope.

My heart broke at the sight of it because I knew how she got here. I didn't need her to explain it but her eyes spoke a thousand tales. I knew she was going through an internal battle and wished she could unsee certain things.

"What can I do to make you feel better?" I leaned closer and whispered in her ear.

She didn't respond for a few seconds, contemplating what she really wanted. Food, toys, hope, everything had become a need for survival. She had nothing and by the looks of it, she hadn't been here for very long.

"I just wanted a bit of food." Her voice slightly cracked at the end.

My own eyes filled with water from such a simple request. I

picked her up and carried her in my arms, walking to the gardens that were starting to wither away. There was no fruit or life there anymore. Everything had become dull and dead.

I have been gone for way too long.

I extended my hand in the direction of the spiritless gardens. Waving my free hand as a painter moves his paint brush. I could feel the enchanting life come from my hands.

I feel free.

I feel alive.

I had missed this, putting my magical powers to use. The powers slowly creeped into the garden, leaving life wherever it flowed. The golden life swirled around and went everywhere. The walnut trees began to bloom once again. The flowers seemed to come back to life slowly, the fruit growing besides them.

The pond filled with overflowing water, drinkable once again. The water seemed to be so many different shades of blue yet it was clear at the same time. You could see your reflection off the water and it was memorizing.

I looked at the Lahja in my arms and was warmed by her reaction. She kept closing and opening her mouth as if she couldn't believe what was happening before her eyes. She probably didn't know that I had powers which always surprised everyone once they found out.

She looked at me, her small arms around my neck, my heart was overfilled with love and passion. She wiggled slowly out of my arms. When she stood, she froze once again. Compared to the garden, she looked like a butterfly. As she took a small turn, admiring everything that had been made, I also looked around. It never got tiring and I never was bored by the ability of doing this.

It sparkled and was filled with life. And it was like for a few moments I could hear all the laughter that has ever happened in the garden. The love that was intertwined with the flowers that were blooming everywhere.

The other kids came behind me, rushing and almost pushing me to the ground, I laughed at their happiness. It didn't take much to make these kids happy, they were simple. They knew the difficulty that we were going through and didn't ask for things they knew we couldn't give them. My people knew how to be happy even with the little that we were given.

I stood there watching the kids run around and fill their faces with each fruit and vegetable that they could get.

Sat around a table on the floor, they began to laugh and give thanks for what was given. I couldn't help but smile. How could you not smile and cry from such a selfless request.

They opened the fruit with their bare hands and eyes closed as they moaned at the flavors that burst in their mouths. Fruit after fruit they filled their stomachs, they talked with one another between bites.

Then I felt a tickling on my feet and when I looked down at my bare feet, I was surprised. The small patch of grass that I was standing on was bright green with tall wildflowers. The grass had become long and was tickling my legs as I stood there.

A voice drew me out from the precious moment. "The counsel is waiting to speak with you."

My childhood best friend, Alizeh, stood there with a smirk on his face. He was leaning against a tall walnut tree that I had brought back to life. It slightly shaded his face as he stood there. He looked at me with a sly look on his face.

"Well well, look who it is." I smirked at him, as I slowly walked in his direction. My insides fluttered to see him again.

My friend, my brother.

He had a playfully frown. "Well Sor, I thought you would be more excited to see me than that."

I ran the rest of the way and gave him the biggest hug I could with the little strength that was left in my bones. His arms wrapped around my waist and spun me around like he used to do when we were children. I felt a bit weak since I just used my powers after so many weeks of not being able to.

He hugged me back as he chuckled, "That's more like it."

I have known Alizeh since we were babies, we were cut from the same cloth. We supported each other in everything except my marriage. He didn't want to see me go off to a man that I hated.

"It's our people, Alizeh. I must sacrifice myself" I told him *after trying to convince him it was a good idea. That it was the only idea that had a chance of saving us.*

"But it's not worth your happiness and your life, Soraya. I would prefer to lose my own life if it meant to keep you here with me." His eyes glistened because he knew what this meant and the danger that came along with it.

He wrapped me in his arms and didn't let me go until I was forced too. I have never seen him cry but this time he had no shame in it.

I let go and looked to his bright bluish green eyes, "I have missed you so much."

I pulled him into another hug. Soaking in these moments that I knew wouldn't last. I had counted hours before I had to go back on that small boat.

"I have missed you so much." He pulled away and squeezed my hands.

He looked at me like he couldn't believe that I was here. His eyes told me how proud he was and even though we weren't related by blood he always showed how he saw me as a little sister. I saw him as my big brother, always there to comfort me when he could because I knew he had his own family to take care of.

"Do you know how boring it gets when you're not here for me to annoy you?" He smirked as we walked side by side.

His arm was on my shoulders as he gave me a brotherly side hug. My parents never had another child but I don't think I needed one because I had him. Through thick and through thin, and even if he didn't agree with what I was going to do, he always supported me.

Walking deeper into Uosulia, I noticed how drained it was looking. The garden was only a small glance into the plunging darkness that was around us. It seemed to get worse and worse the farther we walked inside.

My gaze kept drifting over the dying pomegranate trees, the pumpkins and squash wilted in the hot sun. The wells dried from clean water. There were sword marks on the trees, telling me that they were invaded a few times. I wasn't surprised by that but what hurt me is that I didn't know about this sooner.

They were dying. My eyes filled with tears as I took that all in.

My mind wondered how the people were feeding themselves and how they were sleeping at night. This place wasn't what it once was. I looked down to my feet, the grass springing back to life wherever I stepped.

I hate shoes, I smiled to myself. Enjoying the tickles on the souls of my feet from the soft plants. I gazed behind us and the path began to slowly come back with color. The bright green began to spread and whatever was wilted was springing back up again.

"Did you hear anything I just said?" Alizeh bumped me in the shoulder. Shaking me back to reality, I was so lost in my thoughts that I didn't even hear what he had said.

"Not really." I mumbled to him as I looked into his round eyes.

His eyes were no longer those bright blue and green eyes

that were filled with life and brightness. In an instant they had become dull and dark. Under them there were bags that showed he hasn't been resting well recently. That is one of the many reasons that he is a brother to me.

He knows my pain, he sees the pain of the people of our country and yet he tries with everything that he has, to bring a smile to anyone's and everyone's face.

"With every passing day, he oppresses us more and more. Taking our crops, raising taxes and prices, and enjoying our suffering. There isn't much hope left, we can't do much now." His voice was deep and full of emotion.

Whenever I wasn't here to rule or to decide anything, he always took my place. He made sure everything was right and if something wasn't, he would find some way to tell me.

The only things that have ever made him cry was when I left and when he has had to witness the destruction in our land. Alizeh would always tell me that he could support seeing himself in agony or not getting what he wanted but when it came to the people he held closest, that's when he broke.

Before we knew it, we had reached the counsel. The meeting was filled with advisors, counsels, and princes. I knew each of them by name. They watched me grow up and now they help me with everything about my life. They were old and some of them have been here since my great grandfather and they have shown themselves as someone trusted in this kingdom. We rarely ever added someone into this small circle because you had to earn the trust to be able to know about every single detail of this kingdom.

All the men and women were grouped talking loudly in the midst of themselves. They hadn't noticed that I had arrived. Even the magical life that radiated off my body had become unnoticed.

Alizeh whistled so that all the voices would be silenced.

Each man and woman turned around in my direction. When their eyes locked with mine, they kneeled down and bowed deeply. Uttering the same words I had heard my whole life.

Long live the queen, their voices turned into a symphony.

I begged and begged for them to stop over the years but they wouldn't listen. Their response was that reverence is due to where reverence is found.

I turned to the oldest advisor, the one most dear to me, *Zion*.

He was old but he looked like he never aged, he looked the same ever since I was a little girl. He had lived and served my father and mother. Now he was guiding me every step that I needed to take. He was a father figure in my life and I know that I wouldn't be where I am now, without him.

It was as if I could feel a piece of them with me. Zion smiled at me and looked at me with fatherly love. A smile on his face that could warm even the coldest heart, "Your word is our command, my Queen. Give us hope and direction and we shall follow."

Ephraim

Chapter 8

I stared at the red rose inside the ancient glass. As each day passed, life and color were drained away from the petals. The bright red that was once full of life and color had now become a deep blood red. In many ways, I felt that it looked like my soul. Dark, evil, and wickedness but then again, I had no choice.

I have lost myself in the darkness that consumed me, that left me broken. I let myself be taken away into the haunting of the night and the torment of darkness and now there was no way for me to go back. I dug too deep of a pit for me to get out now.

I shook my head from the trance and continued to look at the red rose. It was isolated and alone in the west wing of the castle. This space was abandoned ever since my parents met death. People think it was because I didn't want memories but I never really cared to remember them anyway. It was because of this flower that I wanted everyone miles away. One soul who saw this would have my life and all of this kingdom in their hands.

Spiders had made this into their home, leaving their traces everywhere they went. The glass had become covered in dust, blurring the image of the dying rose. The stand that it was placed up was covered with a once ivory colored linen.

I huffed and glanced away from it, looking at anything except my dying fate. It was comical that my fate was in the petals of a red rose. Elders say that roses in the Kingdom of Aales were rare and precious. That one rose could only be brought back alive by an act of selfishness and love. I never believed in them because that was just fiction, it wasn't real. It would be stories they would tell to young kids so that they would have hope and love in their hearts.

There were 12 petals that had already fallen. Leaving only 24 petals left. Each petal counting my fate, each reminding of the moments I have left.

And even after all these years, I still don't know why they fall. I thought of hundreds of possibilities of why and how they fell and died but I couldn't think of one thing that would make sense.

Every time I have killed someone, I would have been dead years ago.

Every time I have hit someone, I would have been gone the first week.

My mind constantly thought of a possible answer to this torturing curse but I always ended up with nothing. Every possibility I thought about was impossible to me, *I didn't deserve grace or love. Hope was useless to go after.*

I remember the night that old woman came inside the palace and told me of the curse that would be bestowed upon me but she was speaking in riddles. It's been more than 20 years and I still can't find the key. The key that would break me through all of this torment and torture so I began to lose hope.

This rose had been a constant reminder of the curse that

followed me everywhere I went. Reminded me that I had become darkness. That the beast and monster that were inside me, had become my identity. We were one and our thoughts were mixed and I no longer would ever be myself.

That old woman could have been more specific by telling me how to break the curse instead of just giving me a rose, I mumbled to myself.

If someone could give me the answer to that, I would be grateful and give them everything I have. Instead of having answers, I always had more questions. Problems seemed to multiply themselves and the finish line never was in sight.

I bent closer, leaning my elbows on the small table that was placed on top. Once in a while, I would examine it but never touch it. What if I touched it and my body was consumed.

"No one knows you exist," I said as if to respond.

"But you truly are the bane of my existence." It was the only reason I was alive and the only way that I could know when my last breath would be. It was linked to me somehow. I knew when a petal of the flower would fall and when it was closer and closer to death.

I can't believe I am talking to a flower. I truly am going insane.

I turned around, not being able to stand another second looking at it. It made my heart uncomfortable in ways that I couldn't explain. As I walked away, I closed the heavy walnut doors behind me. I took a glance back, admiring the ageless design. The way the multiple metals formed designs and swirls all over the door. The ancient design was something that was rarely made these days but I tried my best to preserve it. To preserve history in all of its glory.

I sighed, remembering when this room was made, *This room was made for my mother.*

I remember her smile when the room had just been

finished and she started to decorate it. Leaving her personal touch everywhere. She wasn't the most modern or someone who wanted the latest thing. She was simple and all she desired was for it to look like herself. She wanted it to reflect her essence.

Then when she died, everything was cleared out because I couldn't stand it anymore. I don't know where her stuff ended up going because I didn't want to look at it for a second longer but a part of me regretted what was done.

Yet if it's out of sight, out of mind.

As I walked away, I felt another pressure of darkness, leaving me feeling heavier. The hair on my skin tensed and tingled, my mind agitated and overstimulated. I felt like a beast inside of me was being awakened and risen from the dead.

I gripped into fists even tighter, in hopes the dark powers that wanted to flow from them would stop. Each day that passed made it harder to hold back. It gripped me tighter and tighter, leaving me angered and irritated. Each day seemed to have a tighter grip on my soul, on my hardened heart.

A servant walked past me, bumming head first. Everything seemed to go in slow motion after that, his body slowly began to tremble with fear. It looked like he would kill himself with the amount of fear that resided in his bones without having to look at me. His gaze slowly trailed up until they connected with my dark gaze. He was looking at me as if I was a beast, which I was. I might look like a man on the outside but the inside was warfare from hundreds of demons that tortured me day and night.

My servants have lived with me for my whole life, they knew what I was like. They knew that even with a wrong glance it was a sentence of death. That patience and me were mortal enemies, like oil and water.

"What do you want?" I spoke but it was like it wasn't me.

The darkness would say what he wanted at whichever moment and I had no say in that. I became possessed in moments like those.

The darkness radiated off me. I fought it with a little strength but my bones tensed under the pressure. The harder that I tried to fight against it, the stronger that it got. My grip began to let loose as the magic slowly began to overtake me.

"My King, I am sorry. Please forgive me. I-I" he began to ramble.

"Speak you fool" The dark magic rolled out of me like a thousand tidal waves. I reached out my hand as the darkness grabbed him by the neck. It lifted him up into the air, his body became an ant against the darkness that swirled around us. The walls seemed to fade away the longer that we were there. The sounds that the palace was filled with went mute.

With each passing second that he didn't speak, was another second that color faded from his skin. He turned deeper than the color scarlet. His face had different shades of blues, purples, and black.

"My king, the queen-" he tried to speak, his voice barely coming out as I was choking him.

"What is it?" I yelled even louder. My voice came out louder and louder. Like a thousand tidal waves in the middle of winter. Herds of lions waiting for their prey. A killer who lures his prey into his trap.

My skin felt like a thousand ants had pricked it, leaving my skin burning. It felt like I was being burned alive, slowly and painfully.

"She is gone" his voice whispered as his body was in its last moments alive. His arms were like twigs, no movement. His legs were in the same state and with my hand still gripping his neck, he looked like a puppet.

In an instant, the power slowly retracted as I stepped away

from his fragile body on the floor. He wasn't dead but if I had just held him for a second longer, he would have been.

"Leave, I don't want to see your face again. Next time I see you will be on your death bed." My voice boomed behind me as I stormed away to find my escaping bride.

It had been hours since the guards had been on their horses searching the kingdom for Soraya. The servants were running around the palace for a missing queen, everyone was on high alert. There was not a single person doing nothing, everyone was desperately trying to find her.

I paced back and forth in the throne room in complete silence, "Where is that woman?" I mumbled to myself.

And as if on cue, the wooden doors opened and there stood my bride with guards beside her.

She was in one of her evening gowns, something simple. I observed every detail, taking every inch of her

Her hair was fuzzy from the wind dancing through it. Her clothes were almost in pristine condition, only the brim of the dress had dirt on them. And when I looked at her feet, she had no shoes.

That left my mind in a tangled mess, *Where did she go?*

"Leave us alone" I spoke to the guards without even looking at their direction. My eyes were focused on her and I wouldn't take them off. She just managed to make the entire palace a mess from a single disappearance. No one was in their place doing what they were supposed to and my entire afternoon was wasted because of her.

"But sir-" one of them began to speak back.

When I looked at him, my eyes spoke words that didn't have to be said, he nodded and turned around. The rest of the guards bowed deeply at the both of us and walked away without taking another glance.

When the thudding sound echoed from the closed doors, I walked closer to her. Her body frozen, her eyes glued to mine. The closer I got to her, the smaller she was and the more she had to lift up her head. Her head hit the middle of my chest so when I was this close to her, I had to look down.

I whispered, "Where were you?"

I don't think I have ever in my life spoken this gently yet here I am. Just a few moments ago, a man that I was holding by the neck was about to die and now I am speaking to her with such softness. Softness that never existed inside of me.

"None of your business. I thought I wasn't important or my whereabouts weren't even needed." she mumbled back, her voice wasn't irritated or angered. It flowed with patience and kindness.

Even with these short few weeks of being with her, I had discovered that she was different but had a sharp tongue when she wanted to. She was the definition of gentle and kind. Even though it angered me once in a while, she never changed. She has lived here for over a year and never once did I see her act any differently than she usually did.

"The queen must be protected and guarded at all times. My queen does not belong in the roads with the poor" I murmured in response, lost in her gaze for a second. I blinked several times, trying to regain myself because I can't believe I said those words.

My queen.

She didn't respond, as if she was taken aback from what I just said. Like I cared about her, which I didn't. I don't know why it came out of my mouth because it would seem like she had any worth to me.

"You never addressed me like that," She muttered. It wasn't a question but more like a statement.

"Address you like what?" I crossed my arms, knowing full well what she meant.

"Like I have some sort of value to you." Her voice was barely audible.

"You don't" I turned around and took a few steps back.

Needing a break from her piercing gaze. Her hazelnut eyes seemed to burn into me, as if she could know my darkest secrets. Her beauty has been carved inside my mind and when I closed my eyes, in the middle of all the darkness that resigned in it, her face always appeared. She has made herself known in this palace and I don't know if I liked it or not.

She nodded her head. Soraya's silence spoke more than words ever would.

Something inside of me twisted, it made me feel something that I couldn't explain. I covered that confusing feeling with stale emotions. I have never felt something because of someone so this was weird to me.

"From now on, you are not allowed to leave these walls unless you have several guards with you or if I am beside you."

She crossed her arms and slightly laughed, "But you never leave these walls."

I huffed. "Exactly."

I never left these walls and all my men were forced to do something at all times. Lazy was for the weak and they were never allowed to feel that. So it would be the perfect excuse to keep her inside these walls where I can see her at all times. I wasn't possessive but I loved control, and this was one way that made me feel like I had it.

Soraya

Chapter 9

I laid in bed as if there wasn't anything for me to do. Like I could rot in bed all day which I could because most of the time, I felt more like a prize to be admired than a person to talk to. The ladies had already come in and out multiple times to try to get me out of bed but I resisted multiple times.

I sat in bed and looked out at the bright sun from the window. I laid down as still as I could so that I could feel everything. Letting my skin feel the wind dance on my skin. Hearing the birds chirp as they signaled all creation the new day that had begun.

My heart already longed to be out there again. To smell the flowers and let myself be led away from everything. I closed my eyes, taking deep breaths to control the sadness in my heart. The longer time I was away, the harder it was for me to recover. My body wasn't ready for any of this, this was far from usual.

"Oh mama," I spoke to the silence.

It has felt like an eternity since she died, more than twenty years ago. People used to say that it would be easier as time went by, but it seemed that each second that passed by, the harder it was not to have her. I was learning that grief would never become familiar, that losing someone I loved would leave yet another mark on my heart.

The flashbacks and the night sweats were the only thing that had lessened over time. I remember the night they were murdered in front of my very eyes. I remember the little girl that was forever changed since that moment and that she would no longer be the same.

I hadn't noticed that the tears were rolling down my face. I barely let myself feel it but at this moment I wanted to remember any good thing about her. The way her eyes shimmered when she talked about something she loved. The way her body melted into my father's arm when he held her tight. The way her laugh would leave goosebumps on your skin. She was life walking on earth. She was love embodied into a person. She was the definition of true love and she was taken away from me.

The sword slid back out, covered in blood. My young eyes knew what it saw but I couldn't believe it. They laid in front of me, breathless. Not a bone was moving but I must have been dreaming.

I am dreaming, tell me that I am just dreaming.

Someone wake me up from this horrific dream, my vision blurred with burning anger.

Anger mixed with many other raging emotions. I felt like a bowl, every type of emotion at full force that was about to boil over. I walked up to them, kneeling before my parents as they laid on the dead grass. Even the garden knew that their masters had died. The color had faded ever so slightly, leaving everything dull and lifeless.

"Mom, wake up. This isn't funny" the words were desperate to come out as I cried before them.

I turned to my dad, "Dad, please."

I placed my hands on both of their pale cheeks. The heat from the body faded away from my touch. They were turning into blocks of ice in this frigid temperature.

Bring them back to life, Bring them back, I forced myself.

Focusing my little energy and young powers to bring my parents back to me.

I opened my eyes once again yet they laid there dead. I tried again and again and again but there was nothing. I tried everything that I knew how but it was useless. It's like the breath inside my lungs were also giving into the panic.

My body slumped against the ground. Drowning in the river of tears that were coming out of my eyes.

"I guess I missed one" a man's voice drew me back to life.

I opened my eyes to see who it was but his face was covered. He was dressed in all black, he looked like a living shadow.

Might as well, I thought to myself. What was the point of living on?

"Leave her" another man pulled the man before he reached me.

"Why? She is a testimony" He hissed

The guy slapped him in the head, "Use your head, idiot. She doesn't know who we are. Plus, grief will slowly kill her over time."

Even under the dark mask I could tell that he was smirking. His eyes were filled with mischief and darkness. My death brought pleasure to him.

His voice sounded familiar.

It was one of those voices that was unmistakable. Those

voices that felt like it was from the devil himself. That left your skin crawling, that voice that made your heart turn stone cold.

I couldn't put a finger on who it was or where I recognized it from. I would have known if I could see his whole face and not just his eyes.

They laughed with wickedness in each beat. As they walked away, they spilled poison on the floor. Then with a final glance back, they threw the torches on the floor. In an instant, everything began to burn.

My heart twisted in anger and hatred for whoever had just killed my parents. Whoever they were, their hearts were filled with such bitterness that they left me there to die.

Fire swallowed the whole garden but left me and the bodies beside me untouched. If the power of life was big enough in a royal, fire and death didn't have the right to any harm. The powers that flowed within me would protect me from anything and everything.

But at that moment, I just wanted to burn away.

"What are you thinking about?" a deep voice drew me away from my thoughts.

I looked to the direction of the sound and was startled at Ephraim standing there. He had his arms crossed which seemed to be his only position. His eyebrows were knitted together, showing his confusion. His hair was a wild mess like he ran his fingers multiple times through it. He had black shoes, dark pants, and a shirt that had the top buttons loosened.

"Nothing," I responded quickly.

It had been a day or two since my escape and the soldiers around me had multiplied. Two soldiers were closer to twenty.

He walked around and sat at the edge of the bed. He studied his reflection for several moments. I thought he only came to check if I was still in the room, but then his voice broke the silence, "You're lying" he mumbled as he crossed his arms again.

I looked at him, "No I am not."

"Yes, you are. Lying, deception, and death are written into my bones. I can sense when someone manages even a small fake white lie." His jaw clenched and I could see that his hands turned into fists.

Then he finally lifted up his head and looked at me. His eyes widened for a split second when he looked at me. I don't know what I looked like but I hope he couldn't tell that I had been crying.

His lips parted for a second before he closed it. He took one step forward and then another step back. I could tell that he didn't know how to deal with a woman who was crying.

"Are you feeling alright?" he asked. This man confused me. His appearance and voice was closed off but he questioned my well-being. For the first time since I lived here, he was asking me something about myself.

I blinked at him several times, probably making myself look like a fool.

"I'll be fine" I croaked out, it seemed that I had lost my voice because of a man that never until this moment asked how I was.

"Have you eaten?" He questioned as he leaned against the wall.

I shook my head and with that he stepped outside the room. I could hear his footsteps start to become quieter as he walked away. From the distance, I could hear him yelling at someone to get the chef and I wondered why he was in that state if I didn't matter.

Why did he want me to eat and why did he come to check on me if we didn't care about one another?

I began wondering about the thousands of possibilities that made him act this way. Ephraim twisted my mind and confused me. He was yelling and killing somebody and the other moment he rushed to make sure I was fed.

I took a few moments to fix my appearance. I straightened the bedsheets and fixed the pillows behind me. Then I grabbed my hair and quickly braided it into a loose braid. I couldn't see if my makeup was smeared or if my face was swollen, but I didn't have time to fix that.

When the door opened once again, I straightened myself and sat in bed.

I don't know why I am trying to impress him. You don't even like him, I thought to myself.

He came in, pushing the door open with his back. When he turned around, he had a tray full of food. I couldn't even see what was on the plate. My mouth already watered from the aroma, as it filled the space.

His eyes didn't leave the tray in front of him. He was balancing everything in one hand while the other one had the pitcher.

"May I?" He looked at me for a quick second with a questioning look in his eyes

I nodded once again, all the words taken away from my mouth.

He placed everything on my lap and the pitcher on the table beside the bed. He then took several steps back and spoke with authority, "Eat. I won't leave until you eat everything on your plate"

He sat on the chair that was across the bed. His feet extended and rested on top of the bench in front of the bed. His hands were folded behind his back, leaving him looking like he was much more relaxed.

He is trying to kill you without you realizing, I reminded myself.

I had to remind myself that this brooding man in front of me who I had to marry was not someone I could fall for. His looks didn't help at all with the situation.

Then he smirked and looked at the plate on my lap.

Why did he smirk?

"Maybe stop looking at me and start eating and I won't have to be here for that long."

I could feel my cheeks start to burn from the embarrassment. His grin slowly faded and went back to not being able to read a single emotion on his face.

Inside the golden tray, there was a cup of freshly squeezed grape juice. The aroma of the grapes left my mouth watering. There were dates, figs, and apricots. There were different types of jams and dips for the bread.

I began to rip apart the Barbari bread. The steam intensified and left my face and hands slightly warm because of it. The garlic and olive crept into the seams of the bread. Once the bread touched my lips, it was like I had reached heaven.

The saffron and the garlic made my tongue dance in happiness. I could feel myself lean into the pillows as I savored each second. There were so many flavors that it made me hungry for more.

I didn't know that I was this hungry. What time is it?

"If I knew that you were that hungry, I would have told the servants to make more" He grunted.

Ephraim's lips curled slightly up but he didn't smile. It wasn't quite a grin or a smirk.

"You asked them, you didn't yell at them right?" I responded back at him as I shoved another piece of food into my mouth

"No, I commanded them to do it because they should be prepared for anything and everything." He shrugged his shoulders and continued to look at me as I devoured and savored each piece of food.

I stopped paying attention to him for a bit as I continued to savor the flavor in the food. The fruits had just been picked, they were completely ripe. The juices from the apricots poured onto my hands as I opened the fruit and popped it into my mouth.

This is so good, my eyes rolled back from the flavor that burst in my tongue.

"What is it?" He asked once again.

He wasn't a man to give up and would continue to ask about something until he got an answer.

"Nothing is wrong, just not so good memories" I whispered. Hoping that he wouldn't ask any other questions.

"If someone touched my queen, I swear that man will," Before he continued his threat I interrupted.

Extending my hand for him to calm down, "No one has touched me."

I took a shaky breath and decided to ask a question of my own, "Why do you care about what happens to me?"

He stood up and straightened his clothes. Looking at me as if saying he was caring about me was the worst possible comment he could have received.

"I don't care. My men would simply die if they touch anything that is mine."

I am his?

Ephraim

Chapter 10

I was really thinking of killing these men and the pros were starting to over power the cons. I knew they were helping but if they only knew they were adding fuel to the fire. Inside my mind was a raging war, two battlefields.

What should I do?

Do I kill them now or later?

In front of me were more than twenty men arguing and pointing out things that I already knew way too well. My shoulders were tense from the weight I felt on them.

Problems, wars. Killing everyone would be much easier, I thought to myself.

"The Apiritah kingdom has once again threatened to begin another war." Someone's announced.

Another man talked on top of him. "They are finding out things that even we do not know."

I hit my hand against the handrest as I released cuss words into the heavy room. I looked over to the servant that was standing by me and told him to fetch me wine and grapes.

I didn't know how much longer I was going to be able to keep myself together.

"The Apiritah kingdom has slowly attacked us over time. They took my people as captives and have tortured them daily. They tried to break into the palace walls but never were able to because I made sure of that." I stated because it was a fact. Their king didn't want to start a war. He wanted to provoke me to start it and for me to have a horrible public appearance, which I already had."

I signaled for a servant to pass around another round of wine. "Now, he is retreating and I wonder why."

"War is brewing. Might as well prepare for a war." Someone exclaimed.

I had ordered the entire court for a meeting yet we were still in the same place from when we started. We hadn't resolved anything or thought of anything and my patience was running very thin.

There were maps covering the tables in front of me. Maps of all three countries. History books piled on either side to keep them open. I wouldn't be surprised if the palace library was practically empty from how many books there were here.

I sat at my throne with my eyes closed, trying to think of a possible solution. My head felt like a thousand drums beating at different beats, which was causing me a headache.

"Shut up, let me think." I yelled.

In unison everyone shut up, giving me a moment of silence and sanity. I rubbed my sore temples and begged my mind to focus.

Give me an idea that is not killing everyone that I see right now.

I opened my eyes and noticed that everyone was looking at me the entire time.

"You know when I say shut up, I don't mean to keep

looking at me" I grumbled and looked deep into each of their eyes.

When I stood in front of the multitude of maps, my eyes searched for answers or something to guide us in the right direction.

They took something from you, take something from them, a voice spoke in my mind.

"How many years have our countries been at war?" I asked everyone.

No one responded for several moments. Some of them kept looking at me which meant they had no clue. Others were trying to count on their fingers.

"Hundreds of years" some men finally responded back to me.

I rubbed my stubble, thinking of how this idea was going to come together, "We need to find their darkest secret for me to hit where it hurts. I need someone there to report back information."

I looked back at their faces, hoping that they would catch on to what I was saying but they looked at me as if I was speaking another language, their faces displayed confusion.

"Mavros, my tolerable friend, what do you think?"

He leaned against the table, arms folded and an evil smirk on his face. Both of us were much more reckless than the rest of the men.

Do anything to get what we want.

End anyone who got in our way.

We had the same vision and thank goodness that he didn't annoy me most of the time.

"Hit them where it hurts. I have men who are ready for your word."

See, that's a man with vision.

I nodded in agreement, "Then it is settled, does anyone have anything against it?"

If you did then prepare your funeral because that meant you wasted my time and had probably had an idea all along.

A man raised his hand and began to speak. I didn't bother to remember anyone's name because they were not of importance to me, "It better be worth my time or it will be the last thing that you say."

He cleared his throat and raised his voice for all to hear, "What then? What do we do when we find what you are looking for?"

I rolled my eyes, thinking that my plan was obvious enough, "We look for it. We find it. We end them. No one will be left alive."

Vengeance. That's what I want. Vengeance for my mother.

The only thing left on my mind was death. They took the one person that mattered to me. Now I am going to take everything that has ever mattered to them.

I don't care if they never did anything wrong or they keep telling me it wasn't their fault. Everyone rebels at one point or another and I wanted to end them all. I had nothing in my soul anymore, darkness had consumed it.

If they die, then let it be a painful long death.

Ephraim

Chapter 11

---◆---

Endless nights.

Turning and turning, not finding rest. I haven't been able to sleep correctly in so many years. Demons haunting me night and day, leaving me gasping for air in the middle of the night. The darkness seemed to consume me and the silence was never an option.

Even from a distance, my mind replayed the sounds. Crashing glass, screams and yells, and the sounds of whips and hits. The sight of my own mother in front of her husband. People always thought I had assumed what he did to my mother but I saw it with my own eyes.

My own father made me watch him hit her, saying that women would never learn. That they were nothing.

A woman is nothing more than simply for pleasure. So learn to keep their mouth closed, they are in no place to voice it, he would yell at me in between the yells.

I gripped myself from the torturing dream and was awoken by the sound of me gasping. My chest kept rising and falling at unsteady beats, leaving me gasping for air. My lungs felt like someone was compressing it, leaving me strangled and on my knees.

I turned to see Soraya deeply asleep. I was grateful she hadn't witnessed my heartache. I abruptly stood up, my body swayed side to side. My face almost came into contact with the floor.

My hands brushed against my chest, making sure I was still in one piece. My hands trailed into my hair, soaked in sweat.

I was losing it.

The darkness had crept away from my control, overtaking every part of me. Leaving me a hopeless beast. The darkness swirled around me, I could feel it gripping onto my legs. Trailing and leaving its mark on me. My mind felt paralyzed, my body couldn't fight back.

What was happening to me, I thought to myself.

I could barely keep myself from yelling and waking up the entire palace. I wanted to scream and see if the darkness would run away yet even my voice seemed to be silenced.

Where the darkness had chosen me to be the sacrifice, there was never an escape. It was like the light at the end of the tunnel would always disappear whenever I would find it.

Then something touched me. A pair of small hands touched my back, giving me a gasp of air. When I looked behind me, Soraya was looking at me.

She is beautiful.

She was the first time that I thought about something good. First time that I could see something good in someone.

Her long chestnut hair framed her small frame perfectly. The loose waves made her eyes shine in a captivating way. Even in the darkness, they seemed to shimmer in a way that I couldn't comprehend.

The darkness and death inside me seemed to be scared of her. I felt the grip that it had on me become less and less the longer she touched me. Her touch made me feel alive in ways that words weren't enough to express.

"What is wrong?" Her voice intertwined with kindness. Her voice was softer than usual, probably because she had just woken up.

It seemed I had lost my voice with the simple act of her touch. Her touch made me lose it all. I touched her on purpose multiple times, to show people that we tolerate one another. But this was the first time that she touched me. Her hand was gracefully on my bicep, leaving my arm paralyzed once again.

Her eyes kept trying to find answers in mine but when she found nothing, she turned to face me and placed both her hands in mine. Our hands fit perfectly with one another, as if they were made for one another.

And for a second, I felt normal. For a moment, I felt my mother by my side once again. Her laughter, her joy, and her peace. Soraya wasn't her in any way but she radiated peace in a way. Soraya and my mother weren't the same person but they seemed to have the same thing inside them, something that I didn't have but I wanted.

Soraya led me back to bed without saying anything and once I laid, she placed the sheets over me. As she turned away to leave me alone I whispered out, "Stay with me."

I begged and I wasn't a man to beg but just this night. Just this night I wanted to sleep in peace, without demons fighting over me. A day where every haunting dream was thousands of miles away.

"You are not in your right mind, Ephraim. Tomorrow you will hate me because I listened." She responded but stood right where she was.

I know I wasn't because I was under so much influence. Darkness, death and a whole lot of wine. I wanted to forget the pain, forget the problems and just have a sense of peace. Even though I will never reach a complete sense of peace.

"Just this one night I want to sleep in peace. And just by a touch, you calmed down the raging storm inside of me."

With that she turned around, looked me once more in the eyes and nodded in response. Before she laid in bed, she added more fire to the fireplace. The crackling sound of the fire slightly calmed the uneasiness inside me. It filled the silence around us.

She slipped back into bed, her back facing towards me. Her hair was loose and laid perfectly behind her.

From such a short distance I could smell her hair. Her hair smelled like frankincense and myrrh. I didn't know anything about this woman but at this moment all fears and demons were miles away. For the first time in years I was able to sleep without worrying about if I would make it out alive.

The thunder from the dark clouds drew me from my dark sleep. The flashes of light illuminated my room as I gripped my chest.

Breathe Ephraim, just breath.

It had been 12 days since that old woman had been here and it seemed that each day was more difficult than the last. The dreams gripped me to my deathbed. Darkness swirled around me constantly as it became my only companion over time. No longer did happiness and life radiate off me. Darkness was my new power.

I yelled loudly, trying to call my mother. She didn't answer.

"Mom." I yelled once again.

No answer.

Her room was beside mine and I knew that if I breathed

differently, she would come rushing in. So why is she not answering? Where is she?

I got up from the bed, my legs not being able to support my weight. That woman didn't tell me that the curse would affect my health.

I wobbled over to the door that connected our rooms, *Locked.*

She never left it locked.

I opened my front door and there stood a guard and one of the masters in my father's court. They had somber expressions on their faces, my heart plunging. The guard took off his hat and held it in his hands.

"Where is my mother?" I demanded, trying to push myself through but they wouldn't let me.

I was tall and strong for my age but they were much stronger. They took a step forward, blocking my view from anything behind them.

My mind raced and my heart pounded. My lungs were desperate to try to find air but none was found. My vision became blurred, the men multiplied into many and then back into two.

What was happening to me? I thought desperately to myself.

I tried once again to push myself through but they insisted once more.

Then I saw several pairs of feet passing behind them. Two men were walking backwards and another two walking forward.

No, it can't be.

"Where is my mother?" I yelled at them.

My voice cracked with despair. My eyes burned with pain. My lungs cried in suffering. But no man, no boy is ever ready to hear the painful words that came out of their mouths.

They both bowed deeply and said in unison, "She is no longer here, my king."

My rule started with bitterness and revenge. I had the power in my hands from a young age and I needed to figure out the rest on my own.

When I woke up, I felt like another man. I wanted to open my eyes for the first time. I didn't wake up with a haunting feeling, so I decided to take advantage of it. I could never live far from it, it followed me everywhere that I went, it had become a part of me. Leaving me immune to complete cure.

I turned around to see Soraya but the bed was empty. For a moment I had thought that I lost her once again but it was impossible. Most of my army would be dead in the blink of an eye if they let her out of their sight. If she was harmed in any way, it would be their fault.

I got up and signaled for the servants to come. They rushed in here faster than a blink of an eye. They began undressing me and putting on official king attire. The way the dark navy and black suit complimented my dark wavy hair. The badges of honor and jewel dangled from it, leaving me feeling like a king.

King. What I was born to do. What I was born to become.

I love my black clothes, it left me looking presentable and nice but didn't make me look like a fool but today was an exception. Today we had to take our official paintings to hang on the wall. My picture would hang right beside my parents', a constant reminder of how I failed like them.

When I arrived downstairs, everything seemed to be in a rush. People running from one side to the other. Giving me a headache because nothing stayed still. Everything was in chaos and therefore causing me a bit of stress.

The painter was already ready. His oil paints spread on the wooden pallet. The white canvas was prepared to be painted. He was the only calm and ready person there. He waved his hands, demanding a cup of wine to be served.

"Where is the queen?" I demanded.

All eyes laid on me and a wave of bodies bowed deeply at my presence.

"She is coming momentarily. Mavros went to go get her" a servant responded as she extended a cup to me.

I waved her off, not in the headspace to be drinking this early in the morning. Which was a surprise because I depended on alcohol to keep myself slightly sane.

"My King, your queen has arrived" Mavros' voice spoke behind me.

When I turned around, I could have sworn it was an angel in the middle of the darkness.

Soraya

Chapter 12

He looked at me with a different look. His eyes shined in a different way. Today they weren't dark and full of death. Today they looked like the summer sea. With just a glance, you could see that there was something different in them.

I know I wasn't supposed to use my powers on him yesterday but I couldn't help it. I was startled awake when I heard the sounds of silent screams and panics. When I looked into his eyes last night, he was gasping for air. Looking for a place to run and hide. It looked like he was being chased alive.

It doesn't matter how badly you treat other people, no one deserves to live this way. No one should always feel like they are on the run. Nowhere to hide and nowhere to call home.

Broken people will hurt others. I remembered my mother teaching me that at a very young age.

At that moment, all I wanted to do was to help him fall back asleep. Staying here drained my powers and made me feel useless, might as well put the little I had to use. I had to set aside our differences, our background to help him. Despite the hate and opposition I felt, it all needed to be put on a pause.

When I laid in bed again, I stayed as still as possible. Letting my powers radiate off my body and calm the darkness that haunted him. My skin glowed slightly in the dark but I hoped he wouldn't have noticed. Even after a few moments, his breathing slowed to a steady pace and he was in deep sleep.

"Your queen has arrived." Mavros said beside me.

I had started to get used to him being beside me wherever I was. I still didn't like the idea of being assisted everywhere I went but it wasn't as bad as I thought. He was kind and respectful and understood my point of view when I decided to speak.

When we had fully descended the stairs, I stood in front of Ephraim. He took me in, looking me up and down before locking our eyes again. My cheeks felt hot and I wanted to squirm away from the attention I was receiving. He had a small grin on his face.

"Everyone is looking at us" I whispered to him, breaking the ice between us.

He smirked slightly and whispered as well, "I don't think anyone is looking at me."

My heart melted slightly at his comment. So when I saw smiles on everyone's faces as they looked at me, I knew he was right. I never had so many people look at me this way because at home I always wanted to be treated like anyone else.

His arm extended in my direction, waiting there for me. I slipped my arm inside the crook of his as we walked. We never really walked together like this so it was something new.

The ballroom had been directed for the painting session. Flowers hung off the walls. Pillars of gold placed with precious brass items on top. There were so many types of metals around us. There were grapes cascading down a bowl in the background.

The man who was going to paint us waved his hands together, "Stand closer together, my king and queen."

There was a good foot or two between the both of us. We both took a few steps closer but not touching each other yet.

"Closer" he said once again. He kept moving his hands closer and closer together.

We took a few more steps closer to one another.

The painter sighed and walked up to us. He pulled me gently against Ephraim's chest. He grabbed Ephraim's hand and placed it on my hips, leaving the skin burning under his touch.

A million butterflies flew in my stomach. The fluttering feeling in my heart started. My heart seemed to be pounding as strong and as fast as a drum. I didn't have any romantic feelings towards this man but I didn't know why he made me feel this way. Why with just a touch, he made my feelings go crazy. With just a glance, he made me blush. With just a word, he made me want to fall.

"Stay like this, don't move" he rushed over to the canvas and began to paint us. It's like creativity sparked inside his mind and now he rushed to get the ideas onto the canvas.

This might take a while. Keep yourself composed, Soraya, I reminded myself.

I took this small advantage and noticed the way he was much taller than me. The way his arms felt on my skin. The way his breaths were slow and peaceful. And as time passed, his body relaxed and he wasn't so tense anymore.

The painter popped his head from behind the canvas and looked at me, "Smile my queen."

I pushed myself a bit more to give him a genuine smile even though I was dead tired. My insides felt weak and my body felt like it had been left out in the desert sun. My heart was slightly pounding from how tight the ladies pinned my hair today. My breaths were shallow from how tight the dress was.

It has now been a couple of weeks since I last went back to Uosulia. Everytime I went back there, it was like I was recharged. Like my powers and my mind were recharged and were able to withstand whatever came my way.

I rarely used my powers like this because I didn't want to feel like I was manipulating someone's emotions. Keeping someone at peace, drained me.

So when I did it, it left me sleepy. It made my eyelids droop and bribe me to close them even for a few seconds.

"Lean against me" Ephraim whispered against my ear.

"It's okay" I responded as I smiled a bit bigger and stood a bit taller. I couldn't be seen as weak.

"Stop being a stubborn woman and just listen" He pulled me a bit closer to him, forcing me to lean against his tall frame.

And I let myself lean against him. I let my sore body rest against this infuriating man.

His arm around my waist gripped me tighter as he held my weight. I glanced at his hand, his thumb stroking the violet fabric that hugged me. Butterflies erupted in my stomach, leaving me weaker than before.

You are playing a dangerous game, Soraya.

When the painter was finally finished after several hours, he took a step back and sighed. He leaned his head to the right, then to the left and then he smiled. His pearly white teeth showed that he was satisfied with the result.

"My King, I must say that you have the most beautiful bride in all of Aales. No other woman compares to her."

He bowed down in front of us and then turned back to the painting. He grabbed it by the dry edges and turned it around for us to see.

That can't be us.

In the painting, it looked like we belonged together. The way he was painted made him look like an angel. The way he painted me made me look like a precious jewel.

He made me look perfect. He made us look perfect and we are far from that.

Even from a great distance you could see each brush stroke. The color of crimson swirled into the background made the both of us pop. The way my dress made me look beautiful.

The way Ephraim looked made him look desirable.

I took a second to look at him. The way his body towered over mine. He was a good foot taller than me, making me barely hit his chest.

In the painting, he was looking forward with a slight smile on his lips. The way that his eyes were perfectly captured. They were like bright little stars on his face.

I turned to Ephraim, he was a bit closer than I thought. I could feel his breath dance against my skin. I shivered because I could sense the effect he was always leaving on me, "What do you think?"

I held myself still as I awaited a response. He looked at the painting then to me and then back to the painting. His hand slipped away from my waist, coldness replaced where heat once radiated.

He shrugged his shoulders, "Good Enough."

With that, he commanded them to leave it out to dry and to hang it later that week.

I stood there baffled, I didn't know what to say or what to do. I knew that the heaviness of a kingdom was on his shoulders and his own torment didn't make anything better but I could see the battlefield in his mind. It made me appreciate moments like last night and this morning a bit more.

Then the painter stood beside me, he was looking at the direction that Ephraim had just left.

"You know, he wasn't always like this" he spoke quietly beside me so that no one's ears would hear.

Curiosity struck me, "What do you mean?"

He looked at me with sadness in his eyes, "I have been with the royal family since the reign of his parents, may they rest in peace-"

He stood quiet for a moment before he continued, "There was one dark night, everything changed and ever since then he hasn't been the same."

I felt my body tense with those words. I could feel the haunting darkness around us just by the mention of it.

What happened?

Was he hurt?

What happened to his parents?

My mind thought of a million questions but I shouldn't care. I shouldn't care about what happens to him. He is trying to kill me without knowing.

But a small part of me wants to help him. A small part of me went against any opposition I felt towards him. I wanted to find out what happened that night.

I wanted to find out why all the joy, happiness and love of this man was taken away from him in only a fortnight. I wanted to know who was so cruel to rip away from someone the pleasure of life.

Ephraim

Chapter 13
Flashback

---◆---

I cursed under my breath. Sometimes I wish I could just get what I wanted in a blink of an eye but that doesn't happen. Life isn't fair with anyone and you had to sweat blood and tears to be able to get what you wanted. If I ever wanted something, I had to work for it, earn it.

I would indulge in wine and alcohol imported from all over the world. I would allow myself to get drunk and happy. I would invite a girl to comfort me at night, whispering sweet words into my ears to quiet the dark thoughts within. All in hopes to keep the dark evil voices and thoughts away. Instead of those things softening the darkness, they made it grow. It made the wretchedness inside me become more powerful than my thoughts.

Now I was alone, brokenhearted, drunk and with no one to comfort me. The woman that I was going to crown queen, that I had convinced myself that I loved, traded me for my closest friend. From that moment on, I promised myself that I wasn't going to trust anyone or anything, that I was going to have to find strength within myself.

The doors creaked as I slipped myself outside in the dead of night. I couldn't think and no woman brought me comfort. The trees swayed back and forth in the cold winter wind.

I swayed back and forth, unable to keep my balance before I crashed into something, or someone. Whoever I was leaning against was much smaller than me, so it couldn't be a guard.

I turned my heavy gaze and my eyes came into contact with a woman.

Her face was covered and the only thing that I could see were her beautiful eyes. They were captivating to say the least.

"My king, are you okay?" she still had a small hand on my arm and the other one extended outwards. Ready to catch me if I fell but I knew if I did she was going to go down with me.

"I am fine" I slurred a response.

I shivered when another breeze brushed against my skin and realized that I had no shirt on. I turned away my gaze and pulled myself away from her grip, wine splashing on my hand due to the harsh movement.

"Do you need a guard or someone?" her voice was filled with worry. She took a few steps closer before coming to an abrupt stop when my hand extended out to stop her.

"I don't need anyone." I grumbled.

Because I don't have anyone.

You don't have anyone and you never will, you wicked demon, a dark voice spoke out loud in my ears.

I knew no one around me heard that voice because I was the only one tortured by it day and night. It was the voice that led me to become an assassin, led me to become a drunkard, my life was in its control. Whatever it was, it had me like a puppet.

I turned around and looked at the woman again. Her face was mostly covered and when I let myself take her in, I noticed her simple clothing. Either she was from the town that was trespassing in my palace or she was a woman of high standards who thought herself of very little worth. Whichever is the case, I didn't know who she was and why she was here.

"Who are you? For I can't recognize a woman with only her eyes."

I could tell that underneath the face covering she grinned, "I am one of the women that has been forcefully brought here for your choosing, my king."

Oh what a pain. I was so drunk that I totally forgot about that.

I forgot that Mavros decided on my part that I needed a new wife. That I needed someone that was going to help me get over my disastrous engagement. Someone who captivated me and the people. Someone who brought me pleasure and wasn't a headache. The biggest part on that list was that they didn't give me a headache because I think I already have too much of that from my daily life.

"What is your name or shall you hide that from me as well?" This game she was playing was entertaining me. Usually women would beg to talk to me and now I stand before a woman who won't even show her face.

Her eyes closed slightly like she was smiling, "I won't say it my king because it wouldn't be fair to the other woman."

I huffed and took a long sip of my wine, "Then how then will I know it's you who I talked to tonight? What if I want to see you again?"

She placed a hand over her heart and bowed, "You will simply know. I must go before I am written down as missing."

I quietly laughed as she turned around and gracefully strolled back to the palace which now had four guards stationed beside it. They were all staring at either me or the woman who was walking in her direction.

I sighed because I couldn't even have a moment by myself. There was always an eye watching or an ear listening. Everyone was close but at the same time they were distant. People started to be scared of me, no one felt safe and I didn't blame them because of that.

That wasn't my life. I inherited the darkness that I hated in my father. The man that I swore I would never become is the man I am now. The things that he did that I swore to myself, were the same thing I did constantly.

Alone and wretched, maybe there was still hope left for me but I doubted it. So I have learned to accept it, to accept the demon I have become. The king that everyone feared and hated at the same time.

I drank the rest of my wine and slammed the cup against the stone table beside me, almost falling onto the table. I held myself with the little strength that was still inside my bones and continued to walk.

I didn't last long before I felt my body slamming onto the floor and the darkness surrounding me, tightening me in its grip. I could hear voices from miles and miles, they asked if I was okay and for someone to find the doctor.

For a second I had a choice, to go into the light that a part of my soul wanted to go to or go to the darkness. Darkness is the only thing that I have grown to know and become friends with. With a sigh, I could see myself walk back into the darkness, back into the very thing that captivated me and tormented me.

Soraya

Chapter 14

I was already awake before the sun even came up. I decided to dress myself because I didn't want anyone asking me thousands of questions or telling me what to do. So my hair was loose and free, just the way that I liked it. There weren't any shoes that were hurting me with every step that I took.

People said that when I had my hair free, that I looked more like my mother. She was one of those people that didn't care about what other people thought about her. She didn't care if she was up to royal standards, she was free. She loved when her hair would dance in the wind and her clothes weren't glued to her skin. She wanted to be free.

Unlike me. Sometimes I felt like a prisoner bound in chains.

I walked down the steps and down the grand staircase. To this day I haven't even been everywhere. The palace was way too big and no one left me alone long enough. I was always swarmed with maids and guards telling me what to do and when to do it.

When I fully descended, the palace was busier than usual.

People were standing in the middle of the hallways, and talking in groups. No one had noticed that I arrived, everyone immersed in their conversations and for a moment I appreciated feeling unseen.

For a moment, I loved not having to beg someone to stop having to bow down to me. Or feeling every eye was on me.

Until, the guard by my side, cleared his throat and announced me, "Queen Soraya, Wife of the great King Ephraim" his voice boomed loudly.

Everyone turned their bodies in my direction and bowed in unison. Their voices became one, "Good Morning, Queen Soraya."

I nodded and continued weaving myself through the maze of people.

I turned to the guard, "Where is the king?"

He looked down at me, "He went out on business, My Queen."

I nodded. "Then why are these people here?"

"The king has commanded a feast." He was giving me cut and dry answers.

"For what reason?" I questioned.

"I am not permitted to say." He looked forward and avoided eye contact with me.

It wasn't unusual to have a banquet but something was unsettling, something was off. Someone would have told me beforehand. If it was just a banquet then I would be preparing everything with the maids, but I wasn't. I wasn't complaining but something just seemed weird.

"Okay then." I responded quietly.

He took a step in front of me, his eyes searching for something or someone, "Would you like breakfast, your Highness?"

I shook my head, already predetermined what I was going

to do today. "No, I am going out to get out of these walls for a while."

His body completely tensed up as he turned around to look at me. His eyes wide in fear, "I must object, my Queen. He will not only kill me but also many others. Your safety is my reason to stay alive."

I put my hand on my waist. Angered at the way I was being treated as a baby, that I couldn't take care of myself.

"Who commanded such an order?" I sounded furious and he was squirming under the pressure.

"The King did, madam" he stuttered, not knowing how to respond to me formally.

"Well, he isn't here and I am more than capable of taking care of myself. Plus you will be there and we will be back before he returns. He will never even know I left."

I smirked and awaited his response. I didn't care what I needed to do to get a break from here. If I couldn't see my own people then I was going to go outside and act like I belonged. If I couldn't spread life around this palace, then I was going to use it and help the people.

Even if it was against principles and rules to use powers outside my country.

No one was here to stop me now

He sighed deeply, "Let me get some other guards and then we can leave."

After much insisting and feeling like a child, I had convinced the 20 men around me that a horse was not necessary. It would bring too much attention to me, not like twenty guards surrounding me didn't bring enough attention already.

The goal was to meet the people, help someone and slip

back into the palace before Ephraim even notices anything. I don't even think he would notice that I was gone.

When I stepped outside the palace gates, I didn't expect this to be the first thing I saw.

Families were starved and skinny, their skin covered with grime and dirt. The kids begged merchants to give them food but they were given no attention.

My steps had slowed slightly as I took it all in. My heart breaks with each thing that I saw. Fathers and mothers who only had a single serving of bread and had to split it between their children. Elderly women grabbed onto the nearest thing to be able to stand up straight. People passed without giving a second thought into helping them out, looking at them as if they were bugs.

This was sickening.

My stomach turned and turned, this nauseated me. We walked deeper into the crowd, people taking steps away once they saw me.

Some of them looked disgusted at the sight of me and I couldn't hold that against them. I barely left those walls and when I did, it was to go back to my own country.

I have never taken the time to meet these people and that made me feel even worse. I looked to my right and there was a little girl who was beautiful. She looked like an angel and I was in awe of her beauty. Even in ripped dirty clothes, her beauty couldn't be denied.

I stopped in my tracks and knelt to look her in the eyes. Ocean blue eyes and instantly I was lost in them. They looked like the ocean on a spring day. Multiple shades of blue swirled in her eyes; *completely mesmerizing.*

They looked bright and still full of life. Eyes were the first thing I noticed in a person. The eyes of a person were the portals into their hearts. It showed what they were feeling at that moment.

I smiled at her but she didn't smile back, "Hi" I whispered to her.

She waved her hand but said nothing. I didn't know if she was unable to speak or if she was just scared of me.

"Are you hungry, little one?" I asked.

I noticed the way you could almost see every single bone on her arms and legs. The way she had hollow cheeks and bags underneath her eyes. The way her clothes seemed to swallow her entirely.

I reached out to pick her up but let my hands hang in the air for a moment.

"Can I pick you up sweetheart?" I asked.

She shook her head and quietly stated, "I am dirty."

My heart melted. "I don't care about that. I care about you. Clothes are simply clothes, people are more important."

Her eyes filled with water as she walked into my arms. I picked her up and placed her on my hips. She was stiff in my embrace for a second but then she relaxed, her head slowly leaned against my shoulder.

"My Queen, you should not be touching such filth." I turned around and looked at the guard. He was the only brave one to speak up and look at my face. The others were looking everywhere and anywhere except me.

"Who commands what here?" Very rarely did I use my voice of command but I needed to remind him of his place.

I continued to hold onto the little girl in my arms, who had now made herself comfortable. She played softly with the edges of my hair.

"You, My Highness" he responded and stood a bit taller as he said that.

His eyes showed how much fear he was in. That if Ephraim knew what I was doing, the cost would be their lives. I would get a yell and a hard look but they would risk their lives completely.

"If the king has any problem with that, then he can come to me." I said to him as I walked around to the nearest food stand.

The people were no longer looking at me with hatred but with curiosity. They wondered what a queen was doing in their midst. The look of question and wonder were all over their faces.

I am here to show them that I am not any better than they are.

We continued walking in the midst of the crowds and the smell of food began to infuse the air. The seasoning started to get stronger and stronger. The sound of people was getting louder and louder. More people were around us as we struggled to get through.

We were close, I could tell.

"Where are you taking me?" I looked at the little girl and saw that she had become unsettled.

"To get you food. Where else do you think I was going to take you?"

I thought that was obvious.

"No one has ever gotten me food before" she whispered in my ear. When she said that, my heart broke into a million little pieces.

What?!

I stopped myself in my tracks and looked down at her, "Little one, do you have a family?"

She shook her head, *heartbreak.*

"How do you feed yourself?"

Did I really want to know the response to that question?

116

"I usually eat what is left on the floor. People call them scraps."

I held on to her a bit tighter as I tried to not break down in the middle of the busy street. It was already a scandal that a queen was here and I didn't need another reason for Ephraim to yell at me.

My heart broke at the thought of this young girl having to survive on her own, and the thought of it broke my heart. In fact, she probably hadn't eaten a full meal in years.

The only downside to my powers was that I felt. That my heart didn't have a limitation to feelings. My heart would leap with joy at one moment and the other it felt like someone was ripping out my soul. My emotions were more than usual, they were intensified. That came with good and bad things and one bad thing was that I got emotional over small things.

A lump in my throat had formed, leaving me unable to speak. And maybe that was better because I couldn't be responsible for what would happen if I said anything right now.

As if to distract me, my stomach let out the loudest sound. It was letting me know how hungry I actually was. The little girl thought it was amusing and I was glad that my moment of embarrassment was a moment of laughter for her. And I had a feeling she rarely had moments like these.

"What do we want to eat?" I asked her as I looked at the many merchants offering freshly baked food.

From a distance you could see the leavened flatbread steaming. The aroma drew me closer. The hints of rosemary and olive oil made my mouth water. The fig jam made my stomach turn in hunger. There was a merchant who was selling stews of all kinds. Lamb, beef and chicken stew, which used to be my father's favorite. I never loved it as much as he did but I always ate to feel like I was closer to him somehow. Just the smell brought back memories of him and his favorite dish.

"Is food ready?" My father would yell from outside for the millionth time

"Not yet my love, I will call you when it is ready" my mom yelled back as she cut the meat and vegetables.

I looked at her from the floor, where I was playing with my wooden dolls. People used to say to me that I looked like her but her beauty was incomparable. Even if she was covered in flour or her hair was braided messily, she was still beautiful.

She was beautiful inside and out. One moment she was a queen who acted with love and the next a mother who cooked with love.

She was perfect in my eyes.

It hadn't even been 5 minutes before my father walked in with a smirk on his face. He tiptoed behind his wife, signaling me to be quiet.

He whispered into her ear, "Is dinner ready?"

Her body jumped up from how startled she was and then she burst out in laughter. My dad hugged her from behind, as they swayed side to side. Her laughter didn't die and the smile on his face didn't fade.

This is love, I thought to myself.

Love isn't money, fame, or multiple women. Love is when you live in young love even after 20 years of marriage. Love is when you do everything and anything for the person despite what you feel. Love is when you wake up to them and the thought of leaving them appalled you.

My mom turned her head to look at me, "My precious daughter, I pray to the God above you find a man that loves you like your father loves me. A type of love that doesn't depend on status or anything that is vanity. A love that leaves the angels in awe."

I nodded at her and put them in my mental drawer. When you're that young, you never really understand things like that. All the advice they ever gave me was secretly kept with me. Where I would have them with me for eternity.

Where they would be engraved in my mind, they would help determine my footsteps.

This was one of the best moments of my life.

I arrived in the castle and was beyond grateful that Ephraim wasn't there. I told the maids to take a day off, as I slipped into the bathroom and thought about everything that had just happened.

The little girl was just a small part of a much bigger problem. The problem was that there was no life in the kingdom. There was no joy, no love and no purpose for the people to keep on living.

My thoughts turned into a ball of snow as I slipped myself into the hot water. I sat there in complete silence and let my thoughts loose once again.

It all made sense. The king enforced slavery as the only way to survive and eat. It gave people no hope and so it gave them no reason to live.

The darkness that abided in these walls oppressed the people who lived within it and outside it. The people needed to find a reason to live, a reason to keep pushing before it was too late. The way a king felt about his people was the way the people were going to act.

I saw in their faces, the way they held themselves with little regard and importance. Finding food was the greatest challenge of their day. The way they had to pay to drink fresh clean water and if they didn't then they would drink filth.

I don't regret a single moment for seeing it all with my own eyes. It was one of those things that you couldn't believe was real until you saw it for yourself.

It was one of those things that really put into perspective the different ways people live life. There was no one who was more important than the other. We all do the same thing during a single day yet we can be treated differently just because of status.

In the midst of all this, there was not a single person who I saw that wanted to help. A person that wanted to go against the current and make a difference. Bring hope back and give people a reason to live.

I will be the vessel to help these people.

If no one was brave enough then I will. If I sacrificed my life for the better of those around me then may my life be the answer to many unanswered prayers.

Ephraim

Chapter 15

◆

I could feel the storm inside me begin to ramp up. My mind began to throb from all the hours I had spent in front of these papers. The only thing that was keeping me sane was that things were beginning to move along. The people in the country were beginning to sway in the direction that I was forcing them to go. I was taking anything and everything from them.

I didn't care what they thought about me. That was the least of my priorities. I just wanted everything and everyone gone, no wars or headaches.

I had decided two days ago that the best thing to take my mind off it was to have a banquet. Where I could purposely lose myself in the alcohol, where people would dance for pleasure and that there wouldn't be a worry in the world for a few short hours.

It was the one place where papers, documents, problems and wars couldn't creep themselves into. It was an escape from all that, where I could just get myself drunk and out of my state of mind.

A knock came at the door, "Come in."

The door creaked open as Mavros slipped himself into my office. My body slightly relaxed that it wasn't another servant to come in and bother me.

He poured himself a cup of alcohol and sat across from me without saying a word. When he finally sat down, I noticed the papers in his hands.

My hands were already covering my face, prepared for whatever he was about to tell me.

"What do you want now?" I asked, my hands muted my voice.

"It may come as a surprise, I am not here to bring bad news but an idea." he responded.

I slowly took my hands off my face and crossed them, *he rarely came in here to tell me just an idea.*

"What is it?" Trying to make this go as fast as possible.

"Tonight we are having a banquet."

Thanks for stating the obvious, I rolled my eyes at him because he wasn't saying anything new. Mavros knew how I hated for things to be repeated multiple times.

"What if Queen Soraya was not to attend today?"

I sat there frozen, *Why would he ever say such a thing? He knows that if the queen doesn't attend banquets that the king holds, it will cause a mess.*

I looked at him and tried to find out why after all these years of bringing me facts and strategies, he would say that?

My mind rattled all the possibilities that would make him say that but my mind came blank. Thousands of problems constantly ran through my mind, I didn't need something else.

"Why?" I questioned him.

He cleared his throat, "The queen is tired and she needs time to rest."

I huffed at that because even I knew how stupid that

sounded. I haven't spent much time with her since the night she helped calm me down. She has been going to sleep before or after me and I have been waking up before her. Our paths weren't really crossing one another and I don't know if I liked or hated that.

I was a hundred percent sure that it was because today someone had told me that when I was gone, she ended up outside the palace walls. There were cheers and chatter as she walked in the midst of the people. One of my guards told me that she was carrying a little orphan girl and feeding her.

When I walked past her in the halls, I pretended that I knew of nothing and kept it to myself. Nothing that happens inside these walls ever gets past me, there is not a single thing under my nose that I don't know about.

If I tell her that I don't want her to leave these walls, it seems to give her even more desire to do so. It was as if, telling her to stay and do nothing all day made her hate me even more.

"Sure, whatever. Just leave me alone." I ran my fingers through my messy hair. It was a tendency that I had, to run my fingers through my hair when I was nervous or deep in thought.

"I will leave in a second my king, now I have some things for the banquet that I need your stamp of approval on."

He said it with a small smirk on his face, and I skimmed over the papers and quickly signed it with my ring.

The time had finally come where I could throw the papers to the side and let myself free inside that ballroom. The party was already beginning as I cleaned myself up in my quarters.

All day I had been wearing my study clothes, which were all black and metallic details. When I left the bathroom, I noticed that Soraya was inside the room all along. She was standing on the balcony, looking into the star filled dark sky.

Her hair was loose and wild. She had no shoes, and her nightgown glistened in the moonlight.

"What is wrong? Do you not have what you want? Do you want me to fetch the newest dress or maybe another jewel for your collection?" I asked her as I buttoned my shirt.

No Response.

"Did you hear me?" I asked once as I stepped closer to her.

Nothing.

"Queen Soraya?" My hands dropped to my side, aggravated that she was ignoring me and giving no remark to anything that I asked her.

She turned her head slightly, "That's the first time you have said my name. Even if you made it sound so appalling."

It wasn't a question, more like a statement.

I wanted to speak quietly and softly but the darkness that controlled me gripped my throat. Her words seemed to dig into my heart. A few words that clogged my throat, leaving me speechless.

I tried to clear my throat, "Sleep in your own room tonight. You know what, stay there until I call you."

I looked down, avoiding her glance as I finished buttoning the wrists.

"Okay." With that, she bowed her head and exited the room.

Her one worded response left me there in utter silence as I began to replay the events in my mind.

I feel like this has happened before, I thought to myself.

Then I remembered, this is the same way that my father used to treat my mother. Even after so many years, trying not to be like him, I still was.

I had become a monster, I thought to myself. Maybe I

hadn't become a monster, maybe I always was. I tried to be different but I think that I tried too hard. That my strength alone wasn't enough to be different.

The day that started it all replayed in my mind on repeat. All the hitting and the screams were my lullaby to sleep. When it was quiet, that's when war had begun.

The sun had barely risen. The sky was still dark and the stars were still visible. From a distance I could hear my mother quietly crying. She rarely cried out loud, but I had noticed over the few years of my life that she held it in until she couldn't. I knew she didn't want to appear weak in front of me, she wanted to keep herself together but as each day passed, I could see that her heart was breaking even more.

I slipped myself out of the sheets and tiptoed out of the room. The creaks of the door gave me away but through the crack of the door, I could see my mother curled on the floor.

Her head was stuffed into her lap, her cry muffled by her clothes. She didn't look up when I sat down beside her but she knew it was me. I was the only one who worried about her, that cared about her. All the other people that worked here only cared about their jobs and riches.

"Are you okay mama?" I asked her as I brushed back her damp hair away from her face. Her skin was slightly too hot, her hair damp with sweat and tears. Her small frame was shaking slightly as she tried to recollect herself.

She didn't answer or look at me for a bit. Her breaths began to slow down, her body stopped trembling. Her hands were used to stop the tears from flowing as she lifted up her head.

With the saddest smile on her face she looked at me. The

way she looked and the amount of tears she cried, could break anyone's heart. Bright ocean blue eyes were exchanged for darkness. Dark bags encircled them, showing how long it's been since she slept a full night.

Even in the midst of all that, she was still beautiful to me. Nothing could make her ugly and someone would be a fool to not treat her like she deserved.

I didn't have the courage to say it to his face but my father was the greatest fool of them all.

"I will be fine, my son" she tried to speak but most of her voice was already gone. The sadness inside of her soul seemed to mute her, to make her keep the pain to herself.

I wrapped my small arms around her neck as she pulled me into her lap. Her arms were around me as she started to cry once again, this time uncontrollably. I held on to her a little tighter trying to tell her that it was okay to cry. She didn't have to build walls around me to protect me, I was here for her.

I always thought it was okay to not be okay but as time passed I realized that there were different levels to that. There were so many moments that she was so burdened with the torment from her own husband and it shouldn't be okay to deal with that. No one should have to deal with that.

Yet my mom wasn't like that, she was different. She would keep holding it in as if she was immune to pain. She would hold it in and when she couldn't take it anymore, she would release it all with a cry. And in a second, her tears would be wiped away and then there would be a smile on her face as if nothing happened.

"My son please don't be like your father." she mumbled into my shoulder.

Her body shook from her raging emotions. They were screaming to be seen. They were yelling to be heard. Her emotions were being demanded to be felt and understood.

I wanted to cry even though I didn't go through what she did. Even though I never was abused physically by him, I wanted to cry for her. Her emotions were rooted, they were deep. They were as deep as the ocean, as strong as a lion. Her heart could make even the strongest walls come down. She could make the coldest heart tumble without even having to say a word.

"I promise I won't momma but-" I pulled back to look at her.

Her hair was all over the place, covering her most beautiful facial features, "momma, what about you?"

She smiled and placed both hands on either side of my cheeks. Her thumb caressed over my cheeks as her eyes looked deeply into mine. Her hands were warm and soft, they felt like home to me.

I guess it was because her hands reminded me of how I got here. Everytime I would fall, she was there to pick me up off the ground. Those hands protected me from the evil that lingered in these walls. Her hands were covered with stories, the true definition of a mother.

"Don't mind me, I will be alright but you-"

She tried to smile fully but failed, "You will be the difference that this kingdom needs. Simply don't walk in your father's footsteps and there will be endless possibilities."

Mavros peeked his head into my private chambers, "My King, are you ready? The feast has begun."

I shook my head, to bring myself back to reality. For a moment, I was able to feel emotions. I have become one with darkness. Emotions that once lived inside of me disappeared.

Every time I tried to feel, care, or even love, the darkness in my bones would tighten at the thought. It would make me repulsed and disgusted. Immune to the weakness that came along with emotion.

There are some days which I wish that I could rewrite the past. Yet that isn't in my control, nothing is.

Mavros interrupted my train of thought once more and I had a sudden urge to kill him but as quick as it came, it left.

"My King, are you well?" In the blink of an eye, he was standing in front of me.

His worried eyes looked at me as he awaited an answer, "Yes, I am good. Let's enjoy ourselves tonight."

He smirked, "Let us enjoy ourselves and forget the problems of a kingdom."

I could already feel the wine in my veins and the darkness in my heart.

Ephraim

Chapter 16
Flashback

Locked another night in my room, there was no way I could even keep track of how many times this has happened. Each day passed was another day that my father got worse.

He had become the devil himself ever since the old lady walked into these palace walls. Each word that she spoke had come to pass.

Another party was being thrown for no specific reason unless it was to pet my father's ego. He always used the best decoration, the best food, the best wine. This time it was longer, and these walls were the only company that I had.

Every time there was a party, my father would demand the guards to lock me inside. His words were, *"He is too young and doesn't need to see anything. That it isn't his business."*

He used the best wines from the stolen crops, concubines who would throw themselves at his feet. He was naive to think that I didn't know what happened at his parties.

Meanwhile, as he danced and drank the night away, me and mother were locked inside our rooms. We were fed what was left and the guards treated us like we meant nothing. Those nights, our titles meant nothing. The place was filled with wickedness and you didn't need to be the smartest person to recognize that.

I didn't have powers but I knew some way my father did. Nothing that he did made sense, it felt like it was all controlled. The way he automatically got anything he wanted. The way everything would fall at his feet. People acted like puppets around him, their emotions controlled by the darkness that was in him. I didn't know how he did it but I was determined to find out.

I searched my room, looking for a way to get out. A way to escape these walls that seemed to get tighter as the time passed. The doors were locked and guarded at all times. The door to my parents' room had been locked from the outside. At first, I couldn't think of any other way to leave the room.

My eyes looked for a small escape and when I was about to give up, I found a way. The windows were slightly open. The fabric which covered the windows was blowing slightly in the wind.

Perfect.

Thank the heavens that my room was right on top of a balcony. In case that I took one wrong step, I wouldn't fall all the way to the ground. The curved entryways, several ledges, and domed shaped ceilings. There were several places to walk and jump on.

One step in front of the other, I walked slowly to the nearest window that was opened. My breath held, my heart pumping faster and faster. My legs and arms are shaking profusely. The wind would blow against my face, my clothes blew in the air.

When I finally slipped myself through and landed with a quiet *Thud*, I exhaled. I treaded quietly as I walked to the doorway but then I heard voices coming in my direction. I cursed underneath my breath as I swiftly found a place to hide.

A princess walked in with servants that followed shortly after her. I could tell she was a princess by the way she held herself, like she was better than everyone. She commanded everyone to do things that she could have done herself.

Great, another spoiled brat, I thought to myself.

My father also had the tendency to marry other women because it would strengthen the relationship with other nations but he couldn't fool me.

I knew me and my mother were never anything to him. There was no belief that he ever cared for us but he still kept me around. I was the only true heir to succeed but I had a feeling he would fight anyone to keep that crown on his head.

As for me, I didn't care for the crown because I saw what it did to people. Made them into selfish people, centered in their ego. Whatever was hidden inside the soul would always be revealed.

I hated people that thought they were better because of a stupid golden crown.

Before the door closed, I slipped my slim body through and quickly crept down the stairs. The stairs slightly creaked, signaling that someone was coming but the music was way too loud for anyone to notice. There were barely any servants walking around, they had been forced to stay until the party was over. Hundreds of guards wore stationed around the palace, so there was no one looming behind me.

When I reached half way down the descending staircase, I sat down on the velveted floor and peaked between the bars to see what was happening.

My stomach turned and turned at the sight, it was worse than what I had expected. My father had thrown himself onto the throne, letting the women throw themselves on top of himself. One of them was feeding grapes as he whispered something into their ears. He played with their long locks of hair and whispered sweet nothings to them, making their cheeks turn bright red.

The ballroom was filled with drunk men that had no right to be there. The king's court, highly ranked men, and drunk married men had flooded into the palace. My stomach hurled at the thought of women and children at home thinking their husbands and fathers were working.

"Cheers to pleasure" my father yelled out drunkenly.

His body swayed side to side as he tried to regain his sense of balance but he didn't. He was so drunk that when he tried to walk, he swayed once again and fell to the floor. His body fell to the floor with a huge sound, heads turning at the second.

A collective gasp came from the throne room, people circling around him to see what had happened. I took a few more steps down the stairs to get a better view but I regretted it. I was beginning to believe that I shouldn't have been there yet I still was. My eyes witnessed every detail.

The physicians of the palace came rushing in, trying to awaken him. They shook him, threw water onto his face, and yelled into his ears. The physician leaned his ear against his chest and used his fingers to check for his pulse. Only for a short moment, his face fell. He slowly reached for his hat, his gaze focused on the floor.

He was dead.

The moment he was declared dead, a black magic lifted off his body. Darkness seemed to be ripped from deep within his dark soul. The color of it only turned darker and darker until it looked like a black abyss. Hundreds of eyes followed that dark smoke. The darkness swirled and danced around the throne room, waving itself through people as if it was looking for something.

Slowly it got closer and closer to me. I fumbled to my feet, trying to run away. My foot kept getting stuck on the carpet which made me plummet to the floor. Before I could escape, I was trapped within the dark smoke. People wanted to come closer and save me, but were petrified they would be touched as well. The mysterious black cloud, people whispered amongst themselves, no one knew what it was. It wasn't to my surprise that no one dared to save me after all.

Somehow I knew what it was, like my soul already could feel the presence of the darkness and death. As if I had already been used to it and its characteristics.

People slowly faded away, the thickness of the smoke intensified. It crept into my skin, gripping onto me. I let out a cry of pain from the claws that were being dug into my skin. It seemed to freeze me, not letting me go for a single second. Never have I felt so powerless like I had in that moment. Inside of me, there was no ounce of strength to fight against it, it was darker and greater than I ever was.

Hisses danced across my ears, thousands of voices that I have never heard before. They set a shiver down my spine, a petrified fear settled into my heart. I didn't know if I had died or if I was still alive. Maybe I was being killed alive slowly and each feeling was being intensified as seconds passed on.

I looked around for a way to escape, a sliver of hope. My vision had darkened, I couldn't even see my own hands. My head throbbed in agonizing pain, there wasn't just torment from the outside but now on the inside. My body had become a battlefield, my mind a war.

But then I heard dark voices that seemed to be coming from all directions. Voices from different pitches, and frequencies. Yet they were all saying one thing, they all wanted one thing, "You're ours now."

Soraya

Chapter 17

*L*ove. *What even is Love?*
　　I have asked myself that one question more than the rocks in the sand and the stars in the night sky.

"What is love?" I asked one of the ladies that was tightening the dress around my waist. It had become our daily ritual. After months of being locked within these walls, I got to know her more than most people did.

Mehra.

I had told her countless times that her name was beautiful. Even the meaning embodied who she was. Kind, loving, and gentle was who she was and I have found a friend in her. She didn't know half the woman I was but yet I seemed to have found a close person to confide in.

Her daily reminders were that I am the queen and she is just a servant but I have always reminded her that there is no such thing as someone being more important than another.

"Love, your highness is a beautiful yet dangerous thing." Her voice softened just slightly. I could tell by the way she said it, that it meant something to her.

Was she in love? Did she ever have a lover?

I bent my head back to try to look at her but she was focused on getting a curl pinned correctly, "Have you ever been in love, Mehra?"

Her hands froze mid-air, but she had yet to look me in the eyes. I pulled her up by her elbows but when I looked into her sweet eyes, they glistened. They glistened and showed all the emotion and the answers that I would ever need. No words needed to be spoken, her eyes said it all.

"No one inside these palace walls has ever called me by my first name." She answered me gently . Her voice sounded like honey, sweet.

It was then my turn to be taken aback, *No one?*

"You must be joking with me? How many years have you been working here?"

I could feel the anger begin to trail up my body. The heat flooded my cheeks. My hands turned into fists and my body turned into stone.

"No, my queen. Everyone addresses me by you, servant, or a peasant but never by my first name." Her voice was barely above a whisper. She spoke such heartbreaking words with such delicacy.

"A little over 5 years, my Queen" She answered once again but her gaze was now on the floor. I knew she was nervous from me asking hundreds of questions but I wanted to know more about her.

I paced back and forth, trying to let the anger roll off my back. Unkindness and belittling someone was against every foundation I ever stood on. Lies that opposed my every belief were the key to my downfall.

The powers inside my veins no longer were calm but they felt like lightning. My body trembled with the roaring emotions. Breathing in and out, trying to keep my mind together. Part of me wanted to go to that stubborn man and gave him a piece of his own medicine.

"Please don't say anything, my queen. The king would have my head on a platter if he knew that I was talking with you." She began to eat the inside of her cheek, clearly distressed at the thought. Her eyes were searching for security. All you could see was fear within her eyes, and at that the anger slightly dimmed.

I exhaled, "Have you ever been in love, Mehra?"

I asked her again, avoiding that I had almost lost my temper.

No one in this kingdom knew that I had powers, that there was golden magic flowing inside my veins. If I didn't control my emotions, then I could kill others and myself. And I couldn't tell anyone my secret, no one was allowed to know because I was the very person they were trying to kill.

Uosulia has been enemies with Aales for thousands of generations. When kingdoms began in tents and prophecies were the only source of hope. I never really understood how our kingdom came to be but I always felt the history inside my bones.

My parents knew that when I became queen, people would try to attack me and kill me. So ever since I was a baby, I have been hidden away. No one outside my country knows what the queen of Uosulia looks like but I was always in danger, despite any precautions I took. Almost losing myself for a second, risked the chance of not just my life but an entire nation.

I loved too many people, I loved my country too much to do that to anyone. I already sold myself into a marriage to protect them as much as I could and if I needed to die in their place, I would. We were one, we were united.

"A while ago but he is now living with the saints now." A single tear fell down her cheek and all I wanted was to reach out and comfort her. I touched her shoulder to bring her a sense of comfort and allow me to make that sadness fade away faster.

"How did he die? If you are comfortable telling me?" I questioned but I didn't know if I was pushing her boundaries. The scar on her heart might be too new.

She shook her head and refused to answer the question, "I am sorry, my queen but it is too painful to remember. And you have no reason to hate the person who did the crime."

Her fingers went back to the fabric that flowed out in all directions. Her hands worked at the speed of light. They created magic and I wondered how long it took her to learn to do that. To create beautiful pieces with a piece of fabric and a needle. Powers didn't compare to the ability to create a masterpiece with little material.

"How do you do that?" My curiosity was getting the best of me today.

Between the both of us, I had the most tendency to talk to her. She reminded me constantly that I didn't need to know anything about her life or her personal ideas but I wanted them. It gave me a sense of normality, a friendship.

"Do what, my queen?" her hands kept working their magic.

It was like each time she helped me get ready made me feel more beautiful than the last. I had lost count how many gowns she had made me with her bare hands. Each was more beautiful than the last, each more special. This one was a deep purple with accents of gold. She told me that dark colors went well with my tanned skin.

"Call me by my first name please. How many times have we gone over this?" I smiled to tell her that it was okay to call me by my first name. That I wasn't going to let any harm come her way because of it. She wasn't the only one that wanted someone to call them by their chosen name, their given name.

All I wanted was to be called *Soraya,* not queen or anything else.

"How many times have I said that I don't want to die?"

With that we both burst out laughing. It wasn't funny, death wasn't something to be played with but it was the way we bickered with one another. We acted like we knew each other longer than we actually had, like we were sisters. When our laughter died down, I told her the reason I wanted to be called by my name.

"My parents gave me that name because it means star cluster. They told me that I was the brightest star in the night sky but they aren't here anymore. Now they dance among the stars."

I smiled at the thought of them looking down at me.

What did they think about me now?

Have I made them proud, did I put a smile on their face?

"Everyone calls me, my queen or my highness but never just my first name and I desire that more than anything. It gives me a sense of normality."

In my voice you could hear how much I desired that. To hear my name be said by someone who wasn't me. Because in a weird way, it feels like home.

"You aren't normal, you are queen after all." She laughed at her small remark but I didn't. I don't think anyone was going to ever see me for the way I wanted to but instead how society did.

When she read my face that it wasn't just a silly comment, Mehra took a breath in and continued talking. Her voice filled the tension filled silence, "Does the king not call you by your name in his chambers?"

Oh.

I forgot that everyone thought we were in love, that we married not just for law but for love. They thought we have laid with one another but he hasn't touched me once unless it was to remind me of my place. His intentions and emotions are clear and I didn't have anyone to tell me how Ephraim felt about me.

Love, I thought once again. Was I worthy to find it? Was I worthy to know what it feels like?

Those are questions that I don't know if I ever would find the answer to but my mother said that when powers and love mix together, that person would become unstoppable.

Love was the greatest weapon that one could heave, that one could hold. The only problem was that you weren't given love. No, you had to search and find it and then fight for it for the rest of time.

Soraya

Chapter 18

I sat on the floor with all the elders as we tried to find a
solution to the problem. I took value in each person's
opinion and their views because they could always see
something that I couldn't. They have been doing this for so
many years, it was as if they were born into this. Most of the
time, I would keep my thoughts to myself.

The last time I was in Uosulia we didn't have enough time
to talk about everything. I couldn't stay here for long because
then Ephraim would get suspicious. Even with the short
amount of time that I was gone, He still sent hundreds of
guards to look for me.

It was like I was a baby, under constant watch.

I picked up another tart that was freshly baked from the
celebration everyone had thrown in my honor. Anytime that I
would come to visit, they would throw a small celebration in
my honor.

I loved these people so much.

Alizeh had already lost all interest and was playing with the
children in the garden. Running after them, acting as if he was

the big bad guy. The kids screeched and yelling in excitement, their hot pink cheeks gave away how much they were loving it.

Every few minutes he would look at me and give me one of his blinding smiles. His pearly white teeth and dimples were on display. I smiled back at him every time and got distracted by the way he was playing with the children.

"So what do you think, my Queen?" someone asked me, pulling me away from my daydreams.

"I agree." I automatically responded, receiving chuckles and laughs from all over the table.

I smiled, happy I was able to make everyone laugh. When I refocused myself, the ancient ones explained the same thing again. For some reason, my mind couldn't comprehend anything being said. It was like my body was here and my mind and heart were miles away.

"Look I promise I tried to focus but I need a break. Let's have an hour break and re-group." were the only words I could manage to say.

I sighed and lifted myself up, my head exploding into a hundred pieces. I rubbed my temples, trying to process everything that was being explained to me.

Yet I was frustrated because I couldn't. I tried paying attention but my mind would daydream and be amongst the stars. These were the moments that I felt like I couldn't do it, like I wasn't meant to reign my people. It was a constant fear that if I didn't do my best then they were going to perish.

Ephraim could finally get what he always wanted if I simply gave up which I was so close to doing. There goes our history, my powers, our life. There goes my entire life, the reason for living. I walked back and forth on the sand near the water. The crashing sounds of the waves filling the silence.

What can I do?

What can I do?

"You're a wonderful queen and my best friend. Don't let the thoughts try to blind your true worth." Alizeh spoke behind me.

His paces were slow but in the blink of an eye he was standing in front of me. His crystal ocean blue eyes were glued to mine and in his gaze I found home. Not for the reasons one might think. I found home because he has been through thick and thin with me. He breathed the same air I did, born on the same soil, cut from the same cloth.

Our childhood wouldn't exist without one another. Words didn't have to be spoken so that we would understand what the other person was going through. And I didn't have to put up a mask with him, he could see right through me.

"I am getting tired of this." I mumbled through watery eyes and a clogged throat.

He placed either hand on my cheeks and drew my gaze back to him, "You're taking on everything by yourself. Let me help. It kills me to see you like this, Sor."

"I know but-" I placed my hand over my eyes to try to stop the tears, "I miss them. I feel so lost."

I couldn't say anything else, I just cried. My words were the hundreds of tears that rolled down my face. My silence was worth more than gold. And all he did was just hug me. He didn't repeat things over and over again but he stood there in silence.

I was glad to have him as a friend, as a brother. I wouldn't trade him for anything and I knew that he would always be in my corner, supporting me through whatever I went through. His support was what I needed. This brotherly love was what my soul desired.

With a final hug, he went away and left me alone to think. He knew that my brain needed space to think, to breathe. Before he left, he repeated once again that he would always be by my side and if he needed to kick anyone's butt, he would.

I was so lost in my thoughts that I hadn't heard Zion approaching behind me. My heart jumped a few beats as I yelped when I felt a hand touch my back.

"You're very jumpy today my dear, what is wrong?" His voice was soothing. It sounded like a thousand crashing waves.

Without waiting for me to respond, he gave me a hug and I melted in his embrace. I haven't hugged my father in several years but Zion had the same embrace. Where I could let myself cry and turn into a puddle. He knew me and what I was feeling before I knew myself.

I miss my father and mother more and more every day. It was like a piece of my heart went with them, but I am glad that Zion is here with me. I don't know where I would be now if he wasn't.

"Talk to me my child" he gently directed me to the nearest rock where we could sit together.

When I looked at his eyes, you could see all the wisdom and love in them. The wrinkles and grey hair don't make him look old in my eyes, it makes me admire him even more. I knew he would always be with me to teach me and guide me, he was always listening to me.

"I don't know what to do." I whimpered.

The tears were coming down on a steady beat. Emotions overwhelmed me most of the time but today they felt over-bearing.

"Many of us don't know what to do. I even feel lost sometimes."

He stared into the distance, admiring the peaceful sky.

I huffed, "You? I can't believe it."

He turned to me with a sad expression on his face. His hands folded on his lap, "My child, no one comes into this life knowing what to do. It's our first time living, our first time thinking-"

He took a breath in, "It took me very long to realize that I needed more help than I thought. I needed to learn more, listen more. Your father was my closest friend, a brother. He taught me, guided me, and took me in."

I could feel another wave of tears coming because of the way he talked with fondness. He never said anything against my father and even if he wasn't here anymore, Zion would always defend him with honor. Being his friend was his honor.

"How did it all begin?"

He smiled and a single tear rolled from his eye, "Our brotherhood? Well that my little one is a long long story."

Zion

Chapter 19
Flashback

———— ♦ ————

We ran away like there was no tomorrow. Like there wasn't a coronation to be planned, or treaties to be sorted. Played like we were teenage boys again and not in our twenties. And laughed like there was still hope in our lungs, and strength in our bones.

When we reached the end of the forest, it turned into a lovely beach. Where the ocean looked like a painting from the story books and the sand looked like mini crystals. Our laughs made our stomachs and cheeks hurt. Trying to breathe once again, our lungs gasping for air. I closed my eyes to soak in this moment and to remember the feeling of being free. Where there weren't countless problems being thrown onto my lap. Where Amauri and his parents weren't in a constant fight. The feeling of being with my friend, my brother once again. No eyes watching us or prohibiting our next action.

Amauri broke the silence and asked, "What do you think life will be like after I am crowned king?"

I sighed because deep down inside I knew what would happen. I knew that responsibility and kingdom would come first between the two of us but I didn't want that. I didn't want to let go of our friendship but in a way I had to. He was about to become king and his job was more important than anything else.

It was going to be more important than me.

"I don't know, my friend" I responded not wanting to break his heart with the truth I have come to peace with. I might be thinking too much into this. Maybe I always thought of the worst and it wasn't going to be how I imagined.

He smiled up at the bright blue sky. It almost looked fake from how perfect it was. There wasn't a single imperfection. I had to remind myself to be grateful for everything I was going through.

"I don't care how much power I am given or how many problems I need to solve but I need you in my life, my brother." Amauri spoke with such confidence and belief.

We looked at one another and spoke with our eyes. We knew what would initiate when he sat on that throne. That the power and all the magic that was within this land was going to be inside him. But I knew he wasn't going to get hot headed and prideful with all that power. Despite all that, I didn't want to get in his way. His parents already hated how close we were together, how much we cared for one another.

"But you do know we won't be able to be together as much as we used to. That our childhood is long behind us, entertainment will be forbidden." I needed him to be realistic.

He laughed as if I had said the funniest thing, "Zion, why are you always looking at the negative and not the positive. If that ever comes, our bond will become tighter and closer. I will never allow power or the kingdom to come before us."

He slapped my back in a brotherly way like has always done. Before I could respond, we were spotted by the banquet coordinator. He yelled at us to go back to practice. He said we weren't perfect and that there was much to do.

"Wanna race?" He asked, determination in his eyes. His feet were already grounded and ready to run away.

I grounded my feet as well and yelled, "Ready, set, go"

Every time we ran I would always out run him but this time I didn't want to. I ran a bit slower to process the roaring thoughts in my mind.

What if I do lose him?

What if I lose my best friend, my brother?

What will become of me, where will I go, who will I be?

I shoved those thoughts aside, not letting myself waste this moment. If I was going to lose him, I needed to soak in these last moments. Freedom and enjoyment had to be the only thing on my mind, and the problems could come later.

Yes, the problems come later if that's what you desire or it can come now. The way you plan your future is the way it will be.

Soraya

Chapter 20

When he finished telling me the story of how they were friends, how they grew together, and then how he watched my father die, all the tears had run dry. There was no strength inside my bones to cry anymore but my heart throbbed. It felt like someone had ripped a piece away and left it on the floor.

"What happened?" My voice trembled as I asked him the hard question that I was dying to know.

I didn't know if I wanted to know the rest of the story but I wanted to know more about him. I wanted to know how he dealt with that pain and ache. Maybe it was going to give me insight.

"I saw him die and then I saw you, the way life faded away from your beautiful face in an instant. I wanted to run and protect you. I wanted to hide you away but they had held me captive."

He was crying, which wasn't the first time I had seen him cry. It made me admire him all the more, he was true. He was wise and the way he talked, it overflowed with understanding.

"What should I do Zion? I don't know what to do anymore. I have married our enemy, that is trying to kill us as we speak. There is no one that I can trust and there are ears everywhere."

Was I over reacting?

Paranoid?

He took both my hands in his and looked at me deep into my eyes, "My child, I can't tell you what you should and shouldn't do. Only you can know the right path to take but I will say something-"

He paused for a moment and I knew that I might not like what he was going to say, "You have to stop coming to visit us. Sneaking away and disappearing for hours will become suspicious to the king. You might be putting us in more danger than you realize."

I hadn't thought about that and in a way it was proof to me that I wasn't ready to lead. Maybe I wasn't the queen everyone thought I was but despite what I thought, I took his words to heart.

With a nod, he gave my hands a little squeeze, "But I have no doubt you will make a good choice. You are like your mother and father. Selfless and brave."

We sat there a moment before someone came calling us to come back. My country needed my help and I hadn't figured out a solution yet. I married a man that was trying to kill me without knowing.

I sat on the floor looking for the nearest servant. Here they weren't servants that were treated poorly but they were treated like me. We were all treated equally and fairly.

"Could you please get me a cup of wine?" giving him the faintest smile that I could manage.

The young man began to turn around before I called out for him again.

"Instead of a cup, just bring the jar," I said with a weary smile. I rarely drank because I saw what it did to people and I opposed being like them. The times where I indulged more than a cup has scarred me forever.

Too many awkward experiences.

I was unpredictable under the influence of wine but I drank it when the time called for it. Yet now I felt like I was going to need it more than anything.

Hundreds and maybe even thousands of ideas were repeated multiple times. All the ideas were pointing to only one solution, one thing that I had to do. I didn't want to do it, I could do anything else except it.

Please don't make me do it.

"So what you are all saying is-" I began to speak, the voices hushed around me.

"I have to gain king Ephraim's affection and persuade him into falling in love with me. To then convince him not to kill our people. Am I hearing you all correctly? Please tell me I am not and I simply have to clean my ears."

No one responded, it was completely silent. You could even hear the leaves dancing in the breeze.

Zion looked at all the men before raising his voice, "My Queen, sadly that is what we are saying. So far that is the only possible solution we found that has a chance of working."

I covered my face and moaned, "Do you really think I would want to make such a wicked man fall in love with me?"

"Didn't you marry him because of us?" someone pointed out.

I slowly slid my hands away from my face and looked at Zion. He had a straight face but I knew he was reading my every emotion.

"I did, didn't I?"

He nodded, a small smile on his lips. I grunted because I

knew that this was our only hope. Not only did I have to persuade him not to kill my people. Not only did we both hate each other and kept each other at an arm's distance. Not only were thousands of lives on the line but my life was on the line.

What if I did persuade him to fall in love with me, what then? What would happen after that? I couldn't trust myself around him. The unsettling feeling of what if all this didn't work settled in my stomach.

Snap yourself out of it, Soraya.

You can't fall in love with him. He is darkness and death embodied in a person. You're light, life, and you have powers of life at your fingertips.

Dark and Light don't mix. Life and Death don't mix. So it is forbidden for the both of you to fall in love.

Make him fall in love, guard your heart and when everything is over with, leave.

It seemed to be easier said than done and I had a feeling that nothing was going to go like I planned.

Ephraim

Chapter 21

◆

"We didn't find their queen. We spent hours and hours-" the spies responded after weeks of no news.

I yelled and threw the closest object. My body began to tighten and I began to lose myself to darkness once again.

The darkness inside me had taken over and I was going to let it.

That magic inside my veins shot out and gripped both of the spies by the neck. Their faces were horrified. It was like they had seen the devil face to face. Their pale skin began to turn into purple, the life inside them began to leave. I don't think I even had to kill them, the fear inside them already did.

"Weeks are not enough. You are not to come back here until you find her."

I gripped onto them even tighter, "Then pray tell me, why would you show your worthless faces here if I told you that I am not to be disturbed unless you find something." I yelled at their uplifted faces.

They tried to nod but struggled. My grip tightened slightly

but when I let go it was a second to late. Their bodies dropped to the floor like rags.

I stopped and yelled to the nearest guard, "Clean the mess up and tell Mavros that I need him in my studies."

Before he walked away, I yelled at him "Bring me a few jugs of wine as well."

I stopped and before I arrived at my studies, I passed the one room that haunted me. The darkness only feared the thing that was locked away from any eyes.

The rose.

I hated that rose with such passion but I wouldn't get rid of it. I didn't know what would happen if I did. If I threw it away, would I die and would it be so bad if I did?

I slipped myself into the room and slowly proceeded the rose. When I bent to look at it at eye level, another petal had fallen. It was like it knew when i was near and liked to torture me.

But why does the petal fall? What is the reason?

I don't know why I bothered with it when I already knew my doomed fate. The darkness that consumed me would continue on until I became dust.

I sighed and walked away from my fated destiny but before I looked back, I took another glance. Even in the darkness the rose slightly shimmered and glowed.

"You seem to mock me without any words."

I am mocked and reminded of this dreaded curse by a rose. A blasted rose is the bane of my existence.

"Finally you arrived," I huffed like a beast.

Mavros smirked and continued to waltz into my private studies. No one came in here and left alive yet he was tolerable.

"You called for me and you said to be here soon, it's been thirty minutes."

He drew out his words to imply that I was making it more dramatic than it had to be. Mavros took a giant gulp of the wine before sitting down in front of me. His long legs extended in front of him as he leaned into the chair.

"What do you need from me?"

I rolled my eyes. Sometimes he acted serious but other times he acted like a boy. He knew that I didn't like to be messed around with.

"Pull yourself together" I hissed at him

With that he sat upright in his chair and looked at me with a serious gaze. His brain must be putting the pieces together and then he spoke up, "What happened? Did they find anything?"

I could tell that he was curious, hungry for new information,"No. They said they searched for hours and found no sight of their queen." I stood up, the chair scraping against the floor.

"What now? What did you tell them to do?" His gaze followed me.

"Oh, they are dead. I need new spies now that I thought about it." Their death didn't bring me much discomfort, there was too much blood on my hands to be bothered with that. I took a moment of silence to pull my thoughts together.

What if they were two steps ahead of us? Oh how I hated when that happened.

"What if they know that we are searching for her? Maybe they are hiding her from us?"

He rubbed his hands along his bearded jaw, "Better yet, what if they are hiding her in plain sight? Where we least expect it."

My eyes widened because I hadn't thought about that. I

froze mid step drink. That wasn't an idea which was impossible and it could be true.

Blast, I had already killed the spies before I could even figure out if they saw any other women. Any clues or hints that could lead me to find her.

I paced once again, back and forth as if it was going to help me think of an answer, "We need to find the queen or we will continue to have war for the rest of our lives."

"Yes but-" Mavros wanted to interrupt but I continued on, "We can't forget about Apiritah or they will take advantage of this moment."

I wonder why they have been so silent, I thought to myself.

Mavros simply nodded his head and continued to think in silence. When my plans didn't work at first made me want to burn it all.

I needed a plan that was going to get what I wanted without risking anything. Without risking my kingdom, wealth, or loved ones.

Wait, I have no one left.

Soraya

Chapter 22

S creams and terrors ripped me away from my slumber.
My eyes blinked several times as they adjusted to the
dark room, a dark and lonely void.

Maybe I was only dreaming.

While the screams were not my own, they felt like they
could have come from my own pounding chest. I leaned back
against the cold bed and stared into the suffocating darkness.
The weight on my shoulders seemed to grow heavier.

Despite knowing what was best for me, there was a
lingering ache in my heart from Ephraim's absence. He hadn't
called me in days and I wished that all I felt was relief.

Sighing, I lifted my hands into the air and admired the
miraculous powers that flowed through my veins. The golden
light lit the void. My heart ached knowing that there were
people who could benefit from it but I couldn't do anything.

How could I enjoy this life in this grand palace, keeping my
gift to myself, when all those townsmen were without food or
water? I was riddled with guilt for not thinking of a solution

yet. Somehow, I felt paralyzed and useless, which made me feel so small.

I waved my hand around to see the gold lights flicker and move, like brilliant orbs of starlight. While they were mesmerizing, no amount of watching their magnificent display caused me to fall back asleep.

I was exhausted and the enormous bed was as comfortable as they came, but it was far too cold and lonely to sleep. The darkness felt as though it were swallowing me whole, filling my mind with dread. While the fire was only a few feet away, its dying embers did nothing to warm the frigid room.

Just as I was beginning to drift off to sleep, ignoring the loneliness I felt, there was a knock at my door. Groaning, I turned in the bed, but the knocker continued relentlessly.

A small whisper filled the quiet space, "My queen, the king needs your assistance immediately." Whoever was speaking, spoke with urgency.

I wrapped a robe around myself and ran to the door, it swung open hastily. "What happened?"

Why should you care? Ephraim is trying to kill me without him knowing.

"I don't know my highness. He won't say. All he said was that he demanded your presence in his quarters."

The servant was much shorter than me yet he walked much faster than I did. As we were walking there, I tried to fix my hair and look presentable with the few brief minutes I had.

When we reached the quarters, I took a shaky breath in and flung the doors open. My knees wobbled as I stepped inside the pitch-black room, filled with swirling darkness so sense that I couldn't see anything. Blindly, I stumbled forward with my arms stretched outward to avoid bumping into anything.

With a soft whisper I called out to him. "My King?"

Nothing.

"My King?" I whispered slightly louder.

Where was he?

"Ephraim?" My voice slowly grew louder as I shouted out into the swirling darkness.

I continued to blindly search the room, hissing every time my foot hit something. With my eyes closed shut, I allowed my touch to be the guide I needed.

Wood, I thought as my hand brushed against the uneven grooved surface.

Brass, the rings on my finger slightly chimed at the soft impact.

A hard, breathing bare chest.

My throat went dry, and my body froze but my hands remained. They rose and fell with the movements of his heavy breaths.

"Who are you?" A dark mystic voice surrounded me.

It sounded nothing like Ephraim, yet I knew it was him somehow. Somewhere within the void, he spoke to me.

"It's me. Your queen, Soraya." Soraya." I answered, voice soft and low. The shadows lessened, seeming almost soothed by my presence. The darkness faded just enough for me to see his face, pale as a ghost. The color in his eyes was completely faded, replaced by two dark, haunted voids.

Underneath them were shadowy circles, making him look like he had been through hell and back.

"What are you doing here?" His voice was weak, filled with exhaustion. Ephraim's body swayed side to side making it clear how much he drank yesterday. Tendrils of darkness burst through his chest, swirling around him in angry wisps that consumed us.

My lungs trembled as I drew in a breath. Against my better judgment, I looked up into his eyes and placed my shaking hands back on his chest.

I shouldn't be doing this.

Using my powers outside of my kingdom was forbidden, but I knew those rules needed to be broken for Ephraim. Desperately, I needed to see him whole again, even if it meant breaking myself to make it happen.

"You need me." My voice broke as tears filled my eyes. I couldn't stand to watch him suffer, and I knew that if I did nothing, I could never live with myself. My heart exploded into pieces at the sight of someone suffering.

Ephraim continued swaying, "You should leave, Soraya. It was selfish of me to call on you when I can't even think right. You shouldn't see your king like this."

I smiled slightly at the comment, "But shouldn't that be a reason for me to stay? I want to see you well. Let me expel your darkness and let you rest."

He huffed. He didn't laugh but was clearly amused by my offer. "You know," he paused, almost grinning. "I have tried all the sorcery this land has to offer, yet nothing has expelled the darkness that lies within me. But-"

"But what?" I urged, hoping to take his mind off the shadows that plagued him.

His eyes lowered to my lips as he pondered. "There has only been one night that I have actually slept in peace."

That night.

Somehow, I immediately knew which one he was talking about, unable to forget that night myself. My cheeks heated at the memory.

"We are enemies, and I know that. I am aware that you hate me, and for whatever reason, I am supposed to hate you too. But could you..." Ephraim's eyes remained on my mouth as he frowned. You could tell by the lines on his forehead that he desperately tried to remember what he was going to say. I nodded, encouraging him to continue.

"Could you do it once more? Just one more night, would you keep my monsters away? Please." My heart shattered hearing the desperation in his voice as he begged me.

"But," I blinked, looking down at my hands. "I thought I was just for show, and that I should keep my mouth shut." I whispered to him. I repeated the exact words many people told me in this palace. The words that made me feel belittled and insignificant.

Ephraim grumbled and cursed under his breath. "I am a fool under this influence. Forgive anything I have said and done when I was not myself."

Shocked, I stood there in utter silence. I let my hands fall to my sides, paralyzed by his words. The darkness grew thick and heavy once again. I shuttered hearing Ephraim hiss and moan. His pained face scrunched and his eyes closed, concentrated to avoid an outburst. My eyes traced the hard lines of his clenched jaw, as he fought something that must have been unbearable. Ephraim's hands gripped his chest, his heart pounded erratically.

My eyes looked for an answer, confused about what was hurting him so severely. "What's wrong?"

Other than the pale skin and the dark circles underneath his eyes, there wasn't anything else wrong. Although, Ephraim's next words were unexpected.

His breath was rapid and heavy, "A blasted curse."

Ephraim

Chapter 23

—◆—

I don't know what was within Soraya, or what she possessed to be so gentle but it constrained me. The moment she laid her shaky soft hands on my cold bare chest, the darkness slipped away. Even if it wasn't complete freedom, for a moment I felt free. Where I didn't have to deal with this horrifying curse that tormented me day and night. It left me a prisoner under shackles and I felt useless in it all.

The moment she took her hands off, the darkness intensified even more. The pain and the weariness I was feeling made me almost pass out in her arms.

"I know I said that I didn't want to see you for a few days but please stay with me for the night."

She didn't respond. I couldn't tell if she was still in the room or had run away. Maybe she ran away to yell until the ends of the earth about the monster she married. The beast that lived within these palace walls.

What took me by surprise was that she didn't do any of that. She didn't run away or curse me out. She didn't call me the devil or a beast. All she did was, place her hands in mine and look at me.

I couldn't see her caramel brown eyes and the constant sparkle in them. The way her face seemed to be shaped and carved by something supernatural. The way her beautiful wavy long hair descended like a waterfall and left her uncomparable. I wanted to see her for who she was more than anything at that moment.

"Let me lead you into bed, your highness" She led me to my bed and as we walked with one another, I could almost see a restful night. Each second as she held my hand, the darkness was one more mile away.

She kept one of her hands in mine and used the other one to prepare the bed. Taking the endless pillows off the large bed. Without letting go of her, I slipped myself into bed.

"What about you?" I mumbled.

"Uhh, I will sit on the floor until you fall asleep." she said as if it was the only way.

I shook my head, "Lay beside me. I promise I won't hurt you."

When I said that, I thought she had slipped herself away but in a few seconds I felt the bed move. Without thinking, I turned my body to face her and wrapped my arm around her waist.

She let out a quiet *"Oh"* before her body slightly relaxed against me.

I shifted slightly so her head was right beside mine. So I could be lulled to sleep by her presence and the smell of her ocean hair. It smelt like a day by the ocean. Where you would take a deep breath every time a breeze would pass. That somehow brought me peace like nothing else. And each day she would wear different essential oils but she smelled perfect with each one of them.

Never in my life have I felt such comfort in a person like I did with her but she seemed to bring a side of me that I couldn't. Maybe I didn't just marry her because of her beauty. Maybe I married her because deep within me, I knew she was different somehow.

"Promise me that you won't leave me in the middle of the night" I mumbled against her ear.

She slightly shivered underneath my breath, "Go to sleep my king."

"Promise me, please. I know I don't deserve it but that's all I ask. I just want to sleep one more night."

I could feel her smiling as she moved closer to me. Her hair was now braided to the side. Her clothes were pure silk, amazing against my hot skin. Her fingers trailed up and down my hand, the skin underneath her fingertips felt alive, "I promise."

Those words were the only ones that I needed to fall into deep slumber. Knowing that with her, demons and darkness would be hundreds of miles away.

The night passed as if it was nothing. No fears, no darkness, or death lingering around me. I woke up with the sunshine of the late morning sun and for the first time in years I smiled. Not because I was forced to or because I needed to but because I just did.

I looked at my queen who was lying down beside me. Her breaths were even and quiet. Her body was completely still so it gave me a moment to look at her. Admire every aspect of her.

Without tormenting thoughts night and day, I could finally see her. Her beautiful cheeks that always turned red when she was nervous, mad, or happy. The long dark eyelashes that framed my favorite pair of eyes. Her beautiful full rosy lips. They were in a slight pout and I wondered for a second what was the one thing in this world that could make her upset.

What was one thing that could get her irritated? What was something that could make her happy or fall in love? I have never thought about any of this or asked her.

She shifted slightly in bed and scooted even closer to me. Her left arm was across my chest and her right hand underneath her head.

How could someone look so peaceful even as they sleep?

"What lies within you that makes even the darkness within me flee?" I whispered out loud to myself.

I knew she wouldn't answer but it was something that I would keep asking myself over and over until I found a response.

She seemed to be the remedy that I needed. The thing that my soul ached to have. Peace, love, freedom. Yet when I was under the influence I couldn't think for myself. I couldn't appreciate what she did or who she was.

She shifted once again, before her big brown eyes opened and connected with mine.

There are those beautiful eyes.

She cleared her throat and blinked several times. When she noticed that her hands were on my bare chest she quickly retreated them. She swiftly scooted away from me, giving space between us.

"Thank you" I whisper to her

Those words, *Thank you.* They seemed to be the hardest words that could ever come out of my lips but this moment I felt free to say it. I felt liberty to say it like it wasn't a prohibited word. So I took advantage of this moment and said everything and anything before it's too late.

"What did you say?" She pulled her head back to look at me. She stared at me with unbelief in her eyes like she couldn't believe what I just said.

"Thank you. Am I such a beast that you think I am not capable of saying those two small words?" I asked her but chuckled at the end so she wouldn't realize that it actually was hard. It seemed to be a foreign language sometimes.

She shook her head and stood up, the bed instantly feeling cold. I sat upright as my eyes followed where she went.

"What is wrong?" I asked her, panicking that I said the wrong thing.

I could feel the darkness lurking around the corner. Waiting for the right moment to sink its claws back into me.

"Nothing." she responded as she began to brush her long beautiful hair.

I stood up and walked over to where she stood. The warmth from the silk sheets against my skin was replaced by the cool breeze. I adored how my private chambers had an open balcony. Where I could see the city come alive and watch everything that I have built.

When I reached her, I stood behind her. Making sure there was space between the both of us. I couldn't trust myself around this woman yet something in me always wanted to be close to her.

Our heights were completely different. She barely reached my chest as I seemed to tower over her.

"What are you going to do today?" I pressed, the silence was killing me.

She huffed, "Sit and be pretty."

Those words seemed to be a knife inside my soul because they were the same words my father would say to my mother. Now, it's the same thing I have told her.

She continued to brush her hair in long strokes. Her hand

goes up and down with the golden brush. The waves in her hair started to unite and become tamed.

"Can I braid your hair?" I asked as I looked at her hair.

It would be an excuse to touch her. To have my hands between her hair. So I could have an excuse to be near her.

Her eyes widened just like it had a few minutes ago. "Do you know how to?"

I chuckled, "Would I offer if I didn't know how too?"

She smiled nervously, "I guess not."

I could see how nervous she was for me to touch her hair and I couldn't blame her for that. I never was the most caring and loving person. It was a constant battle field in my mind, something that I had no control over.

I am a monster, that has become my constant reminder.

Then my mind flooded back to one of the first moments that I met Soraya.

My butt started to hurt sitting on this throne for so long. The grapes and bread that were being offered constantly had gotten on my nerves. Chatters and giggles of the ladies were simply fueling the fire.

The sore temples on my face had indents from constantly rubbing them. I don't know how many hours had passed or how long I had been here waiting but I was getting tired of it.

It's been a year since these ladies have been living on the palace grounds and weeks since I have been needing to make a decision. I haven't found one because I didn't want one. And if I was going to be forced to marry, then it at least had to be someone who stood out to me.

Another group flooded into the throne room, whispers between each of them. Most of the women were dressed in their best clothing. Their hair was pinned up and their dresses showed all the blends of culture.

My eyes drifted from one to another. Everyone seemed identical to each other. No one had caught my attention until they landed on her.

Her.

Her.

Her.

I don't know what it was about her caramel colored eyes that stood out to me. Her lack of extravagant clothing or the way even from a distance I could see she had the most simple sandals. The way the head covering was covering most of her face and only her eyes were visible.

Nothing about her screamed, *"I am here."* or *"Notice me! I want to marry you for your money and power."*

And something about her seemed recognizable like I met her somewhere. The way she held herself and the way her eyes shined seemed familiar.

With my eyes still glued on her beautiful eyes, I stood up and walked in her direction. She seemed to be a magnet that lured me closer to her. Even the death inside my bones and the lifelessness inside my bones was lured by her.

Then I was in front of her, barely any space between us. I could smell the fragrance on her soft skin. The way she breathed, nice and slow. The way her eyes were glued to mine and they never broke once. I could tell she wasn't similar to the rest because she wasn't gasping, giggling or acting differently because of me.

"What is your name?" I asked her.

Her eyes crinkled in the corner, "My name is Soraya, my king."

I hummed at the sound of her name. Even her name was beautiful and sweet.

I took a step back and looked at her overall. She was beautiful and would look perfect by my side. The people would love her and she would hopefully settle the constant bickering in the people.

I turned around and looked at Mavros, who was standing beside the throne. He looked at me, questioning if she was the one. With a single nod, he understood and began clearing all the other ladies. The gushes and giggles were replaced by bickering and complaining.

When all the ladies had left and I was alone with her, I turned to look at her. She was still quiet, not a single word had slipped from her lips. Her hands were hidden behind her back as she rocked on both her feet.

"Why do you want to marry me?"

I could already guess her response, *Money? Fame? Power? Riches? Vanity?*

"Who said I wanted to marry you?"

Glued in place, I tried to take in her response. No one had ever talked to me that way, and responded to me so abruptly. With that, I slowly turned around on my heel and looked at her. She stood with poise, no regret at what she had said.

"If you didn't want to marry me then why bother coming here?" I wasn't offended but rather intrigued why she answered the way she did.

She sighed like I had asked the stupidest question, "It is the honor of God to conceal a matter and the honor of kings to search it out."

My mind was long gone as my fingers mindlessly intertwined themselves in her hair. Twisting and turning strands into a complex braid. I couldn't help but think about the feeling of her hair between my fingers.

Every time I moved her hair, a breeze of myrrh and clove would take over my senses. When I finished her braid, I tied it off with a flower. My mother taught me. She let me braid her hair on nights where she didn't have the strength to or when she was physically in pain to even lift up her arms. I took care of her those days and braiding Soraya's hair, even if it was just for a moment, reminded me of my mother. The way her hair seemed to be like silk in my hands. The way her hair smells like freshly picked flowers.

"How did you learn to braid, my Highness?" She inquired.

I smiled, "My mother. Please don't call me my highness or king. Right now, just call me Ephraim."

Her lips weren't smiling anymore, now they were in a straight line, "And what do I call you when you're in a fit of rage?"

Before I could answer, before a word could slip out of my mouth, urgent knocking came from the door. A feeling to kill the man who decided it was a good idea to knock right now.

Why do people need me in moments that I don't want to be needed?

"Come in" my voice demonstrated how annoyed and frustrated I was with the interruption.

Soraya's eyebrow raised just to prove my point and I took that as something to keep me in check for whatever was about to happen.

A guard entered and when he looked at both of us, still in our sleepwear he froze. I had forgotten that I had no shirt on and Soraya was in her silk gown. When I looked at her and her slightly revealing dress, I took a step forward to block her from his view.

His face fell flat as he looked to the floor, "I am sorry my King and Queen, forgive me but this is an urgent matter."

I hissed at him, "Did someone die?"

He shook his head in response, "We have news."

The guard looked up and locked eyes with me. In a moment, without another word having to be said, I already knew what he was talking about. I waved him off, saying that I would be there in a few minutes and turned to Soraya who was curious about the quick exchange.

"What do you think it was?" Her eyes darted from the double doors that the guard walked through.

"Nothing that concerns you" I tried to say, kind and soft but it came off harsher than intended. She looked at me with sadness in her eyes and with a nod she went off to the bathroom. The brass doors creaked behind her, leaving me completely alone.

I sighed knowing that it came off harsher than I had intended to. The weight on my shoulders started to come back. An ached soul replaced the peaceful one that I had just moments ago.

I growled, unable to control myself and stormed off. I didn't want to be like this in a way I felt like I had no choice. I had to be this dark beast that didn't care about anyone or anything. The bloody curse did this to me and I hated it, it turned me worse than the day before. My mind felt like one of a puppet, controlled by someone.

When I reached the throne room, there were few men there. Not the whole court had been assembled which could mean one of the two things. Either it was very revealing news that had to be spoken to only a few trusted people or it was bad that only a handful of people had the bravery to tell me. I had a feeling it was the second.

I took steps further into the room, looking each one in the

eye. When I could finally wake up on my own time, they were always ready to bother me.

It looks as if someone has died here. Was I walking into a funeral? I must be walking into their funeral.

"We must set a date." Mavros spoke to me with such demand. His voice had a small note of annoyance and anger. Something seemed to have tipped him off the edge because he was not one to get annoyed or angered.

"Remember your place." I had to remind him once in a while that who gave orders was me.

Another man spoke up but I didn't know his name because I never bothered to learn anyone's name.

"They will revolt and attack if we do not do something about it. Immediate war is the fastest solution."

Mavros composed himself and spoke up again, "Sorry my king but something has come up. The Usoulians will attack if we do not do something."

I crossed my arms as they continued to speak of things that I already knew everything about.

What they couldn't seem to figure out was the solution to all these problems.

"Apiritath has been quiet. They are no longer sending threats or declaring upcoming war." someone mumbled out loud

I turned to the voice that said it and it was a young boy. No older than twenty five years old. When he noticed that everyone was looking at him, his face reddened. He looked embarrassed and frightened.

"What did you say?" I confronted him.

He struggled to find his words for several moments, "My king, please forgive me if I said anything out of line."

I waved him off. "Nevermind that, what did you say?"

He swallowed, "One of your worst enemies is no longer sending threats, warnings, or anything. They have become completely silent. What frightens me is the reason that they are silent."

By the time he finished speaking, he was trembling violently.

"Finally, someone gives me something that isn't the same bloody thing over and over again."

I turned back again to the boy and asked him, "What is your name?"

He was taken aback, "My name?"

I sighed because he was making me repeat myself, "Yes, your name?"

He smiled, "My name is Azrael."

I nodded, "Well Azrael, since you are the only one who seemed to find out about that then you will be in charge of finding the reason."

He nodded and scurried away before body slamming into a guard. A moan left from both of them. The guard nodded at Azrael and walked closer to me. He had a silver platter on his plate with a single piece of paper on it. It was folded into a small rectangle with a stamp on it. His hand extended with the silver platter as I reached for the note.

I slowly cracked open the wax seal and at that moment my stomach turned ice cold. I couldn't figure out who it was, the stamp on the seal was undetectable to me.

The blood in my veins froze and my body stilled. All the noise in the room went quiet as I read the words on the note. Words that haunted me for the rest of the day.

To the wicked king Ephraim,

I know something you don't know.

Soraya

Chapter 24

I had been walking around the palace for a few minutes. There was nothing to do and I was bored out of my mind. The walls seemed to talk to me and the silence was torture. I enjoyed the silence from time to time but today I just wanted somebody to confide in.

This palace was bigger than I thought. The halls seemed to be never ending. By the time I reached the end of a long hall, I took several moments to look to my right and left. The right side seemed to lead back to the center of the palace yet something to the left lured me. It was dark and there was barely any light but I was curious to figure out what was there. My feet led me in that direction and before I knew it, my hand was extending to open a silver door knob.

Something inside me told me not to open it and that I would regret it but I didn't listen to that voice. When the door swung open, it was pure darkness. There was nothing and it seemed like no one had been in here for years.

Spider webs were in every corner and crevice. A layer of dust covered everything like snow. Drapes that covered furniture that once was on display. Windows covered with filth and broken chandelier lights.

Even if it disgusted me, I kept walking deeper and deeper into the room. My heart seemed to have jumped miles when the door closed behind me. The flooring underneath my feet would creak every time I took one step.

When I thought I hit a dead end, I saw something slightly shimmer. I couldn't tell what it was but it was luring me closer. It was like a siren's song that lured me closer by its beauty. When my eyes finally saw what it was, my mind was left with so many questions.

A red rose.

The dying red rose was placed inside a glass vase as if it was on display for all to see. Yet the rose was tucked away in a dark room from any lurking eyes.

The beauty of the rose was gone, there wasn't any blooming color or life. It looked like the color of dried blood or wine. And I couldn't but help wonder how long this rose has been here and why it was a singular rose.

The glass vase that encased the flower was delicate and fragile. I could tell that it was made specially for this rose. The way the gold swirled around, framing the rose. The small jewels that were carefully placed on the vase, it all seemed to have been carefully hand made. So I wondered, *if it were made for someone then why would they hide it here? Why would one hide a dying rose if they weren't going to care for it?*

My mind tried to think of any possible answers but none would seem right. The only thing that I could think of was to touch it. Even though every part of me said not too, I ignored it.

I slowly reached out my hand and placed it on the cold glass. A cold electrifying shock went through my arms and body.

I tried to bring the rose back to life but it refused. Then I tried again and it refused once more.

"What?" I whispered into the void.

Why won't this single flower accept my powers?

I tried one more time, focusing my strength but was rejected. It seemed to be straight out of a fantasy, the golden swirls and jewels began to move around. It was slowly changing and after a bit, I noticed it was changing into words.

To have change, one must want it.

I took a step back, a small gasp leaving my lips. The message appeared out of nowhere, which made me wonder a thousand more questions. And right when I finished reading, as if it knew, it slowly started shifting back to how it was before.

I took slow steps back, never letting my eyes leave the rose. For *the first time in my life, I wasn't able to heal something.*

When I reached the door, before my hand touched the door knob, I heard a voice. My body went immobile and my breath still. There wasn't just one voice but two. Whoever it was, they were speaking in hushed tones and I knew deep down inside of my heart, I wasn't supposed to be here right now. If they found out I was here, I didn't know what would happen to me.

"Tonight." one of the voices said. He seemed to already be determined and settled.

The other one responded shortly after, "But what plan?"

The first man cursed out loud, "You fool, tonight we kill the king."

I gasped, my hand flew to cover my mouth and both of those voices went quiet for a moment.

Did they hear me?

"What is your plan?" one of the voices started to speak again.

Even from a distance, I could feel the anger that radiated

through him. As if he wanted revenge or payback for something. As I stood in the darkness, hearing every word they spoke, my heart pounded louder and faster.

"Tonight when he drinks and eats his corrupted heart away. We simply change his drink for another. Something that will get rid of that wicked man."

They both laughed and walked away. The voices of those men started to sound more distant which gave me reassurance that I could move again.

Someone is trying to kill my husband.

For a moment I didn't know which I was more stunned by. The dying rose in the middle of a dark room, two guards who admitted to a plan of murder, or for the simple fact that I called Ephraim my *husband.*

My heart settled a bit and my breath went back to normal, so I took that as a sign to leave this room. Yet once I left the room and remembered that I was lost, the overwhelming feelings began to overpower everything else.

The halls were starting to blend with one another, I didn't know where I was. I felt that I had been here before. Yet I didn't know why. My body began shaking violently from the lack of oxygen in my lungs.

"I need to find him." I convinced myself.

I kept running, looking for anyone to help me but I was alone. I might have been running circles and not even leaving where I once was. My legs seemed to be throbbing from the amount I ran.

"Help" I yelled into the empty halls, as if someone would hear me.

Then I remembered that there wasn't anything in my stomach which was why I felt like I was going to faint. My eyes started to blur everything. Surprised I hadn't ran into anything, I kept moving, seeing if there was a way out.

What was happening?

Right before the darkness overtook my vision, and before my head would encounter the floor, a pair of arms caught me. My vision went black and everything was dark but I knew who had caught me.

I knew those pairs of arms that had saved me. A pair of arms I *didn't* want to be touched by, but now? Now I didn't know what was happening to me. The lines were no longer crisp, everything grey. My feelings for the person who held me were changing.

When my consciousness finally gave in, I fainted into his arms as he yelled for help.

Ephraim

Chapter 25

✦

She looked lifeless in my hands. The way her head bobbled back and forth as I rushed her to our room. Her arms swinging back and forth. Her chest slowly rose and fell, barely any air flowing to her lungs.

"Soraya, stay with me," I whispered to her as I ran down the halls.

I gripped onto her a bit tighter like I could protect her. Somehow I felt like I was the reason she was in this state. When I reached our room, I burst open the door with my foot and rushed to the bed. Her small body slipped onto the bed as if she was a feather. The weight and warmth leaving my arms.

I rushed back to the opened brass door and yelled to the nearest servant to grab water and food. I quickly rushed back to her, whispering multiple times to awaken her.

Nothing. I felt as if the past was repeating itself again.

I feel hopeless, I reflected to myself.

She had the power to calm the raging storm inside of me. To make the darkness flee and death fear her. But I couldn't do any of that in return.

195

I couldn't heal her. I couldn't make the pain inside her go away or the darkness around her disappear. She laid in front of me, hanging onto her life as I just looked at her.

When the servants rushed in, my heart seemed to have jumped out of my chest. Their footsteps sounded like a herd of elephants.

My hands gripped onto the cup like it was the only thing to ground me.

"Should I call for a doctor?" One of the servants asked. Her eyes were big and round, glistened with tears.

"No just leave us be" I commanded, my eyes glued to Soraya's still body.

She nodded and without hesitation left the room. I brushed away the loose strands that were covering her face.

My mind replayed the moment I saw her after she yelled out. The way she kept spinning around, looking for somewhere to go. And as if time slowed, her body slowly started falling to the ground and without thinking I ran. I ran with all the strength inside my bones. Right before she hit the floor, my arms slipped around her. The way the color of her skin had become a white color. Like she has seen a ghost or the devil face to face.

I walked back and forth in the room, pacing because I didn't know what to do. My mind couldn't think of anything to get her to wake up or cause any of this.

Whenever I heard any noise my eyes would go straight to her. I didn't know why it brought me so much panic to see her in this state.

What was she doing to me?

She was doing something deeper to me than I thought. Was she breaking down my walls? Was she luring me into a trap? I didn't know.

The only thing I knew was that seeing her like this did

things to me. Something inside me ached because part of me knew I couldn't live without her. She was consuming me body, mind, and soul in ways I couldn't comprehend.

Hours had passed and the day was almost gone. The sun had begun to set, the room illuminated with bright colors. My stomach was turning with hunger but I refused to eat or drink.

How could I?

How could I go and enjoy pleasures when I am watching *my wife* at the edge of life and death.

She has made you weak, an inner voice spoke.

Never did I think this was going to happen to me. Where I was going to care about someone and have my own feelings again.

Mavros walked in without knocking but there was no strength in my bones to yell at him, "Any news on the Queen?"

He asked with concern, his eyes were focused on her before they met mine. His expression changed slightly as he looked deep into my eyes.

"Sir, you look worn out. Go eat something and then return to the Queen."

I shook my head. "I will not leave this room until she is well again."

He sighed, "Well then, I will ask the servants to bring food for you."

"And the queen." I added.

He opened his mouth several times in protest but ended up saying nothing and walking away.

The chair I was seated in grew uncomfortable. Leaving me to get up several times just to walk around the room.

I dragged my body around to the bed, unable to fight the

sleep anymore. As I shifted myself in the bed, Soraya's body slid a bit closer to me. My arm underneath her head as I brushed the hair away from her face once again. Hours ago she was white as snow but it seemed like the color was slowly coming back.

"Wake up, my Jewel." I whispered into the abyss.

My body instantly froze and my eyes went wide.

My Jewel.

I had just called her my jewel without any hesitation. The nickname that fit her so perfectly just slipped out of my mouth. It fit her so well. Soraya was as rare as a jewel. And the only difference was that she was more beautiful.

How could she not be a Jewel?

It has been quite a while since our wedding. I bickered and complained about her uncontrollable mouth. Yet was I so blind to see the kindness that was within her?

Was I so stubborn to see the way she cared for others? The way she asked the servants' names and addressed them like normal people?

My mouth went dry and a sense of blame fell on my shoulders. I looked up at the ceiling for a moment. Having to take a break from thinking about her because she was consuming every part of me slowly.

I admired the ceiling, never in my life have I taken a moment to look at the architecture. The way the crimson color swirled with the gold. It seemed to shine in the sunlight. The ceiling wasn't straight, it curved inward then outward to connect with the walls.

"I have always thought it was spectacular." a voice mumbled at my side.

I whipped my head around to look at her. Soraya's eyes were still gently closed but her face was no longer colorless. Her cheeks were the perfect color of pink.

She was filled with life again.

I didn't respond because all I wanted to do was look at her. Her eyes slowly opened, allowing me to see her beautiful brown eyes. She batted her eyelashes several times before looking at me. And this wasn't like the first time she was with me. The first time she scurried away from my embrace, this time she stayed and looked at me.I don't know what she thought when she looked at me but I knew what I saw.

I saw a priceless Jewel.

My Jewel.

My wife.

"What happened?" Her eyelids drooped slightly. By the way I saw it, she couldn't remember what had happened.

I shook my head, "Nothing for you to worry about. Get some rest before dinner arrives."

Then as if what I said activated something inside her, her eyes shot wide open.

She opened and closed her eyes several times. "Have you eaten something or drank anything while I was asleep?"

My eyebrows knit together, *what caused her to ask this?* She had just woken up and was worried about if I was fed? I didn't know much about other people's feelings.

"No, why?" I replied softly, not allowing myself to get worked up for no reason.

She mumbled a quick response, not fully answering my question. Her hands covered my chest for a second before she scurried to try to get out of my grasp.

I gripped onto her waist and pulled her back to me. Allowing her weight to shift back onto me. She turned her head around and a small *"Oh"* left her lips.

I was starting to like catching her by surprise.

"Tell me what's got you in such a panic, my dear."

Soraya froze for several moments, *my dear* escaped my lips.

Never have I been able to say words like that before, kind words.

She shook her head violently. "You'll kill me if I tell you."

That was when my heart broke into a million more pieces.

That's what she thought of me, a monster. A killer.

When I felt safe with her, she was scared to be with me. When I loved her touch, mine repulsed her. I slowly let go of her, not wanting to force her to be near me. Yet she still stayed close, maybe I was overthinking or hoping she felt the same tension between us.

I shook those thoughts away. "I would never touch you if you don't want me to-"

When I was about to remove my hands, she placed her hands on my arms and gave me a look.

I want you to hold me. Soraya's eyes gave me the answer that I needed to know. It gave me permission to hold onto her a bit tighter and closer to me. Her small hands gently touched my chest.

"Tell me, my Queen. Let me kill what haunts you."

She shook slightly, my grip slightly tightened as if I could protect her from anything and everything.

"I overheard some of your men-"

My body already tensed at those words. I urged her to finish the sentence before she lost all courage.

"Two men were planning to kill you tonight." Her voice trembled with those final words. It was like it took all the strength inside her. She shoved her head against my shoulder, "I didn't want to tell you because I knew you would get angry but I don't want you to die."

She doesn't want me to die.

She doesn't want ME to die.

SHE doesn't want ME to die.

Those were the only words that I needed to keep my head

and feelings at bay. Her honesty was the only thing I needed at that moment.

I used my hand to bring her gaze back to mine and look deeply into hers, "Thank you for telling me. No one will touch you or harm you, they would have to get through me first."

I wanted to assure her that she was safe with me. That no matter what, even despite how cruel I was, her safety mattered to me. It might not matter to the darkness or demons but to me she did.

I sat straight and pulled her up to sit in the same position. The golden tray that had our dinner was right beside us.

"Did they say what they were going to do or use? Position?" I asked, searching for something weird on the platter. Nothing looked out of the ordinary.

"They said they were going to poison your wine. Their words were that you tend to lose yourself with wine and you wouldn't notice anything."

When you think you can trust your own men. This is why I trust no one, I couldn't or it would lead to my grave.

If those men had thought through this plan well enough, there wouldn't be anything untouched.

"Then you aren't to touch the wine. Eat this."

I ripped a piece of the bread and dipped it in the date jam. Before I handed it to her, I took a bite from the bread.

I looked at her as I chewed the food. Her eyes focused on my lips. Soraya's facial expressions went from worried to wanting. Her gaze looked at me like she wanted me, a taste of me. Even if it was just for a single moment, it filled me with a feeling I couldn't express. And I was beginning to convince myself that I would be a fool if I didn't want the same thing.

I extended it to her after taking a longer than needed bite.

This felt different, there was something different between us now.

We have been married for so long but we have never kissed, we have never had these moments before. In a way it was different and I want to know what it was. Whatever power she had over the true me was worth more than anything I had.

Her eyes softened as she opened her mouth to eat the bread. Those big beautiful eyes focused on me. Once it hit her tongue, she moaned at the sweetness of the jam but my eyes had fallen to rosy full lips.

I couldn't take them off her, I was consumed in that moment.

"Are you going to eat?" She asked as she cleaned her lips with the tips of her fingers.

I don't know if I was hungry anymore. Just looking at Soraya go back to herself was enough.

Maybe I never was hungry. Maybe all I wanted was her and I never knew it.

Maybe all I needed was to find something worth more than getting drunk for. Worth more than getting angry at. Had more value than anything money could buy.

Hope? What is this feeling?

Even the wickedness inside me didn't stand a chance against her. Even my doubt seemed to vanish before her presence.

"What are you looking at?" her cheeks flushed bright pink.

I grinned, brushing a stray hair from her face, "Nothing." I whispered, looking at what might be my saving grace.

I was looking at my everything.

Soraya

Chapter 26

When I told Ephraim that someone was trying to kill him, I expected him to go crazy. To throw anything and everything in his sight but he didn't, he just looked at me. His breaths were evenly paced, showing he was at peace or was trying to be.

We might have lost track of time but I took advantage of it. We had barely exchanged any words, our gazes speaking multitudes. The moment he took a bite of my bread it was like a cage of butterflies were let loose.

I now realized a fraction of what he went through. Maybe I didn't know what he thought or his reasons but he wasn't the monster I once thought he was.

When I looked deep into his dark eyes, I realized that there were stories within them. He held me in his arms and fed me. Ephraim didn't allow me to eat anything unless he checked it first. And barely any words left his mouth which surprised me even more.

I kept talking and talking and not a single moment did he

ask me to stop. He either liked or tolerated my voice but I couldn't read anything on his face.

As I talked, his finger tips would brush against my skin, "Soraya."

I looked back at him, "Yes?"

His face focused and determined, "Will you have dinner with me?"

I froze and looked at him with curious eyes, "Why do you want to have dinner with me?"

He chuckled gently, "Well we are queen and king, I think I am in the right to request that."

I shook my head because that wasn't the answer that I wanted. "But do you want to or is it just out of pity?"

Now it was his turn to be wordless. He focused on something behind me while he collected his thoughts.

"I wanted to have dinner with my Queen. Not because anyone asked or because I have to. I want to" he answered sincerely.

That was the first time I ever heard him wanting to have dinner with me. My heart melted because I knew it was the true Ephraim talking to me. It wasn't the darkness, the demons or the torment but it was just Ephraim.

"Of course my king."

He took my hand and gave it a gentle squeeze before getting up, "Not my king, just Ephraim."

When Ephraim said he wanted to have dinner, I thought it was going to be in a few weeks. My mind thought he would mark a day but before he left, he said to be ready by the sunset.

Maids have been pouring oils on my skin and preparing me for dinner. They chattered how exciting this was and they had to do an amazing job. While they giggled and talked, my stomach wanted to explode and my body slightly shook from how nervous I was.

Mehra giggled, "Stay still, my queen."

I looked at her through the mirror and smiled. "I am just so nervous."

I don't know if there was another word for how nervous I felt at that moment.

She smiled sweetly. "If he's taking the time to dine with you and treat you differently, then you'll be more than okay."

She continued to do my hair, giving a moment of silence before she continued, "You must mean a lot to him because he never has brought a woman to an official banquet."

Never?

"How do you know?" I couldn't believe he hadn't asked any other woman to eat with him.

"I have been here since he started reigning. I think he doesn't want to make the same mistakes his father did or he tries to."

"What did his father do?"

She stopped braiding my hair and looked at me, "That's not my story to tell, why don't you ask him?"

That's definitely something I would ask him but not now. I was starting to see him past his defenses and I couldn't push it. Not since we have gotten so far. Not after he started to open his soul with me.

Victory was in sight, the reminder of why I was here came into my mind. I pushed away that thought and let future Soraya deal with it.

Was I doing all this because I wanted to or because I was being forced to? I had to remember what my people needed and not what I wanted.

Mehra walked around me and started clasping the jewelry.

Around my ankles golden bangles clinked against one another. Around my wrist small jewels glowed. And after constantly begging Mehra, she didn't add anything around my neck. The veil that covered my face also covered most of my neck so there was no reason to add jewelry.

Around my body there were endless amounts of sapphire colored fabric. Despite all the jewelry and endless fabric, I felt beautiful.

Maybe it was someone else who was making me feel this way.

Mehra stepped to the side, allowing me to have a full look at myself. She had helped me get ready a hundred times but this seemed different. I didn't know if it was just me or she did it on purpose but I looked like myself. I wasn't hiding behind a mask or what seemed to be another face but you could see me.

I took a step closer to the mirror and saw the carefully placed eyeliner on my eyes. It simply intensified and complimented the color of my eyes. I spun around to look at Mehra, her eyes filled with awe.

"What magic do you possess?" I blinked several times to keep the tears at bay. There was a huge chance I was going to ruin this makeup before the night even began.

"I only complimented what you already have. You're naturally beautiful, My Queen. You don't need anything extra." She extended her hands and did her final touches on the gown. Taking several steps back and right before she said she was finished, a knock sounded at the door and with a nod Mehra went to open it.

Mehra stood there for what seemed like a second too long before rushing back into the room. Her cheeks were now a bright shade of rose, her eyes glimmered slightly.

"Mavros is here" she nodded and rushed off to the other side of the room, cleaning up after the mess she had made.

Clothes everywhere, makeup and hair supplies all over the counter.

"Your shoes." Mehra came running after me with a pair of sandals in her hands.

"No need" I waved my hand and without protesting she walked away.

Mavros waited at the door, with his back facing me. I cleared my throat which made him turn around. His eyes softened for the slightest second before his usual expression came back, "You look beautiful, your highness."

We walked side by side and it felt like we had been here before. Every time I left to meet the king or had an appointment with somebody, he was always the one to exhort me. In a weird way, it was like we were friends.

"Mavros, how long have you been working for the king?"

He looked at me, surprised by such a direct question, "No one has ever asked me about that, your highness. I don't know exactly how many years but enough to know how things go around here."

I was nervous to ask but my mind was too curious to not press on, "Was he always like this?"

He stopped in his tracks, "From what I have gathered, none of this is his fault. What I have noticed is that he is a mere puppet, used against his will."

The wheels in my mind started turning and turning. What did he mean by that? A thousand more questions filled my mind as we continued to walk.

"Do you think he actually cares about certain people?"

"I believe he does, deep down inside he does. He might not show it or say it but the longer you stay the more you will know him."

By the time we finished talking, we had just walked through the front brass double doors of the palace and now we were standing in the gardens. I had been so focused on what he was saying or what I was asking that I didn't even think about where I was being led.

"What are we doing outside, Mavros?"

He grinned, "I guess there is only one way to find out."

He extended his hand in the direction that I had to walk. My heart started to pick up the pace and the butterflies started to flutter. I was feeling a mix of emotions and I didn't know why.

He is making you feel this way, that thought passed through my mind. For a moment I doubted it but maybe it was true. Maybe he was doing something to me.

I walked around the bushes of roses trying to find Ephraim. There were small lights glowing inside the trees and it seemed magical. Flowers were blooming everywhere. The air smelled like freshly picked roses and hibiscus. Surrounded by flowers and trees, I finally determined I was lost.

"Ephraim" I yelled out, in hopes his voice would give me direction.

"Soraya, follow my voice" I heard his deep soothing voice from a distance. When he spoke for himself, his voice was as soothing as a breeze on a summer day. It made any anxiety fade away.

I wasn't anywhere near him

I continued to follow his voice as he kept repeating my name over and over again. When I actually found him, I held my breath.

"You found me." he smirked.

I looked at him and now I know why all the ladies would throw themselves at his feet. He was wearing black on black, pristine clothing. The top buttons were undone, revealing a bit of his tattoo and strong chest.

There wasn't a flaw or wrinkle in sight. His hair combed

and placed to perfection. Those eyes were captivating in every way.

He had a freshly shaven jaw, which showed off his perfect jawline.

I took a shaky breath in and smiled in return. "What is this?"

I looked at the picnic that was set in front of us. A multi-colored blanket laid on the green grass. Jeweled pillows creating a border.

Trays of food and wine in the center. In the corner, a small simple black box which left me wondering what was inside.

Ephraim took a few steps closer to me and from behind him, he pulled out a bouquet of flowers.

Red roses. They looked similar to the one I saw in the vase but these were full of life. Each one bloomed to perfection.

I looked up at him, my eyes slowly filled with tears, "What is this?"

He was silent for a few seconds. "I picked them for you."

I could feel my cheeks become hot, it seemed as if someone had dialed up the temperature. My shaky hands took it, our hands brushed against one another for a moment.

That was the moment the butterflies went crazier. I could feel myself almost float to space. Float amongst the stars. I had to keep myself grounded and I wanted to know if he felt the same thing.

"Thank you," were the only words I could manage to say.

He nodded as his hand slipped to my lower back, heat rushed up my spine.

"Let us eat, My Queen." he whispered, his raspy voice made my legs go weak.

I smiled at him and repeated his same words, "Don't call me my Queen, call me Soraya."

211

Ephraim

Chapter 27

‡

I was never nervous. I had never dealt with anxiety before. Yet my feet are trapped in a constant beat against the floor. My fingers were unable to stay still, needing to fiddle with something.

Mavros turned to me with a smirk on his face, "Excited my King?" I knew he was being sarcastic.

I gave him a side glance that quickly shut him up. A guard finally announced that there was someone waiting for me. I waved the person in as I fixed my posture on the throne. When he was close enough, I extended the golden sector in his direction, granting him his own life.

The young fellow walked in with books, papers and other things that I couldn't see from here. There was so much in his hands that it looked like he was about to fall, barely hanging on.

I nodded in his direction as I waited for him to speak, "I have found some information that I think you would like to know, your highness."

"Then let's talk."

213

A couple of hours had passed and I stood before a table with hundreds of papers. These maps and stories were ancient. Papers which were burned on the edges and had wine spilled on them. Dark ink looked lighter and lighter as the years passed on. They were not about my kingdom but about Uosulia. I didn't have any of these maps which made me curious into how he was able to get it.

I looked up at him. "How did you get all of this?"

He grinned sneakily. "I got a few on my first mission to their land and others were bribed."

I smiled, *at least someone does the job well.*

"So as I was saying, their queen is hidden from everyone. Only the people who live there know her true identity.

He pointed to a picture in a book. It had ancient writings that explained things about their tradition, "Here it says that they have been hiding their queen ever since the death of their first leader."

As if the pieces never connected, it finally started to come together. Not many people know about our history for the simple fact that I don't let people know but I knew every detail like the back of my hand. The way that our founder killed his leader for money, fame, and pride.

In a lot of ways it was clear that I was his descendent. The only thing that changed was that I was worse.

That story was inside a history book that no one except me had access to. It was locked and hidden somewhere inside my studies.

"I have searched for clues into who was their queen now-" he looked at the maps before drawing his gaze back to me,

"But ever since the death of the last king and queen, they have been hiding her like never before."

I wasn't even mad that he didn't have a full answer because

he has done more in a few short weeks than anyone in my court has done in years.

"And what are you going to do to figure this out? The longer it takes the more they rebel against us and the stronger they can get."

He stood straight and pulled out another pile of books with another map, "I have an idea but I need your approval."

He took my silence as permission to continue talking, "I wanted to hide in their land until I found her. I already have a cover story. I will live like them, eat like them and become one of them-"

I finished his sentence, "but in reality you're simply faking it until you find her and come rushing to tell me."

He smiled, "Brilliant plan might I add."

I crossed my arms and thought about it. I didn't ask how he got this information and what it cost because I didn't want to know. This actually might work and I was willing to sacrifice anything and everything.

"Mavros come here" I yelled over my shoulder and saw from the corner of my eye, his tall slim body rushing towards me.

He leaned against the table with hands, "What do you need, my King?"

I trusted Mavros' opinion and sometimes he saw things that I couldn't.

Mavros turned to the boy and looked at him with a serious glance, "What's the cost?"

He shook his head side to side, "Nothing, I just hate the people as much as you do, my King."

"Mavros, what do you think I should do?" I lifted my head to look at him.

He turned in my direction, his hip leaned against the table

with his hands crossed, "This is the answer to their destruction. I would suggest you focus all your attention on them."

I should focus all my attention into killing them.

I slapped him on the back in a brotherly way; even though he was far from that.

"Then do as you said." The ring that was on my finger was dipped in wax and stamped onto the paper.

Now there was no way back.

He finished explaining exactly what he was going to do and rushed off to pack before his journey tomorrow. When he disappeared from view, I slouched in my chair in deep thought.

"What is on your mind?" Mavros asked beside me.

He was drinking a cup of wine and eating the fruit in his hand. His eyes were glued to the door, as if he was waiting for someone to burst in.

"I don't know." I leaned my head back and closed my eyes for a second.

Why was I feeling like a criminal?

Then I looked down at myself and was reminded of why I began to wear black in the first place. It was after the night that I saw my father die in front of my eyes. It was from that moment on that everything changed. Yes he was never the perfect father but I still remember the few times we spent together. That moment where I was cursed for the rest of my life, that's when everything changed but I wondered, *What was my favorite color?*

It wasn't black because I was simply expressing what was inside of me. It's not pink because that seemed to scream from the rooftops that I am loud and fun which I was far from.

Maybe it would be a caramel brown.

"I-" before I continued, four soldiers bursted into the room. They were holding two men that looked completely distraught and in agony. With every step that took, the men tried to get themselves free from the grasp on their forearms.

The guards stopped a few steps away from me and threw both men forcefully on the floor.

One of the guards spoke up, "Your highness, we have found the men that plotted your death trap."

I descended the three flights of stairs to where they were laid on the floor.

"What are the names of these animals?"

The guard stiffened, "One of them is a soldier and the other is the captain of your army."

There are times that I think people don't appreciate the little amount of power and faith I put in them. It always seemed to be the same men who would try to back stab me.

I commanded the soldiers to take a few steps away. Mavros was still behind me, he was like my shadow. He knew what was going to happen and never once was he bothered by it.

The guards have seen it many times but always have kept it to themselves, afraid if they said anything what would happen.

"You vile creatures" I scolded in their faces.

Then the one that was kneeling to the right of me, stood up and faced me eye to eye. He puffed out his chest to make him look bigger even though he barely reached my shoulders.

"I would never bow down to such a despicable king like you."

The dark power that flowed within my bones began moving like a dark storm. The dark waves of anger and bitterness flew through me. My hardened heart that rested inside my chest pounded like a drum.

My hand was around his neck, the dark power flowing into

his skin. It no longer was bright and full of life, it faded away the longer I held on.

"Speak to me with respect." I hissed at him, my grip slightly tightened.

"I would prefer to meet death face to face before ever bowing down to you."

Those were his last words before he died in my hands. Another death caused by me, another soul taken away.

What have I become?

That moment I felt darker than darkness. More evil than the devil himself.

Had I become the devil?

All the life that once flowed through my bones was gone. The joy that I felt in my soul had died.

His body slipped from my grip and fell with a *thump* on the floor. The other guy who laid on the floor was trembling in fear. I think if I had just looked at him he would die as well.

I knelt before him and raised his chin with a single finger, "Where are you from?"

He took shaky breaths as he struggled to speak, "We are spies sent from Uosulia."

I cursed under my breath, "What were you sent to do?"

He trembled once again, "We were once part of the Queen's court. Then he-"

He looked over to his friend that laid on the floor and then raised his eyes back to me.

My 6' 2" body was already aching from being crunched on the floor. He could be the way for me to find anything about their queen.

"He rebelled and wanted to kill you himself. I was a fool to tag along. He lied saying he just wanted to stop the war and famine."

He let his head drop on the floor like he couldn't believe he was saying everything.

"Well I think it's only fair that since you know so much about me that I know something about your queen. I promise I won't kill you if you at least tell me something about her."

He looked at me baffled. Never have I given someone the chance to pick between life or death. He stayed quiet for several moments as he carefully chose what he would say.

After what felt like an eternity, he cleared his throat. "She is different."

I looked at him starstrucked. "That's it. All you're going to say is '*different*'?"

He shrugged his tied arms. "It makes sense when you know who she is."

I stood up and looked down at his small body. Surprisingly, I wasn't in the mood or headspace to kill someone at that moment so I waved my right hand to the nearest guard to pick the man off the floor.

"Untie him" I commanded.

Mavros looked at me, baffled that it was so easy to take information out of him, "Tell your Queen, wherever she is, that I am coming and when I come, I will kill everything she loves."

The way that man spoke made his queen sound like an angel. No one was perfect but he made it seem that way.

Was she perfect in his eyes?

What does 'different' mean?

The man went off with a warning, "*If I ever see your face again, I won't be so merciful.*"

He thanked me several times the moment he was untied.

The man bowed before me without ceasing and it got on my nerves.

Mavros now stood beside me, I could feel his emotions bouncing off him, "Why did you do that?"

I crossed my arms, my muscles sore, "Send two spies after him. Make sure they follow him until they find something."

Mavros smirked evilly, sometimes I felt like he loved my plan more than me.

He nodded and went off saying, "Consider it done."

He swayed out like he was about to enjoy what he was going to do but something inside me turned. My stomach twisted and physically hurt yet I had no clue what it was. Then I think of the man I just killed and my stomach turned even more.

Then my mind went to *her*.

Soraya.

Even if I hated to admit it to myself, she was doing something to me. Which reminded me that I haven't seen her all day. She was probably outside or lost inside the palace somewhere.

I waltzed down the halls and at first I didn't know where I was going to go but then I remembered a certain place I hadn't visited in a while. The thought and the memories brought me back to the past, my temper shifting inside me at the near thought of it.

In a far corner of the palace there was a balcony. It faced the hills and the ocean that was in the distance. I leaned my hands on the silver railing and took a deep breath of the fresh air. In the distance I could hear the crashing waves against the shore. The grass and flowers swayed in the cool wind.

Memories flashed in my mind from my youth. From when there was life in my bones and light within my soul. This would be the place that me and my mother would hide from my father. Where we would watch the sun rise and set day after day.

My soul ached being here once again because it reminded me of her. It reminded me of the night she was taken away from me and how I didn't even have the right to tell her that I loved her once more. To see the way she would smile at a blooming or how her eyes would squeeze shut when she was laughing.

I sighed and whispered out into the silence, "Where are you mother? Why have you left me all alone?"

Then a sweet voice behind me spoke, "Maybe she never actually left you. Maybe she is here with you and all you have to do is believe."

I didn't even need to turn around to see who was talking because there was only one person with a sweet voice like that. Only one woman that can calm down the raging beast inside me.

"I thought you were exploring outside." I whispered to Soraya without turning my back.

I could feel her come closer to me, the way that my body would automatically relax in her presence. Her body lightly brushed against mine as she stood beside me.

"I was but I'm back now. I was visiting this sweet little girl." She spoke with such gentleness in her voice.

"The poor village is no place for a queen." I pointed that out as if it wasn't obvious.

"Is that all I am? Am I supposed to be another prized possession? Something to be bought or shown?" I could feel her gaze burning into my skin.

"No, you are worth more than that."

For several minutes she was silent and I thought she was angry but when I began to lose hope, her gentle voice replaced the silence, "I forgive you. I am not a person who holds bitterness."

With that I finally turned my head to look at her and was glad she wasn't looking at me anymore. She was focused on the breathtaking scene before us.

Everything was dull compared to her.

"Have you ever been to that island?" she whispered.

Her voice was soothing. It was like waves of the ocean. The whistle of the wind and the sound of swaying leaves in the autumn breeze.

I smiled because the answer was yes. I had been there multiple times and it was always with my mother by my side. We would throw pebbles in the ocean, stay up to see the countless shining stars in the sky, and laugh until we couldn't breathe anymore.

What I didn't expect back then, that the life I dreamt of living was far from my current reality.

"Yes, multiple times with my mother. I haven't been there in a while though." I tried to speak with softness like she always did but failed horribly.

She then looked at me and our eyes locked with one another.

Her brown eyes.

Her caramel colored eyes.

They had something in them that made all my fears and darkness melt away. It reminded me of the only other woman that loved me. I knew that Soraya didn't love me and that she probably saw me like everyone else, a monster. Yes she was different and I couldn't tell what it was. Everytime I would try to think of a reason why I always felt so safe with her, my mind would go blank.

Even my thoughts were silenced by her beauty.

Under the sunlight you could see the different shades of

browns that swirled in her eyes. I couldn't think of one painting that compared to them. One painter that could paint something more majestic than those small beautiful portals.

Who did she get her beautiful eyes from?

She smiled, "I got them from my mom. I fade in comparison to her."

I doubt that.

My eyes widened, "Did I ask that out loud?"

She didn't respond but instead started laughing. I was wrong, there might be something more beautiful than her eyes.

Her laugh.

It seemed to intoxicate me. I felt enveloped by such a lovely sound. As it started to die down, she went from laughing to the biggest smile on her face and I was so close to her that I noticed the small details of her face. The way her very vague dimples would show when she smiled. The way her pearly white teeth were on display when she was laughing. The way her hair was shiny and long as it cascaded down her back. I didn't know how hair could be graceful but she even managed to do that.

"Why don't you smile more?" her question took me by surprise.

I don't think all my life someone has asked me that question because it never seemed important.

"Because I don't even feel worthy of a smile. I don't feel like I need to." She probably didn't understand why I answered that way.

I didn't feel worthy of a smile. Neither of a good laugh or true love. I didn't feel worthy of anything good because I was far from being good. I have killed, which made me a murderer. I have enjoyed the company of multiple women and that made me a prostitute. I drank to the point of death and now I was a drunkard.

She slowly lifted her hand and paused halfway to give me

time to reject but I couldn't. I didn't want to reject another moment of peace I always have when she touched me or was near.

She gently placed her hand on my right cheek and looked deeply into my eyes, "None of us are worthy of happiness in life which is why we have grace."

I grumbled, "I don't deserve such a thing."

She stayed quiet for a moment and asked, "Why don't you?"

I shook my head and gently took her hand from my face. I took a few steps away from her, cause I couldn't keep my thoughts in check with her.

The moment my back was faced towards her was when I had enough focus to speak, "People look at me as if I am a monster and I have earned that title with honor. I have killed and have done things you can't even begin to imagine."

I slowly turned around to look at her eyes. Where there once was happiness now was replaced with worry and sadness.

I had just proved my point. Even with my words I could hurt someone with no intention.

"And why do you believe that's what everyone thinks of you? Why have you convinced yourself of a lie which has become your truth?"

I shook my head once again because she didn't know. She didn't know the curse I battled against and never found the end to. She never knew the unending torment I lived with. Her compassion was based on what she saw.

The rose.

The red dying rose was not very far from where we were. It would give her a glance into my broken truth. If she knew about it then she would stop pretending there was any hope for me.

"Come here." I turned and extended my hand for her to

take it. She hesitated for a second before slowly slipping her hand into mine. I took a shaky breath in when her fingers interlaced with mine.

Pull yourself together, Ephraim.

One woman shouldn't have so much affect on you.

We didn't even walk far and before I walked inside, I turned to look at Soraya. Her eyes were glued to the door as if there was a beast hidden behind the curtain. Her breaths were slowed and controlled like she was trying to calm herself down.

"What's wrong?" I squeezed her hand to try to bring her back to reality.

She shook her head, "Nothing."

She was lying.

I nodded my head as I slipped slowly inside the dark room. She hesitantly followed behind me, her grip on my hand tightened. Her body pressed against mine as we walked in unison.

When we arrived in front of the rose I turned to her to see her full reaction. Her eyes widened slightly. Her breathing went from slow to fast. Her hands slipped out of mine as she began to take small steps towards the glass.

Soraya then stood in front of me but her gaze was focused on her feet instead of my eyes. She fidgeted with her fingers as she tried to form words.

Whatever she was about to say left me nervous. There was a block of ice inside my stomach and my brain thought of a million things that she would say.

You cruel and evil man.

I want to leave this palace, leave you.

You are exactly what people say you are, a monster.

What she said took me by surprise. I didn't expect her to say it and I didn't know how to respond to such honesty.

Soraya

Chapter 28

"I have seen this rose before," I whispered to him
I closed my eyes, scared to see his reaction.
Was he going to hit me?
Was he going to get angry and close me off once again?

He placed a gentle finger underneath my chin and lifted my head so that our eyes would be connected with one another. He stared at me which made me slightly want to squirm under his gaze.

"How do you know if this is the first time I have ever shown it to you?" He questioned.

I opened and closed my mouth several times, unable to find the correct words to explain what had happened. I wasn't sneaking around the castle, at least I didn't think I was. I was lost and I was trying to convince myself it was the only reason.

"I was walking around the castle and then ended up lost. When I saw the room, something inside it lured me inside. I saw the rose and then walked away-"

I took a shaky breath in, my eyes flooded with tears at the

thought, "Then I heard the two guards planning to kill you and rushed out."

He sighed softly, like he was glad what I said wasn't what he was thinking it would be, "You ran to find a way out but you couldn't and that is when I found you."

I nodded and suddenly felt a burden come off my chest. I wasn't going to plan to ever tell him but it seemed to just slip out. Dishonesty didn't feel right with me, it stirred inside me and made me feel cruel and vicious.

Yet I was still being dishonest, I hadn't told him the biggest secret of all. It was a war in my mind if I should tell him or not but I knew that if I did my head would be on a platter. And this whole plan of trying to sway him would be burned.

I am the queen of the people you are trying to kill, my mind would yell slightly at him.

I had to wait for the right moment to tell him, to tell him that I wasn't the person he thought I was either.

"Why tell me now?" His voice pulled me away from the mental war I was having with myself.

His hands had fallen from my face and were gently placed on my trembling arms. His eyes were completely and solely focused on me, like he was more worried about me then he was about anything else.

Was he worried about me?

Did he care about me?

I don't know if I had the response to that question but at this moment I felt like something was shifting.

"Because I hate dishonesty." Simple as that.

I hated dishonesty and lies with a deep passion. I have been lied to far too many times. People have been dishonest with me and it felt horrible. Yet at the same time that I hate it, I was doing the same thing to him.

It's different though, I thought. Yet I was trying to convince myself of that lie.

"Just another reason that you don't belong with me" He responded with such conviction.

Before I could even open my mouth, he continued on, "I am dishonest, vicious, dark, evil. I am the definition of a beast but you aren't Soraya-"

He pressed his lips together for a moment, "My jewel doesn't deserve to be treated that way. Yet I can't seem to find any center of peace when I am not around you. I am a monster when I am not myself and you seem to help me find myself in the midst of the torment."

I examined his eyes, he wasn't crying but his eyes were glistening. There was a small pool of water in his dark eyes as he talked. Ephraim's doleful expression was a pain in the heart. I could see in his eyes the way he was afflicted and how he wrestled with himself.

His jaw tightened and in the blink of an eye, his emotions were locked away once again, "You confuse me," he admitted in a husky voice. "I don't want you but the selfish part of me desires you." He took a step closer, our bodies almost touching one another. "Every fiber of my being needs you."

He shut his eyes and leaned his forehead against mine. Our warm breaths mingled together as our hands brushed slightly against one another.

What am I getting myself into?

I couldn't think of how I have gotten here, how I was starting to fall for a man that I knew I shouldn't be. He was being so open yet my own soul was conflicted with the secrets I am hiding.

This is for the people and I shouldn't let my heart get in the way.

Maybe I was risking something far greater. I was risking

hundreds of lives and my heart in the process. The lines were getting blurred between him and I. Nothing was no longer black and white and I didn't know what to think.

"What did you call me?" I had just stopped to realize that he didn't call me *My Jewel*.

He lifted his head and smirked, "I called you my Jewel. Even though I am not perfect I know when I see something perfect and precious like you."

I shook my head side to side because I refused to be called perfect, "Don't call me perfect. No one is perfect and I am the furthest thing from being that."

You don't even know.

He took a step back, "I didn't have a choice to become a monster. I was forced to and now I am bound by the chains of darkness and death. I am held prisoner by chains that you cannot see. Change would be much easier for you then it would for me. Let me call you what I see is true cause truth is a very rare thing I come across."

This man was broken.

His heart was held together by a thin thread and in his eyes you could see that he didn't want to do this anymore. That the strength to fight against the darkness was fading and the boy that was inside of him, was lost. I have learned that no one screams and begs for help if they don't really want it. No man exposes himself to someone if his soul is not in agonized pain.

After all this time, the true man that was locked away behind the mask was finally starting to slowly appear. The crashing worlds inside his mind and the desire for change were becoming visible.

I walked closer to him, his eyes closed and his head hung low. My small frame was petite compared to him, the top of my head barely hit his chest. I slowly lifted my trembling hands and placed them onto his chest. His breathing was empty and desperate, his body in a still state.

"If you mean what you said-"

He interrupted me and whispered, "I mean it with all my broken pieces"

I smiled sadly at him, "Then I won't leave your side. Heaven or earth, rain or shine, nothing will separate me from helping you find yourself again."

My mind became a battlefield because I knew I was putting myself in a position where my heart might not survive. Where my feelings will be mixed and my heart will lean towards a person who might not want me in the end.

I tried to convince myself that my feelings and heart wouldn't be mixed in the middle. That everything would go back to being black and white but I knew that I couldn't promise myself that. Despite what I could and couldn't do, what I should do and stay away from, something lured me to him.

I might have the power of life and have golden light flowing through my veins but that was little, it was nothing. What he needed was far more than a momentary relief, what he needed was something far greater. That even the most despicable and desperate man still had hope. Even if you had to run after it or fight for it, darkness will never be more powerful than the light.

Maybe he would be the answer to my questions. Maybe he was going to help me see something I couldn't. Ephraim was beginning to have my heart. He was changing me in ways he didn't know either. And it's not because of who he is but who he will become.

We stood there for several moments in complete silence before leaving for dinner.

Today it was different, he was slowly changing in ways probably most people didn't notice. He asked me to stay by his side the whole night. And there wasn't a single moment where he got drunk or prideful.

We went back to our room that night and before I went to sleep he insisted on braiding my hair once again. I was starting to adore the feeling. My favorite sensation was his calloused fingers running through my hair and brushing out all the tangles. The way he was gentle and kind with me.

We laid in bed and talked for a few moments before sleep whisked us away. I never thought that I would reach the point of feeling comfortable in his presence. I didn't think I would ever enjoy a single conversation with him or loved the way he grinned. Never in a million years did I think I was going to have him braid my hair or hold my hands.

As each day passed, I was thinking that I had this all wrong. That what I believed about him was a lie.

What I realized was that I didn't have to trick him to fall in love with me or to think that I am perfect. I don't have to be someone that I am not nor think like someone else.

I don't have to act like people think I should. Maybe I was trying to make others happy rather than myself. Making others proud will sacrifice my own happiness. I was beginning to realize that I didn't have everything together and I was going to need change as well.

Soraya

Chapter 29

It's been a long week since Ephraim and I had our last moment together and I would never think that I would miss his company. I didn't think that my heart would ache to talk to him but every time we tried to say hello to one another, something would happen.

Every time he would lay eyes on me from across a room and start coming in my direction, someone would stop him mid-tracks and tell him that there was an emergency. Every time that I desired to seek him out, something or someone would stop me as well.

Right now, he was in his office. He has been locked in there for hours and hours. I began to worry but before I could think of the worst, a servant came and delivered a letter on a silver platter.

Dear My Queen,
I am not ignoring you, and as you have seen
that every time I try to search for you, something

stops me. Malcolm and the court have found problem after problem for me to resolve. I am beginning to think they are making things up.

I don't know what you're doing, but a small part of me wished you were by my side. Since I won't be available for the rest of the week, let me whisk you away this weekend. I will take you to a place that you won't know of until we get there. There I won't be King Ephraim and you won't be Queen Soraya. There we will simply be Ephraim and Soraya, husband and wife.

I wish to get to know you better.

Teach me of your ways and your people.

Your Beloved King,

Ephraim

I whipped my head around to make sure no one had read that behind my back.

These words were sacred to me. My eyes only.

I had the biggest smile on my face, my cheeks were growing sore. This wasn't love and I didn't know if it ever was going to reach that point but this was unraveling to something more. To something that I didn't think it ever could be.

The servant held the platter close to his chest and cleared his throat, "What shall I send to his Highness in return?"

My soul seemed to have jumped outside my chest when I heard his voice. I had also forgotten that I was standing in the middle of hundreds of people. Townsmen walking in front of me and behind me, not giving a care that I was there. I was glad they had gotten used to me and no longer were treating me differently.

"Tell the king that I accept and that I am looking forward to it."

He nodded and turned around to mount himself on the horse. With a light tap of his foot, the horse started to gallop away.

Three days left, I thought to myself.

I wondered about the place that he was going to bring me to and why. I thought of how much I desired for a sweet escape and that I was finally going to get one.

I folded the note back up and slipped it into the pocket of my dress. I refocused myself to what was in front of me with the biggest smile on my face.

Maybe life was changing?

I walked around the booths and the crates of freshly picked fruit. The newly woven carpet hung from the walls on display for all to see.

Tables filled with women's clothing. Each head covering was more beautiful than the one before but when I was about to walk away, one caught my eye. An emerald colored one with golden details on the edges. It was beautiful and simple, just how I liked it.

Mehra had told me that deep jewel colors complimented my skin and eyes. She said I was breathtaking when I wore simple yet stunning clothing. Mehra had become a close friend so I trusted her opinion.

I walked closer to the stall. The lady had her back faced against me, not noticing that I was there.

I cleared my throat and then she yelled, "It's not for free."

I smiled, "I know it's not and I am willing to pay the price."

With that she huffed and turned around. Her eyes widened so much that I thought they were going to pop out.

She brushed her hands against her apron as she tried to find her words, "Please forgive me my queen. I didn't know it was you. Usually the only people who come here try to bargain for it for free."

I shook my head and chuckled, "No worries, I would introduce myself but it seems you already know me."

She laughed, her hand laid on her chest, "You're funny, my queen. Yes, the whole country knows of the most beautiful queen in all the land. You have been making quite the difference, you know that?"

My eyebrows raised because that was new to me,, "Really?"

She shook her head, "Yes and I believe even the king is acting differently because of you. Even though our living conditions are horrible, things are slowly starting to change-"

She spoke those words with so much hope and life before giving me a big smile, "Forgive me, which head covering would you like?"

I turned around, glancing at all the ones she had to offer. They were so beautiful and you could see the amount of care and attention she had put into each one of them. Each one was different from the other which made it even harder to choose.

"Do you make these by hand?" I asked, a simple blush coming to her cheeks as she nodded.

"May I ask you something?"

She nodded once again.

"Why do most women not have one if it's custom to use it?" I hoped that question wasn't stupid but I didn't know.

My country was different because it wasn't something forced but all women chose to use it. It represented inner beauty and modesty. I believed it made a woman's inner beauty shine without having to show off her body.

"Well the simple answer is that most women can't afford it.

I tried to make it as cheap as I can yet families are barely able to buy bread and water for their tables."

Those words were heavy. I didn't feel pity but I felt their pain. I have never been in a position to not have food and water on the table but I have dealt with other things.

I have seen my own parents killed before my very eyes. I have seen little girls sold because their families couldn't pay off their debt. Every single cursed thing that my eyes have seen has made my heart filled with burden. Burden for those people that don't have enough strength to fight for themselves. Pain for people who had to choose between protecting their image and food in their stomach.

That needs to change.

I pointed to the green one hanging to my left, "I will buy that one for myself"

She opened her mouth but I continued on, "And I will purchase the rest for all the ladies in this courtyard."

Her hands were frozen in the air, her body frozen like a statue. The only thing that moved were her eyes which she blinked several times.

I chuckled at her blank response. Her eyes began to flood with tears and her cheeks turned into a bright pink color.

"Blessed is the God who watches over this nation. Blessed are you my queen for showing mercy upon your people."

She started leaping with joy and laughing with gratefulness. My heart began to overfill with the same happiness as I watched her.

I handed over mine to one of the guards by my side and began helping the older lady hand out the other ones. Each woman began to cry and shout with joy and it wasn't long before I started to cry myself.

They told me stories of how they have been praying for years to be able to feel beautiful and safe again and their prayers were finally being answered. The little girls that gripped onto their mother's legs were reaching out to feel the strange new fabric. I watched them all laugh and smile with their new gifts in hand.

At that moment I walked away feeling happier than ever. My heart overflowed with delight and my mind was at complete peace. I could barely contain the tears and the joy.

The guard that was standing by my white horse looked at me with worry in his eyes, "Did someone hurt you, your highness? Does someone need to die?"

He already had his hand placed on the sword that was attached on his side. I extended my hand, signaling him to stop with the foolishness.

"No one hurt me, I am just very happy at this moment. Have you ever cried happy tears?"

He scrunched his eyebrows, deep in thought before he fixed his facial features once again, " I haven't ever cried."

I shook my head in disbelief, "Well when you cry happy tears then you will know what I mean"

He nodded in silence before stepping to the side so I could sit on the horse who was now waiting impatiently for me.

Ephraim

Chapter 30

T omorrow is going to be the first time that I have left
these palace walls in years. I don't know if it was
nerves or anxiety but I couldn't seem to think
straight today.

When I arrived in my chambers late at night, when I was
finally able to get away from Mavros, Soraya was already sleeping. She looked peaceful as she slept and was curled up with the
sheets that almost swallowed her whole.

I couldn't help but chuckle to myself before slipping
myself into bed and falling asleep peacefully at night. Every
time she was beside me there was another night I could sleep.

Mavros had thrown problem after problem for me to
resolve. I was starting to believe that he had an endless list. So
by the time I laid my sore head on the silk pillow, I was already
dead tired.

This morning I felt better but my knee wouldn't stop
bouncing. Everyone's voices kept floating away as I lost myself
in my thoughts.

"My King, did you even hear me?" someone clapped to get my attention once again.

I shaked my head to bring myself back to reality, "No I did not."

The man sighed, "Tomorrow we have a very important meeting planned that you cannot miss."

I stiffened, "No, I have something already planned for tomorrow."

I didn't want to have to change my plans and risk breaking the trust that Soraya was finally building with me.

He sighed and stepped closer to me, "My king, I would never been a person to bark orders to you but-"

I hated the word *but*.

"If you want to get rid of your enemies as fast and as painlessly as possible, this meeting is necessary. There are kings and leaders from other kingdoms coming."

I glared at him because he knew full well that he was backing me up into a corner. They know that I wanted this done as fast as possible, this was the one constant torment in the kingdom that had to be solved.

Get rid of them and have peace, isn't that what you have always wanted, a voice spoke inside my mind.

I had become used to that voice and I knew full well that it was the darkness that lingered within me.

For once I wanted to do something that wasn't a war of decisions. I wanted to decide something for myself but every time I tried to fight back, the voice would just get louder and louder.

I groaned, unable to withstand the pressure their glances are giving me, "Fine, what time?"

244

I reached my quarters and I could already hear that Soraya was in the room. She was singing a melody to herself and from the crack of the door, I could see that she was brushing her hair.

For a moment, I watched her. How her voice sounded so pleasant.

I didn't know that she could sing, but then again I was just getting to know her. I still needed to learn her favorite food, favorite color, and song.

Then it dawned on me that I barely knew anything about her. It ached my chest of how stubborn I have been to not even ask her any of that. And now I was about to break her heart with the news that weighed on my shoulders.

I pushed the door open and then walked into the room. She stopped singing and smiled, "What are you doing here so early?"

I didn't smile back because I didn't have the strength or capacity to.

"I need to talk to you but I could ask the same thing, why are you getting ready for bed so early?" I raised an eyebrow.

"I am too excited for tomorrow" she was practically radiating excitement.

Then the news sunk a little deeper into my heart. I could feel the darkness inside my soul grip me a bit tighter.

"We won't be able to go tomorrow." My voice cracked, it seemed to lose all its strength.

The moment I spoke the words, her hand lowered and the hairbrush dropped to the floor. It fell with a light *thump* sound.

"What?" She whispered.

Her face was a mixture of emotions like she felt betrayed and heartbroken at the same time.

Did she not know that I didn't want to do it either?

I had to take this advantage. The quicker I got rid of the

problem, the sooner I could spend time with her. The sooner I would be free or maybe that's what I wanted to believe.

"There is a meeting that I have to go to and-"

Before I could finish, she interrupted, "Since when has this meeting been marked?"

I cleared my throat because the answer was about to paint me in a horrible light, not like I already was in one, "Today."

Her eyes widened for a slight second before she relaxed her face once again. Her eyes were closed for several moments, with deep breaths she calmed herself.

When she opened her beautiful eyes again, I couldn't read her anymore. I couldn't tell what she felt, if she was mad or angry. If she was relieved or wanted to kill me with her own hands.

"Okay." Were the only words that she said to me before walking to the bathroom and closing the door behind her.

I stood there baffled, unable to move. I didn't know what to say or how to act. If it had been any other person, I would have stormed after them and killed them but with her I couldn't.

I can't find myself to lay a finger on her or yell at her and I don't know how that's possible. How my solid rock heart would beat again when she was near.

How she could yell at me and treat me like anyone else but I couldn't yell back.

The way she could walk away with the final word and leave me stunned in silence.

My mind was left like a battlefield, confusion. I didn't know how to act or what to do now. I felt horrible and wicked by saying one thing and backing out at the last second. She looked desperate to leave this palace a bit and I had just crushed those dreams.

Despite what I had just done, I wanted to make it up to

her. I wanted to make her happy again. I have never deeply desired to see someone smile, but I desired her smile more than gold.

Was I falling in love? I hoped that I wasn't because I don't think I would be brave enough to withstand something I have forbidden for so long.

Soraya

Chapter 31

I have tried to avoid Ephraim at all costs since last night. Although, I found it extremely difficult since he wouldn't stop chasing me around.

"Soraya," Ephraim's breathy voice called after me.

I continued walking away because I don't think I could face him right now. My emotions were still unbalanced because I felt like that past constantly repeated itself.

All the times that my parents would plan something with me and then cancel it last minute. All the times that I was prepared for something and it was all trashed in just a few moments.

I heard his footsteps come behind me but I continued to ignore until I felt a strong hand touch my wrist. He didn't pull me so I would face him, he just held me.

"Soraya, talk to me" His whispered request.

I was about to respond but then servants walked past us and I learned that they had ears for miles. I waited for them to pass us before I would say a single thing.

"I am busy, my king." I responded sternly.

He pulled me slightly, it forced me to take a step closer to him. I turned around and when my eyes met his, I wanted to cry. I didn't know why a simple look at his eyes wanted to make me cry.

Maybe because they reminded me of my father. The way I missed his laugh and how his eyes scrunched together when he was smiling. The way he would always promise me to go to the ocean but we would never go.

His eyes widened when he looked back at me. He looked at my eyes, my face, my arms and then back to my eyes.

"What happened to you? Who touched you?" He demanded to know who it was. His eyes burned like he was possessive and protective over me. Although, the one thing he didn't know was that he had the power to hurt me more than anyone else ever did.

A single tear rolled down my cheek and with the back of my free hand, I wiped it away before he noticed, "Nothing that you need to worry about."

He let go of my hand to give space between us. "What did I do?"

His eyes kept drifting from my eyes to his hands. Ephraim chewed the inside of his mouth as he waited for my answer.

"You won't understand." I was about to turn around to continue walking away but when he spoke, I froze.

"I have a thousand torments day and night. Hundreds of things that I can't control. Let me into the intimacy of your heart and understand you in ways no other person ever can."

I stopped midstep when his voice wrapped around me. The way he spoke wasn't a king speaking to me, or the tortured man that lied within him but it was Ephraim. A man that wanted to be changed. Someone I was growing to know.

I turned around and didn't want to hide the waterfall of tears that drenched my face, "I was looking forward to our outing. Maybe I was excited to escape these walls for a bit. Maybe I wanted to get to know the man that thinks he can't love or be loved."

I took a step back and used both hands to wipe away the tears. "Maybe my father always promised to bring me somewhere new but never did because obligations always got in the way."

He extended his hand to reach out for me but I took a step back. "Don't worry about me, my king. Your duties are much more important. If you need me, I will be in the gardens."

He didn't say anything as he slowly lowered his hand. He nodded his head barely to let me know that I was free to go. With that I picked up the fabric of my skirt and rushed to the garden. I knew that there I could let my tears run free.

I wanted to go back to my country but everything has stopped me from going. Disagreements that are about to cause war. People revolted against the king and my safety was risked because of it.

Ephraim told the guards to ignore my orders of less protection and for that I was constantly watched. In my room, there were always two guards right outside.

Even as I was in the garden, there were guards near the door watching me. I felt their eyes dig into my back and watch every single move that I did but I didn't care. At that moment, I wanted to forget and just pretend I was where I wanted to be. I imagined the kids running around me and laughing with joy. Their faces when I made a new flower bloom once again, the way they were star struck every time.

I wanted to feel the hugs of the ones I loved and cared for but I didn't know the next time I would be able to. I wanted to talk to Alizeh for hours and hours.

Then my mind thought about one of the very first nights that I lived here. Ephraim's words ringed in my head till this day. That there was a slight possibility that he would annihilate my people if they didn't give in.

He would kill every single man, woman, and child if it was to end them all but he still hasn't put it into law.

He still hasn't signed our death and I hoped it will never reach that point. I prayed it would never reach that point but there was only so much I could do.

I didn't have a single idea why he hated my people so much. One night, I remembered it as if it happened yesterday. Two guards were walking past me, they were talking amongst themselves. I didn't even think they noticed me. Then one of them whispered, "*The King is in the process of a law that will finally put an end to the Uosulian people.*"

The other man laughed beside him and responded, "*I want to see them die. Now that would be a reason for celebration.*"

That was the moment that I realized it wasn't just one person who hated me and my people. It was an entire kingdom that wanted us dead for reasons I couldn't comprehend.

When I heard it, my heart dropped to the ground and my stomach felt like someone had just punched me. I wanted to run to Zion and tell him what I had just figured out but I couldn't. I can't send letters because anyone could read it and find out the secret I was trying so hard to keep.

I closed my eyes for several moments, trying to calm my emotions. In a way, it was as if I could feel my younger self. How she was heartbroken because her parents were killed before her very eyes. Her childhood wasn't how she wanted it to be but it was to know how to rule a country. The way she thought promises were something in vain.

I opened my eyes and noticed the flowers around me had slightly dimmed. The flowers were hanging as if they were heavy, like they were replicating my emotions.

I extended my hand discreetly and let the gold powers flow

through me and to the flowers. They sprung back up with life and with much more color than they had before.

I stood up on my two shaky legs and proceeded in the direction of the town. Maybe being with the children would help me, maybe their joy would bring a smile on my face and make me myself once again.

As I walked, Mavros appeared out of the blue and was right beside me, "Hello my queen. What are you doing? The king has given strict orders that you are not to leave the palace without guards by your side."

He wasn't saying it in a way as if he was going to force me to go back inside, but it was like a warning. A warning that I was going to ignore and pretend that I didn't hear.

"If the king has a problem then he can yell at me." I slowly strolled away, not in a pressure to get there since I wasn't going to do anything anyways.

"May I come with you? I will have a better sense of mind knowing that you are safe."

I looked at him and smiled, "Thank you Mavros. At least someone in this kingdom isn't overbearing and tormenting me day and night."

He smirked but stayed quiet, he knew deep down inside what I meant by that. We walked side by side in comfortable silence, neither of us feeling the need to talk or say anything.

When we arrived, as if I was just at home, all the little kids spotted me and came dashing towards me. Their small arms wrapped around my legs as they began to yell my name. One child said that their mother loved the new head covering I had gifted, another child said they tasted bread for the first time in years.

Even if the Ephraim didn't know what I was doing, every smile, every laugh, and the joy on their faces was worth it all.

When I turned to Mavros, he had a face of disgust like these weren't people but bugs.

"You might want to change your facial expressions before you scare everyone."

He looked at me with disgust before fixing his expression, "How long have you been coming here?"

I had to answer wisely because if I told him the truth then Ephraim would know and I would be banned from doing this too. Not like I already wasn't under constant watch.

"If I tell you then you are going to tell the king and we both know how he is going to react."

He nodded and then focused his gaze on something far away. His hands were placed behind his back as the look of anxiety was written all over his face. He avoided touching anything as if he would be unclean because of it.

I smiled because it just proved how different we were from one another. I never quite understood Mavros but I enjoyed his company and odd sense of humor. He was a slightly more gentle version of Ephraim. Boundaries, work, and had their own type of fun.

"Well if you don't think you will be able to handle it then feel free to go back to the palace. If the king asks where I am then try to avoid answering."

He smirked and nodded to walk back to the palace. It wasn't far from here but it was funny to see how fast he walked to get back to the safety of those walls.

Those dark haunted walls.

He was running as fast as he could to be contained inside those walls as I was trying to run as far as I could from it.

I laughed again and then focused my attention to the little ones who were pulling my hands to follow them. I walked behind them, trying to listen to each thing they said. They talked on top of one another, thousands of topics being spoken at once.

For a few hours I forgot about my problems and what I needed to get done. I wanted to live and be in the moment like there was no tomorrow.

But that's not my reality.

My reality is to keep fighting until the battle has been won.

Soraya

Chapter 32

The sun started to set, colors in the sky looked like a painter's palette. Full of different hues of pinks, purples and oranges. The eastern sky beautiful and delicate in every way.

The paintings that hung on the walls were incomparable. It couldn't hold a candle light to the breathtaking view before me.

My back rested on the iron bench, tucked into the back of the garden. Children all around me, shoving their faces with freshly baked bread and food. Baskets filled with fruits we had picked from the trees. Each bite made their eyes roll, you could see the joy in their eyes.

They recharged my dying battery and didn't even know it.

Couples and children danced to the music that softly filled the garden. Happiness spread from person to person; soul to soul.

A little boy dashed to me and extended his tiny hand, "May I have this dance my lady?"

I smiled, my hand waving my face, "I don't think I have ever been asked from such a dashing young man."

Only three of my fingers fit into his hand, his small hand leading me into the dancing crowd. These people treated me like one of them. Nothing expected from me, *finally allowed to be myself.*

A small group of people began playing another song, my heart did happy jumps to the familiar beat. This song reminded me of my childhood, my roots.

The little boy twirled around, not a single worry in our bones. Every beat engraved into me, music expressing my silenced emotions. It brought me and hundreds of others back to life.

I lost track of time, the sky pitch black. Small yellow toned lights strung from the trees.

For something to be beautiful, it didn't have to be extravagant.

The music abruptly stopped, smiles around me faded and heads hung low. My body still spinned in endless circles, unable to see what stopped the festivities.

Then I spun too fast into a hard chest. My eyes didn't have to meet his, to know Ephraim stood beside me.

A deep possessive voice grumbled into my ear, "What are you doing in the midst of this filth?"

His strong hand firmly pressed against my waist, guiding me to meet his gaze. *His husky voice did unspeakable things to me.* Ephraim's hair distressed, curls no longer styled to perfection.

"They are people just like you and I," my wobbly voice answered, "It also seems that you don't care much for me. Might as well surround myself with people who haven't forgotten the essence of life."

His grip tightened on my hip, my teeth dug onto my

tongue. "You are my wife and I don't share you with anyone." His husky voice danced across my skin, a wave of goosebumps arose because of it.

"Well, maybe you would treat your queen like she was something instead of treating her like a trophy. Instead of treating her like she is something convenient. Maybe if you showed a fraction of affection," my eyes fell to his soft lips that were slightly dipped at the edges, "I wouldn't feel the need to search for love somewhere else." My eyes squeezed shut, afraid those words actually came out of my mouth. His grip loosened around my waist, his fingers frozen in place.

A perplexed expression displayed on his beautiful face. A muscle in his jaw twitched, an unpredictable emotion written in his mind.

"Soraya, you have to understand that it wasn't my will to cancel our plans last minute" He pleaded for me to understand.

I found it difficult to maintain my eyes on him. They constantly fell to his lips. I hesitantly took a step back, "Then why did you cancel it?"

If I really mattered, wouldn't he show it?

His fingers instantly ran through his hair once more. *He always did that when he was nervous or stressed.*

"That doesn't matter. What matters is that I don't want you out here alone, especially without me or any guards," he took a step closer. His breath mingled with mine, our lips mere inches from one another, "Especially after I told them to follow you for your own safety and my sake of mind-".

His eyes were filled with a type of desire I have never seen. A type of longing that consumed someone's body, mind, and soul. My mouth went dry at the gaze he looked at me with.

I wanted to convince myself that he truly wanted me and desired me. That I wasn't just convenient to him.

His midnight eyes glued to me, "What are you doing to me?"

His soft husky voice sent a shiver up and down my spine, completely transfixed by a memorizing sound. No words formed in my head, silence my greatest answer. Shallow and uneven breaths, heart pounding uncontrollably.

The plan was not to fall in love. Not to be swept in his dashing gaze.

"Nothing more than what you're doing to me." A breathy response.

His fingers toyed with the dainty necklace around my neck.

His gaze finally came back up to meet mine. The world faded away, nothing else mattered that moment.

I didn't know what he did to me, what this palace was doing to me. My emotions were constantly being challenged. Truths I believed in were conspired against.

I no longer hated Ephraim anymore, maybe I never truly hated him. I pictured him to be something that I learned he wasn't even close to.

He had his own tormenting thoughts like hundreds of people did and had the weight of an entire kingdom on his shoulders. Past trauma that followed him wherever he went.

"I am sorry"

"What?" Ephraim questioned.

"I am sorry" A single tear rolled down my cheek.

His mouth twitched, "I don't think in my 28+ years of life anyone has ever said a sincere apology."

He used the pad of his finger to brush away the tears. Then they came rushing in like a flood. Tears destroyed the hours of work the ladies did on my face. A dam had been broken loose. My hands instantly went to cover my ugly cry but he intertwined his fingers with mine, "Don't hide yourself from me."

I cleared my brittle voice, "So let me into your heart."

He pulled back slightly, surprised by such a request, "A precious jewel like you doesn't need to be exposed to a wretched man like me."

His eyes softened, "Sleep with me tonight. Help the demons fade away so I can be a man again."

I nodded vaguely, strength quickly leaving me. With one quick movement, he picked me up into his arms. I weighed nothing to him, a small feather.

I wouldn't have thought in a million years this is where I would be in my life. Years ago, the thought of marrying a king seemed impossible. The answers I thought I needed weren't the ones that I expected. Each day erased the lines, the guards around my heart, and the plan I was oh so determined to stick with.

Maybe the reason wasn't within me, maybe God had a bigger plan and I had to forget what I wanted for once.

Ephraim

Chapter 33

◆

All tension between us no longer existed. Her head fitted perfectly beneath my chin. Her ears pressed against my chest, letting her hear the uncountable beats of my pounding heart.

Her peaceful soft breaths sounded like calm rushing waters. Soraya's gentle fingers constantly brushed at the nape of my neck, *this woman is mine.* The noise of the busy world faded into a gentle murmur, my mind consumed by her touch.

Unspoken words brought me comfort in so many ways. My mind tranquilized with the sound of her peaceful breaths. My curls wrapped around her long graceful fingers.

The golden doors creaked open, servants swarmed in all directions. *Is the queen okay? Is she sick?*

My hands gripped tighter around her waist. "Leave us alone."

Why won't they stop their constant chatter? Can't they see with their eyes, I want to be unbothered?

The servants tripped over their own feet, tumbling into

one another. Multiple whispers exchanged between them but with one fiery glance, they were silenced.

My back pushed against the red copper doors. A slow creak released as the door swung open, swiftly closing behind me. I leaned down and placed Soraya gently on *our* bed. My eyes slowly trailed up her graceful body, our eyes locked. Her face barely had any makeup, convinced she didn't need any.

She is beautiful.

Months have gone by and I yet to admit that *my* wife, *my* queen, *my* jewel is the most stunning thing I ever laid my eyes on. Breathtaking is an understatement.

She is the only breath my lungs need to survive. The only thing that could satisfy my eyes and desire. No one held a fraction of her beauty, a bit of her grace.

Her heart is more precious than any gem I could ever lay my hands on.

Someone's inner worth is more precious than their body.

"You're beautiful," I confessed, "Nothing on this earth held a candlelight to you."

She resurrected the dead man inside me, the man who once *lived*. The part of me that desired to love and be loved. The part that sacrificed everything for a touch.

Soraya nibbled her bottom lip, deep in thought. Her head furrowed, brows tightly knit together.

I raised an eyebrow, "What are you thinking? What worries you?"

Soraya slipped from underneath me. For several moments, she paced around the room. Her thoughts were silent but loud. When all the pieces in her head were put together, she shuffled to me. Her fingers fiddled with the buttons of the shirt, "I have never done this before but a part of me wants too. I don't know if it's wrong of me to desire your touch and your taste as much as I do."

The worry transformed into awe, my soul sweetened by her honest response. My hands pulled her closer, our foreheads rested against each other. Breaths became one, our hearts pounded to the same beat.

Her bottom lip quivered every few moments. Her fingers never lowered below the first few buttons.

I admire her self restraint but I wanted her to touch me. I wanted to feel her in every sense. My desire is far more than anything she could ever imagine.

My heavy eyes fell to her beautiful lip. The color of her rosy lips made them even more desirable.

Delicate like a flower, it lured me closer,"You better have not done this with anyone else. You're mine and I don't plan on sharing *my wife* with anyone." I grumbled in her ear.

An audible gasp left her gaped lips. Soraya's eyes wide, affected by my possessiveness. Her gentle push didn't move me an inch, "Of course not but-" her grin slowly died, "I don't like the idea that you can have anyone at any time either. It's hard enough to admit that I want this when I have been resenting it for so long."

Her body firmly now pressed against mine, the skirt of her dress consuming the floor around us. Her arms caressed against my bare forearms

I wove my fingers through her silky hair, forcing her to focus on me. I needed to look into her hypnotising brown eyes. My finger grazed her jaw, memorizing the feel of her skin.

I am glad to know I had some level of effect on her like she did to me.

"No woman compares to you, my jewel," a flush crept on her face, "You are a rare diamond I have found and I am all yours. Mind, body, and soul, I belong to you."

I pulled her face a bit closer, unable to think with her lips so close. The way her skin smelled like frankincense, myrrh, and cinnamon had so much power over me

She smelled perfect.

"I might fight demons and satan but I would prefer to die before ever letting another woman touch my body that isn't you,"

Never have I been so convinced of those words. Her eyes glistened with unshed tears, breathtaking portals into her angelic soul. A soul I have grown to desire, grown to need. She wasn't just someone that lived with me, Soraya has become the person I lived for.

"I want to know your taste. I want to know everything about you. Every detail, every curve-" My voice faded away, soaking in the feel of her skin against my hands. My fingers trailed down her sides, stopping at the deepest point of her waist.

She wore a deep green dress with details of gold. It covered her arms and her legs, no skin showing. Even if there isn't any skin to be seduced by, she didn't need it. She didn't need to show her body to catch my attention.

My mind came to the conclusion that whatever Soraya wore on her body would be perfect. Whatever she wore made me yearn for her. Soraya had something inside of her that drove me mad. It made me selfish and greedy. I wanted to lock her away and keep her to myself.

I let my fingers explore to find a way to take this dress off, the rings on my fingers constantly tangled in the fabric.

I grumbled a curse word, desperate to find the buttons of her dress. When I finally found one, hundreds more followed.

Does the world conspire against me?

Her fingers steadily reached the buttons of my shirt. They were slow and gentle. My heart and breath froze.

This woman has me wrapped around her finger and she doesn't even know it.

"Why do you always wear black?" Her breath danced on my hot skin.

Desperation and desire ignited in her eyes. *No,* a voice spoke inside me. I pushed her hands away, *I shouldn't contaminate her with my wickedness.*

I took a stride back, the warmth instantly leaving. Her hands paralyzed mid air, "What? Do you not want me anymore? Am I that ugly to no longer be desired?"

My eyebrows snapped together, taken aback from what she had just said. Instantly, I wanted to silence her doubt. Press our lips together until all logic fails us. Keep lies far away from her heart.

If she could only understand the amount of desire I had. The little self restraint that kept me standing in place.

The dress slipped off her shoulders, exposing the beautiful tan skin underneath. Skin that has been touched by the sun, somewhere I wanted to explore. Soraya is as precious as a rare gem and I have been given the opportunity to know her. To know her and be the only one to have that honor.

I cursed again because I needed to kiss her. I want to get to know her smell, her touch, her body but if I had to risk my happiness and desire to see her still whole, I would do it every time.

"I cannot contaminate you with my weakness. I can't allow the wickedness that lies within me to destroy your purity." *There.* I confessed my greatest fear.

I hope she understood what I meant. I hoped that Soraya could understand the glances and gazes we exchanged.

I didn't want her to know how many women I have slept with. How many people I have killed or what I have done to be here at this moment. A lot of blood has been spilt on my hands.

If my death and silence kept her whole and healed, then so be it. She deserved a man who would treat her with kindness and love yet if any man touched her, I would haunt them from my grave.

If these were the only interactions we would ever have, I would die with a smile on my face.

She has become my only breath and without her I am dead. Soraya is my center of peace, without her I am a puppet in the devil's hands. Soraya is the reason for the change, without her I am a dead man walking.

Soraya took a step closer, slipping her hands underneath my almost open shirt. Light soaking into my skin, her touch is the healing I need. Tingling sensations radiated made my heart beat faster.

Her hand firmly on my heart, *I was going to have a heart attack.*

All consuming thoughts were long gone. I couldn't think of anything else other than the way I adored the feeling of her skin against mine. The way her hand moved every time my rushing heart beat.

"How could you ever say you are undeserving of love if you never have tasted the real thing?"

Time stopped. Everything around us faded away, only specs of colors. She moved her hands to my cheeks, her thumb brushed against my light stubble, "How could you say that I shouldn't want you when you're the man I am married to?"

Even if I didn't want her in the start, I wanted her now.

A sad smile on her lips, knowing I had to make the decision for myself, "Give yourself one night, tonight. I am all yours and if you don't find pleasure or beauty in me, then cast me away but please don't stop yourself from feeling it today."

Those words snapped all self restraint. The voices that spoke, I silenced. The darkness that raged inside my mind and body, imprisoned.

This moment, even if it was going to be one night, I allowed myself to live. I allowed myself to have the person who is consuming my body and mind. If this was going to be the only moment we had with one another then I was going to soak every part of it.

Soraya took off my shirt, her breath caught at the sight of me.

Her fingers trailed over my tattoo that has appeared over time. The first time it had ever appeared was the night I saw my father die. And now most of my shoulder and left chest was a dark tattoo. Designs and swirls covering my tan skin.

I looked deep into her eyes and saw her desire. The way she held herself back. Her gaze made me feel like I was something, like I was someone. Her attention made me feel worthy. If she looked at me like that everyday, I wouldn't need anything else. I would have won all the riches in the world.

She leaned and pressed a gentle kiss to my chest, a small moan leaving my lips. My head leaned back, giving her full access. With each kiss she pressed, blazes of fire erupted.

She pressed another one on my heart, "Those who don't know you would say you are satan himself but I have gotten to know you. You aren't what people say you are, you are a broken man who needs love and attention like anyone else."

My breath quickened at her concession, her words that left my mind paralyzed. I closed my eyes allowing me to feel her every touch, her every breath. How every bone in my body instantly relaxed.

When she took a step back, my eyes slowly opened, peace and hope consumed me. My brain was mush, there was nothing I would rather think about then her.

She played with her fingers, her attention no longer on me. Her brown eyes slightly dimmed, the shine dimmed ever so slightly. Most people wouldn't notice that but I did. I noticed everything in her.

I took a step closer, unable to keep myself away, "Be brave just for tonight. If I repel you, if you hate me, I allow you to never have to see me again. You will never have to lie down with me again but be brave with me."

Soraya

Chapter 34

My mind couldn't think with him so close. A battle against fear and desire in my head. My body trembled with fear and when he noticed, his eyes softened. It softened every so slightly. He reached out his hand, waiting for me to take it. I started at it, it was the most welcoming yet horrifying thing.

No one has prepared me for this moment.

When my hands slipped into his, he slowly pulled me closer, "I desire you more than you know. I desire to know everything about you,"

Ephraim gently squeezed my hand, "What makes you afraid of this moment?"

My vision went blurry because this was the most humiliating thing to say, "No one taught me what comes after. No one prepared me for this night and I am scared."

Several emotions flashed across his eyes. Feelings that he never showed anyone else. *For the first time, someone desired me.*

He didn't think I was stupid or dumb, he still wanted me.

He still desired me despite all our differences. He pleaded to know me, *Who desired this more?*

With one long stride, his body pressed up against mine. His hands were always in contact with my skin, somehow it made me feel grounded. His touch made me feel safe.

His hands slowly went up to my hair, mumbling underneath his breath because of the thousands of pins tangled in it.

"I can do this myself. There are hundreds of jewels and it's a pain in the neck to take them out." My hands already fiddled their way through the complexity of it all.

He placed his hands above mine, stopping me from removing them. His chest rising and falling rapidly as he chuckled. His breath danced against my face, completely sensitive to him.

My soul left my body when I heard his husky deep whisper against my ear, "Give me the honor. I want to be the first man to do this, I want to be the only man. Those maids shouldn't even be doing this."

I burst in laughter from how serious he said it. Ephraim gently took out every golden ornament from my hair. Every time he would touch my hair, he was beyond gentle. Treating me with a level of kindness that no other eye saw.

The way his fingers slowly brushed through my hair as he undid the braid made my stomach flutter. The jewelry would ring every time he dropped one onto the table.

Shortly after, my hair was released and I have never been so grateful for my hair to be set free. A small uncalled moan left from my lips as he massaged my scalp.

A smirk on his face, his hands at the next button, "May I?"

I nervously nodded against every opposition. Any fears that tried to stop me from living this moment were put on hold.

He slowly unbuttoned the dress. Every button bought me

a bit more time, time to compose myself. It helped me remind myself that I am married and I can and should feel desire.

But should I feel this much desire?

When he was finally finished, the dress slowly slid down my body and fell to the ground. My body froze, unable to think what to do next.

Maybe I wasn't what he expected.

The silence in the room was my greatest enemy. Hundreds of thoughts passed through my mind. I got nervous, I whipped around to look at him. My hair whipped behind me and hit my eyes.

His eyes took me in like I was the last cup of water in the dry desert. His eyes burned with the fire of passion, his body slowly leaned closer to mine.

His eyes glanced over at me, a flush coming to my cheeks. "You're so beautiful."

His voice was raspy and thick, which made me want to melt into a puddle. My heart did flips and turns, thousands of butterflies swirling around. It's like I drank all the wine in the palace, high on the feeling of his attention. I was his soul focus that moment and there was nothing greater to that.

He took a step closer to me, hands on either side of me. His breaths had slowed down, our souls in another dimension.

"What now?" I nervously questioned. The desire ran through my veins. The desperate feeling of wanting to be loved ran deep in my veins. The need for his touch made my heart pound uncontrollably.

"This is something for you and I, something we learn together. I promise to be gentle." He spoke softly before his lips finally captured my own.

Ephraim

Chapter 35

I couldn't think of anything except: *Soraya.*

What we experienced together is far better than anything I could ever imagine. My brain couldn't comprehend anything else. From that moment on, I regretted every mistake I made in my past. For not waiting, for not only wanting one woman in my life.

I decided that I was hers from now on. No one would ever capture my attention like she has.

Soraya was deep in slumber, cuddled against my chest underneath the covers. Her arm laid against my chest, not letting me go. She rarely moved during the night, always glued to my side.

My mind replayed everything that happened the last few hours. How we were able to know each other on new levels. The way I felt free and liberated from all torment.

This was different and special.

She slightly shifted her head, her hair pointing in all directions. I grinned because even as she slept, her beauty stunned me. My calloused fingers brushed away her soft hair, avoiding anything that might awaken her. *I didn't want this moment to end.* I wanted to be with her for the rest of the day and for the rest of my life.

The whole world could forget about me.

I leaned in and pressed a kiss to her cheek, then to her forehead and then to her sweet lips. It tasted like honey and the sweetest figs.

She softly moaned, her lips instantly kissing me back, "You should stop before I get used to this attention."

I smiled and leaned closer to her. I knew she loved when I whispered deep into her ears, "Maybe I want you to get used to the attention. Maybe I have decided that I don't want this to be the only time you're in my arms."

She grinned widely, her fingers playing with the hair at the nape of my neck, "Good Morning, my king."

I flashed her a grin, placing another sweet kiss on her lips, "Good Morning, my sweet jewel. How did you sleep?"

She grinned, "After the night we had, it was the best sleep I ever had."

Before I could respond, a knock came from the door, a familiar voice followed, "My King, may I come in?"

I looked at Soraya, who now fully covered herself with the sheets. I peaked underneath the covers to see her eyes filled with fear. *Stop it,* she hissed before shoving her face into my arm.

I laughed loudly, "You can come in."

I laughed even harder when Soraya hit my chest underneath the blankets. She scrunched herself closer to me and gripped onto the sheets for her dear life.

Mavros turned the corner and noticed that I was still in bed, a grin creeping on his face.

"I didn't expect you to be awake my king, how did you sleep tonight?" he said with a wink.

"You know what Mavros, I haven't slept this well my entire life."

He smiled again and placed a stack of paper on my desk in the farthest corner. The stack only grew. "Any specific reason or person that made such a difference?"

I could hear Soraya under the covers whisper, *don't you dare tell him that I am here.*

"That's private information" I smirked because all three of us knew the reason.

He nodded and before leaving he reminded himself of the reason he came, "We need you in your studies my king-" right before he walked out the door he announced loudly, "Good morning, my queen."

When he left, Soraya peeked her head to survey the room. She turned and looked at me with a fake angry expression, "Did you tell him I was here?"

I smiled, running my fingers through her long hair. Her scent was intoxicating and I loved it. Her powerful touch made me weak.

"I have never once woken up happy like I did today and all the credit is to you."

She blushed. Her cheeks now a beautiful rosy color, "All the credit is mine? So that means you're in my debt?"

I smiled and leaned down to whisper against her lips. I have learned that I have an effect on her when I do that and I plan to take full advantage of it. Savoring the feeling of her lips, "I owe you my life, my dear."

She pulled away, her pointer finger trailing up and down my chest. She had a fascination with my tattoo, always gliding her fingers across it, "There's so much power in my hands now," She brushed my messy hair back, "You have to go and do kingly duties."

With a sigh she began looking for her robe but before her

hands even touched it, I extended my hands to intertwine my fingers with hers.

"Just 10 more minutes" I grumbled in her ear.

The kingdom can wait. The word can stop. Soraya is my sole focus right now.

She giggled, "I hoped you were going to ask."

When we finally got up, my chest felt lighter. My head is in a good sane condition. Soraya and I got ready together, taking care of each other.

She buttoned my shirt, as I clasped the jewelry around her neck. Then we stood in front of the golden mirror together. My tall frame towered over her. Even if I seemed to be a shadow, we were perfect. Everything about us was perfect.

She said a few things that I couldn't even try to pay attention to. All my mind thought about was how many hours until tonight. How many hours until I could shut off the world again.

And if anyone tried to keep me working all night, I wasn't going to give in.

When she noticed that I hadn't been paying attention, she huffed and walked away, "You're not even paying attention to me."

"Oh my dear, you have more than my attention."

I grabbed her by her wrist and spun her around. She collided firmly against my chest, grinning at the rising blush on her lovely cheeks.

"Let's go to the beach. Let's escape all this for a bit."

She looked at me like I had gone crazy. Her arms crossed, "You can't, remember."

I grinned, "I may or may not be the king of this kingdom

and I may or may not be able to persuade the counsel to give me three days to be with my wife."

Her head slightly leaned back, giving me a quick moment to kiss her. She hummed with eyes closed, "I love the sound of that."

I kissed the soft skin of her shoulder, "Then pack your bags my queen because it's going to be just me and you for hours and hours."

She giggled and after much hesitation let each other go. She told me that she was planning a banquet and needed to put everything on hold so she could pack. I wished I could be there beside her but I had to deal with the law. *I am the law.* I felt used and pushed to the extremes but needed to remind myself that I signed up for this. Which meant everyone needed me all the time.

I needed to be present all the time and I am now starting to realize how tired I actually am. The feelings that I have buried for so long started to appear again. I didn't want to allow myself to become numb or allow the demand of a kingdom be what keeps me busy and tired for the rest of my life.

I was going to feel and live. As long as I had Soraya by my side, I was going to be okay and I would have the strength to fight against all darkness.

When I arrived at my studies, Mavros and a few other men were waiting for me. They heard me coming in so they began to find their chair and settle in.

"What is it?" I questioned, examining everything laid on my table.

"You're smiling." Mavros stated.

As I walked around them, they kept looking at me. Their

gazes followed me around the room like they were scared for my next move. A servant that was in the far corner came to bring my wine but I shooed him away.

"What happened to you?" Mavros asked, his hand brushing against his beard.

Soraya happened to me. Her smile, her laugh and her touch has made me into a new man.

"Nothing. Now what did you wake me up for?" I asked, leaning back against my chair with my legs on my desk.

All the men came closer to the desk and as always Mavros was the leader, he was the first to speak because I trusted him the most.

"A spy has returned and he has let us know some surprising news," Mavros plopped himself into the chair across from me, "As the spy was coming back to the palace, he found a man clocked and covered. He looked like he was sneaking around."

I laughed and it boomed off the walls. "And that's what you want to tell me? You wanted to tell me that someone decided to play hide and seek?"

Mavros shook his head, "No, my king. This man isn't from here."

Ephraim

Chapter 36

—— ◆ ——

"What do you mean that he isn't from here? Where is he?" I looked around to see if there was anyone unusual but ended up just seeing guilty faces all over the room.

"When the spy figured everything out, it was already too late." Mavros stumbled over his words slightly. He had a tendency to stutter when he was nervous.

I stood up and placed both of my hands on the desk. My fingers curled around the edge of the table, the wood digging slightly into my skin. I could feel the darkness inside me start to rage and the anger boil but then I thought of her.

I thought of the way she made me feel. The way with just a look in her eyes, I would feel seen and heard. It was something I couldn't explain, something worth so much to me.

When I opened my eyes, I gazed at Mavros, "And why are you here telling me this instead of going to try to find him?"

He smirked like he already knew I was going to ask. Maybe Mavros was finally learning to be one step ahead instead of aggravating me any second he got, "The spy has already gone undercover and once he finds this man, he will alert the guards and bring him to the palace."

I sighed, because that's not the answer I wanted but I decided to let it slowly roll off my back because nothing was going to take away my excitement for my trip tonight.

"What about finding the queen of Uosulia?"

Their deadpan faces were the only answers that I needed. Some of them were rocking on the ball of their feet and twiddling their thumbs.

It felt like forever when a man finally decided to raise his voice instead of mumble amongst the others. "The man you sent to figure that out, has been slowly finding more information. He still hasn't seen the queen personally because it seems like she isn't there."

I massaged my temples and cracked my tense knuckles, "And where might she be?"

He slid the letter on my desk about all the information that they have found. I skimmed over it, not having much patience to deal with this. As I skimmed over the words on the page he continued to talk nonstop in my ear, "She isn't anywhere on their island. One might infer that she's either at the Apiritah kingdom or she might be hiding here."

I slammed the paper onto the desk as my dark eyes shot up to look deep into his petrified eyes, "What do you mean that she might be here?"

He cleared his throat and by the way his body shook told me he was nervous, petrified maybe. His skin started to turn a bright shade of red and he kept patting his forehead from the amount of sweat he was drenched in, "Don't worry my king, I have already sent a few men to go look for an unusual activity."

I stood up to face my back against everyone else, taking a moment to take several breaths. My hand on my head like it would protect me from any headache that might arise. My temples were sensitive from the amount of times I rubbed them during the last few minutes. I didn't know if this was exciting news or just a big headache.

Then they decided to jump to another topic because they *wanted to live.* Unsolved and solved situations were being thrown at me, more unsolved than anything else. My ears felt like they were being burned off because of the nonstop noise. The constant chatter and debate between them sounded like a hundred birds at once.

When they finally quieted, I opened my eyes, "Sometimes I debate if I should throw a dice to see if I kill all of you yet by my surprise you are all alive."

Some of them gave a vague smile, not comfortable with my joke. There were others whose eyes were about to bulge out,"I am taking a three day trip. I don't want to be annoyed or bothered at all. So I am leaving Mavros in charge."

When they began to argue and ask thousands of questions, I lifted my hand and in a second they were all silenced, "That is the reason why. I will bring guards with me but I am not to be disturbed because if I am-"

I looked each of them deep in the eye, "I don't think I need to say what will happen," I turned to Mavros "Make sure that everything stays at least semi-functional while I am gone. You have my approval for any necessary actions."

I lifted up and in unison they all bowed deeply before me. I walked around my desk but stopped myself from walking out the door. There were bookshelves to both my right and left, most of them weren't even hard to reach because of my height. I took a quick glance at each and every one of them, picking each book wisely. When I was satisfied with the ones I had picked, I left with hope in my chest.

As I walked down the hall, the guards were beginning to switch posts. Each one of them bowed as I walked past, a type of satisfaction filled my lungs seeing everything organized and scheduled. Once I turned the corner, from afar I could see a piece of paper taped to the wall. Without any thought, I began to walk a bit faster. Scared that anyone else would read that note because deep down inside I already knew what it was. When I was close enough, I ripped it from the wall and grazed over the few words on the small piece of paper.

You're not rid of me. I know of your every move, every plan, and every desire. Say Hi to the Queen for me and make sure you enjoy that three day vacation of yours.

Sincerely, Your Enemy

I crumpled the paper in my hands and cursed loudly, *there was a rat inside my palace.* I didn't even know if there was just one or multiple and at that thought, a knot formed inside my stomach.

I stormed away, not wanting anyone to see the distressed look on my face. My mind began remembering all the other notes I had ever received. No one knew about it so the torment was only to and for me.

You're a failure. You will never amount to anything. You can't even destroy one enemy. You can't even keep your own palace and kingdom in check.

I slammed the door open and when I walked in, Soraya had her hand gripped to her chest. She looked like her heart was going to come out and when I noticed that I startled her, my heart broke.

I dropped the books onto the floor and dashed to her, "Please forgive me, I didn't know that you were in here."

When I wrapped my arms around her, her body slightly

melted into my embrace. I pulled back, our eyes always automatically connecting with one another, "Are you okay?"

She nodded, completely disregarding her small heart attack. "I am fine but what happened? How did they react?"

I shook my head, my eyes trying to find something to focus on. I instantly noticed how Soraya wasn't wearing shoes despite the amount of times she has been told to. There are protocols, certain appearances that we need to uphold.

Yet she seems to destroy every type of expectation I have.

I put that in the back of my mind to ask her later, "Nothing that you need to worry about. Are you ready?"

She answered with the biggest smile on her face and a simple shake off her head, "I even packed something that I bought specifically for this trip."

I hummed, my mind already going a thousand miles per hour. Every thought consumed by her once again, "What is it?"

She shrugged her shoulders, "Oh you'll find soon enough." She gave me a quick kiss on the cheek and strolled out of the room once again leaving me speechless.

She kept talking about how she was excited to see the ocean and the beachside. How she always desired to go somewhere far from the noise that constantly rang in her ears.

Her voice started to become my wine. With my eyes focused on her and only her, her voice was more soothing than anything else. Wine didn't compare to the same effect she was giving me.

I sat at the edge of the bed, watching her walk back and forth. The servants had already packed everything that I needed. There nothing else for me to do except wait for her.

How much does one woman need for three days?

Once Soraya was finished, we walked downstairs and went outside the palace gates to where the horses and the golden litter awaited us. The white horses were drinking and eating before the long ride before us.

Servants had everything ready and they all stood beside one another, waiting for their next orders. I extended my hand out for Soraya as she entered the litter.

Once she sat, I entered behind and sat across from her. The litter was a bit small for two people, our legs kept touching one another.

I smiled despite the slight heaviness I was feeling for some reason, "Are you ready?"

Soraya

Chapter 37

I shook my head, so many feelings erupted constantly in my stomach. My heart seemed to pound at a hundred miles per hour. I kept rubbing my sweaty palms against my dress.

Ephraim and I have been married for a while yet it was still odd to call him husband. He has called me a few nicknames but when I went to call him other than his name or my king, my tongue would freeze.

When we passed the gates of the palace, I stuck my head out and waved to all the children who were waving back. Some yelled that they would miss me and that they were already counting down the hours until they would see me again. Others were running behind us, wanting to follow us until the last moment.

"How long have you been sneaking out?" Ephraim asked beside me, he peeked his head out to see all the noise. He glanced at both sides and then fixed himself in his seat.

"A few months" I responded quickly, hoping that he wasn't going to ask any more questions.

He mumbled something to himself but it was barely audible for me to hear. His hands crossed against his chest, eyebrows knitted together. My attention was still focused on the people but from the corner of my eye, I could see his eyes set on me.

Once all were out of sight, I fixed myself to sit comfortably in the chair. I knew he was still looking at me and every move that I made, but I refused to look back at him. I knew if I did, I was going to melt at first glance.

Was it illegal for a man to look that good and act like it was nothing?

I raised an eyebrow and squinted my round eyes "What are you looking at?"

He shrugged his shoulders, "Nothing, just looking at you and thinking."

"What are you thinking about? Is there anything you want to ask me?"

He leaned closer, his body rocked side to side as the litter rolled over rocks, "Why don't you like wearing shoes?"

I didn't think that he would ever notice because no one ever did. I have been doing that ever since I got here and until now I thought that no one had noticed. The dresses I usually wore would drag along the ground, leaving my feet completely unseen.

"I just don't like them." I answered broadly because I didn't want to tell him, *that's how I grew up. Where I live, we are able to dress how we want and be free but you don't know that about me. In fact, you're trying to kill me without realizing that it's me.*

It has been killing me not to tell him that I am the heir of the people he is trying to annihilate. During our most intimate times, I almost spilled the secret but I couldn't. Zion made me swear that I wouldn't let him know because if he didn't have unending affection for me, he would end my life in the blink of an eye. It didn't matter if I was his queen or if it would cause war, you could always be sure that someone was going to die because of it.

"Can I ask you a question?" Maybe I would get the answer to a question that I had been dying to know.

"What is the question?" He grinned. He leaned closer to me, his elbows rested on both his legs.

"Why do you want to kill the people of Uosulia and Apiritah?"

He sighed and leaned back. "Apiritah has always been an enemy to me, since the beginning of time. That is the reason for my constant headache," he stopped and looked out the window for several moments before he continued, "Uosulia will revolt any moment. After everything I have taken from them, they are bound to fold at any moment."

I took a deep breath in because I knew that wasn't right. Yes there were a few people that wanted to start their own revolt and cause war by themselves but that never crossed once in my mind. I hated war because that's what caused my parents to die. If there was any way to avoid war, I would.

To this day I don't know who killed them and I don't know if I am ready to face them. I don't know if I would be able to keep my emotions in check or talk like a civilized person.

I blinked several times to bring myself back to reality and forget about the questions that I have given up finding the answers for, "And that is seriously the only reason you need to be convinced to kill them? What about the babies and the mothers? The children that are yet to live a full life?"

He looked at me with a question in his eyes. I prayed to God that he wouldn't ask a question that would put me into a corner, "Why are you standing up for them?"

I crossed my arms, "I simply don't think that killing a whole nation for lack of reason is wise. I hate war and I would like to avoid it at all costs."

He mimicked my position and expression, "And why do you hate war?"

Anger bubbled inside me but I gripped onto myself a bit stronger. I was not going to burst in anger every time that topic was mentioned, "Because war killed my parents"

He simply froze as I continued, "It killed my family before my very eyes. They not only had the audacity to kill them in front of a child but to mock me as well."

He cleared his throat and looked to the floor, "And how old were you?"

My vision started to blur because I don't think I ever realized how much it actually hurt. How deep it was within me and how hurt I have been all these years, "I was less than 12."

I have been on my own for over 14 years. I have had to learn how to rule a kingdom by myself and how to become a woman by myself. Zion was there to help guide me in kingdom aspects. How to rule a people, how to make decisions, when to avoid and start war, I knew it all like the back of my hand but sometimes I felt like I didn't know who I was.

I ran around the garden, the golden powers in my veins feeling alive and free. It was late afternoon where the sun was still glowing in the beautiful sky. The trees danced underneath the blowing wind. The fruits and vegetables that hang from trees and bushes would shake and a few fell from the highest branch. I ran over and grabbed the sunkissed ripped fruit into my hands. I placed them inside my pocket so I could eat underneath the starry night.

"Soraya" I heard my mother yell.

I rolled my eyes and moaned. When she yelled my name that way I already knew that she was going to ask me to do something and to stop playing around.

"Yes, mother" I faked enthusiasm.

A few moments later, she appeared beside me with her hands on her hips and a stern expression on her face.

"You are supposed to be with your father in his meeting."

I rolled my eyes at her and sighed, "But I don't want to. All they talk about is everything and anything political and when I think it's finished, they think of a million other topics."

She smiled, "First off, you do not roll your eyes at me"

"Sorry," I spoke softly.

She then knelt down and looked at me at eye level. She was very beautiful and had the prettiest eyes. My eyes were brown which I hated all my life but had those eyes. Those eyes that could stop an entire group of people. Those eyes that seemed impossible to have, they were rare which made them even more beautiful.

Her tanned skin that left her glowing, there wasn't a single blemish or mark on her skin and she looked like she stepped right out of a painting.

Sometimes I wondered if she knew how pretty she was and if I would ever be as pretty as she is.

"One day, me and your father won't be here to take care of you anymore. You will have to learn to take care of yourself and you'll have to learn how to rule our country by yourself."

Everytime she would say that to me, I never liked the idea or the message she tried to tell me. I never wanted to live a life without her in it or have to figure out how to be a queen without my dad. Even if I didn't want to ever accept that idea, I also never knew how close that day would actually be.

I didn't know that the next day would be the first day living my life alone.

"Soraya, are you okay?"

I slightly jumped when I felt him touch my arm and I knew my face was drenched in tears, "I was just remembering the last day I had them with me."

He looked at me with fire inside his eyes, "Who did this to you?"

I sadly smiled, "I don't know. They were masked and never told me who they were but they are long gone now."

He looked out the window in silence and didn't say anything for several moments. Ephraim's eyes didn't meet mine for what felt like forever and when we arrived at the dock for the boat, he helped me out but still in silence. Not a word came out of his mouth and his silence made me uncomfortable.

I climbed into the boat and waited for him to come in but he didn't at first. He went to the guard who was stationed beside the horse and whispered something into his ear. I tried to read what he said with his lips but I couldn't make out pretty much anything.

Once we were settled on the boat and were almost to the island, which was getting closer and closer, I looked at him once more in hopes that he was going to say something to me.

"I will find whoever did that to you and kill them." He looked at me like he was sorry. As if he did it, I knew he didn't and he was beating himself that he didn't stop it earlier but how could he. When I was little he wasn't much older, we never knew one another and we were sworn enemies.

"Don't kill yourself slowly because of that, it wasn't your

fault." I whispered to him even though no one could possibly hear.

"I know but no one touches what is mine."

He called me his.

He called me "mine".

I don't know if that was supposed to give me as many butterflies as it was supposed to but my stomach felt like it was turning and flipping around itself. I wanted to puke from the rocking of the waves but blush from being called *his.*

It was already late at night, the sky was no longer bright pastel colors. It was replaced by a dark blue color, illuminated by bright stars all across the sky. It was absolutely magical and perfect.

We already set up everything and there was already a fire going that one of the few servants set for us. Ephraim said he wasn't going to bring many people, only enough people to not let Mavros go insane.

The three servants that were with us, were in the farthest corner of the small island, eating amongst themselves but still in eye reach. The two guards that came were stationed on either side, not taking their eyes off the ocean. Food that we had brought from the palace was being heated by the fire and a pot of tea was being boiled as well.

I wouldn't change anything about this night and I was grateful that I took a shower before leaving because there wasn't going to be any time when we arrived.

"So how are you?" Ephraim asked, he was on the other side of the fire, leaning against the pile of pillows and looking at me above the flames.

"This is amazing and it's only the first day. I don't know

how this could possibly get better." I sighed with satisfaction in my lungs because this is what I wanted and what I desired.

Simplicity. I didn't need much to be happy, I didn't need jewelry or fancy gowns. I had my own life and that was a blessing in itself.

"I just remembered the night I came to the palace" I smiled because even though back then I would cry at the thought of having to be queen, I made it out okay.

"Why?" he asked, eating a grape that was on his plate of food and taking a sip of the drink in his cup.

"All the girls were gossiping about how much and which jewelry they were going to use to meet you. I don't think they realized how much time would pass before they first arrived when they would actually meet you."

He laughed, "I honestly thought that I was meeting the jewelry and the dress instead of the woman wearing it."

We laughed out loud together, our voices mingled together creating the perfect laugh. I don't know how that was possible or if that even made sense and even if he was a bit under my calming influence, I adored this moment.

Where I didn't have fear of who he was and what he would do. Where you could see in his face that he was relaxed and there wasn't torment in his mind. At that moment, I didn't have to wear the most expensive jewelry or shoes, I could simply be myself even if no one knew the true me.

"What was the funniest moment you remember?" I asked him as I popped a fruit into my mouth, savoring the flavor.

He laughed before even speaking, "A girl wore so much jewelry, I swore she had stolen the whole safe. Every time she would move, the jewelry would jingle nonstop."

I chuckled. "I remember her, she took hours and hours to pick out the right pieces. I guess she wasn't picking which one, she was seeing how much she could add on."

He laughed once again and I couldn't help but freeze. His laugh was intoxicating, in the best way possible. It was like a breeze on the hottest summer day. It was like a warm cup of tea on a rainy day. It felt like the goosebumps you would get after hearing something memorable. I don't know how to describe it other than, it was perfect. I haven't heard him laugh like that before, where it was loud and was a statement.

He slowly stopped laughing and looked at me with the biggest smile on his face, "What is it?" he asked

I smiled, "You have a beautiful laugh, you have never once laughed like that before."

He grinned, "Maybe you have something to do with that."

We continued to chat as the fire slowly began to die down. He would tell me something to make me smile or laugh but I realized that he never once said something painful from his past. I wanted to know something that hurt him, that caused him to be the way he is but I didn't want to pressure him into saying something when the pain was still new.

He avoided any conversations about the kingdom and the latest news but I didn't even care much because I couldn't be bothered to be worried about that. I laid down on the pillows and closed my eyes, resting for a quick second. I don't know how long that lasted before I was being carried by someone else.

Ephraim whispered gently, "Go back to sleep."

I nodded against his chest, not arguing because I would never think in a million years that a trip like that would take out so much of me.

I remember when I first arrived at the palace, I must have been so nervous that I didn't sleep for the entire night. This time, I was struggling to keep my eyes open and stay awake. Maybe it was because lately I haven't been sleeping entire nights and for good reason.

A few moments later, I felt the comfort of something fluffy and soft underneath me. I cuddled to my side and dozed off. I woke up slightly with the feel of something messing with my hair and then a voice spoke "Go back to sleep."

I nodded once again and minutes later, the bed underneath me sank with the weight of someone else laying down.

I hummed and scooted closer to Ephraim, he felt like a magnet. His arms instantly embraced and hugged me. We fell asleep together in one another's embrace.

In the middle of the night, I could feel him getting up to do something. I could hear myself moaning from the pounding headache. Shortly after he came back with some medicine and laid back into bed, right beside me. I was too tired to ask where he had gone and why he kept getting out of bed repeatedly. I didn't ask because I noticed that he eventually always came back. His lips always brushed against my ear for me to fall back asleep.

The rays of sunshine flooded into the space and woke me up from my deep sleep. When I turned around to see if Ephraim was there, he wasn't. The sheets were pulled up and the pillows neatly organized. I whipped my head around, searching the entire space but he wasn't anywhere to be seen.

I got up and stretched my hands above my head. The

headache that began in the middle of the night was already gone and now had enough energy to conquer another day.

Something funny about my powers was that they needed to be charged once again. The more I used them and the farther I was away from my roots the more distressed I got and the more tired I was. I couldn't be myself when I felt life being sucked out of me constantly but what kept my mind at peace was that I was using it for someone's good. I was using it for Ephraim's center of peace and there was nothing I would rather do than that.

I breathed in a breath of gratitude and began dressing for the day. Mehra packed more comfortable dresses, dresses that I had space to breathe in. After much debate, I chose the dark pink dress. It reminded me of ones I used to have at home.

I tried my hardest to tie the dress in the back but struggled. There were multiple strands, impossible to know what I was doing.

With a huff, I let go of the strands and stepped out of the tent. My eyes searched everywhere for someone but everyone seemed to have disappeared. I kept walking around and calling for someone but no one answered.

It was like an eternity passed when Ephraim finally appeared. He had his back turned to me and was deep in a conversation.

When the guards noticed me, they stiffened and whispered something to Ephraim. When he whipped around, he smiled for a moment but then noticed me gripping onto the dress for dear life and the sleeves that had slipped off my arms, his smile quickly faded.

He came rushing towards me, you could hear his stomps even in the sand. His hands pushed against my back and into the tent. Ephraim closed it behind him and without a word began to tie the dress.

"Where did you learn to do this?" I wondered out loud.

His hands froze for a moment. "Nothing you need to worry about."

Once the dress was tied, I could finally let go of it.

"I don't want you to ever do that again." He growled beside me.

I drew myself back. "Do what? I wasn't outside butt naked."

He dragged his hands across his face like he couldn't believe what I just said, "You showed your shoulders and anyone could tell your dress wasn't on properly."

I sighed, "The only reason that I went out there was because I was trying to find you to help me with my dress."

He huffed, several breaths in and out before he spoke again, "Finish getting ready for breakfast."

I looked at him as he walked out the room, his voice slowly becoming more quiet. I was frozen, unable to understand what had just happened. I didn't think I did anything because we went to sleep alright but then we woke up he seemed different. Like something had happened during the night that left him without peace, like his mind was in a battlefield.

Even if everything inside me told me not to snoop in his stuff, I did it anyway. I looked through his clothes that were lying down on the ground, searching in pockets and his satchels. Something inside me protested like I knew what was going to happen without knowing what I was going to find.

I kept looking but couldn't find anything in sight. There wasn't anything out of the ordinary and when I almost gave up looking, was when I heard something. It sounded like paper. I took a few steps back and found where the sound was coming from. When I reached in, it was a crumpled piece of paper. With a shaky breath in, I opened the paper and slowly read what was on it. My stomach plumped into a cold state.

You're not rid of me. I know of your every move, every plan, and every desire. Say Hi to the Queen for me and make sure you enjoy that three day vacation of yours.

Sincerely, Your Enemy

This might be a reason why he isn't well but what made my stomach turn was that whoever this person was knew who I was. He knew that we were on a vacation and we were going to be all alone.

I wanted to vomit, unable to contain myself. I hid the paper back where I found it and continued to get myself ready but my mind kept going back to that note.

Who wrote that?

Who was it?

What was I going to do?

This battle might be way bigger than I originally thought.

Soraya

Chapter 38

W e were finally eating breakfast but it was weird. Ephraim was silent and he couldn't pay attention to eating for more than 5 minutes. He would look around several times like someone would jump out and scare us. A guard came and pulled him to the side about twice and you could tell, no matter how many times that he denied it, he was troubled.

It wasn't just him, I was troubled as well. I didn't know how to feel about the note I had found earlier and it wasn't just because of that. It was the unsettling feeling inside me that I had invaded his privacy and found something that looked like it was being hidden.

What if there were other notes like these?

What if this wasn't the first one that he mysteriously received?

Has he found out who sent this one?

My mind thought of a bunch of questions that I could ask him but if I did, he would know that I snuck through his stuff and would lose trust in me.

So breakfast was accompanied by an uncomfortable silence that I was starting to break under but before I said something I would regret, he broke the silence first.

"I need to resolve something." He stood up, he brushed against his pants.

"You promised me that you wouldn't work on this trip." I whispered quietly, trying to not act like a child.

He looked at me with defeat and a big sigh, "I have no choice." and walked away.

I sat there alone and in silence, eating the rest of my food all alone. So far today was nothing that I had expected and I now don't know what to do for the rest of the day or maybe even the rest of the trip.

What could possibly be so important that you couldn't sleep because of it or even eat for 30 minutes? Then I thought again, maybe I didn't want to ask myself that question.

Each second of the day seemed to be worth an hour. The time wouldn't pass and the day wouldn't end. I knew I was going to spend the whole day doing nothing and being all alone, I guess that's what you sign up for when you're queen.

After what felt like an eternity, the sunset finally peaked between the clouds. There were no buildings in the way and barely any trees clouding my view. The ocean reflected the beautiful colors and it seemed like I was inside a beautiful painting. I always compare a sunset to a painting but how couldn't you? They looked like something beyond this world and I loved every part of them.

When I felt like there was nothing I could do for the last few hours of the day, I got an idea. I rushed into the tent and changed into swim wear. I looked at myself several times in the mirror because I wanted to make sure it wasn't showing more than it was supposed too.

I never felt so self conscious then when I was wearing something that showed a bit more skin. I felt exposed in a way, all my imperfections showing, like they were on display for the entire world to see but in reality no one cared who I was. No one was going to remember me when I died or when I was no longer here. I was a breeze of the wind, one moment I am here and the other I am gone.

I brought myself from the rushing thoughts that seemed to be a chain, leading me into a spiral. I glanced at myself one more and with a smile, I walked back into the ocean.

I dipped my toes into the water to my surprise it wasn't frigid. It had been sunkissed. A deep steady breath filled my lungs as I dove into the water. The water swallowed me whole like I was nothing but it was comforting in a way. Surrounded by water in all directions made me feel like nothing compared to it.

My head above water and took a deep breath in. This was wonderful and I couldn't believe I haven't done this before. Escape to an island and be free for a few moments. I guess that's all I ever really wanted to feel, free. Where there weren't any laws binding me in what I could and couldn't do. There weren't any lies being spoken to me or any decisions I had to make. Here I was just myself and I didn't have to worry about outside appearance.

I dove back into the water, swimming a bit further from shore. I swam a bit closer to the sun, and a bit farther from reality. When I looked at the crystal deep blue water around me, I took another deep breath in and let myself sink, where I was surrounded by it from the top of my head to the bottom of my toes.

Waves, a soothing sound and the feel of animals passing somewhere, were what I felt.

I opened my eyes under water and for a reason that I didn't know, my eyes didn't burn. I could see everything around me. Every single beautiful creature that swam past me. Whales and fish came and went in small groups, like they were little families.

I smiled, turning around slowly in the water. Then I was caught by surprise when I noticed small glowing jellyfish around me. They glowed purple, pink and blue hues. An unexplainable beauty. I don't think I have ever seen it up close but I was memorized by it. The way their tentacles would go out and then back in as they swam. There were absolutely beautiful creatures.

Breathtaking.

When my chest began to tighten, I went back up to the surface. Taking deep slow breaths as my mind replayed what had happened. I glanced behind me to see I was slightly farther away now.

No one was screaming for me or following me. I had left unnoticed and part of me wondered if anyone even cared.

There were only a few last moments before the sky would go dark so I soaked it in. If I had to recharge my battery alone, so be it but I wasn't going to trade this for anything.

My feet treaded in the water to keep me afloat. My arms began to burn from the work. When I was about to turn back to shore, I felt a familiar pair of arms wrap around my waist. My back fleshed against his chest. His breath was heavy from the swimming he had just done. I didn't even need to turn around to see who it was, the flutter in my chest already gave it away.

I wasn't mad at him but slightly upset because of what had happened today. I wanted these few days just to be us. Where I could go back to my roots and get to know him a little bit more. When he was this close to me and when his breath danced against my skin, I couldn't think straight. My brain didn't function at his touch.

I couldn't be mad, upset, or dismissive of him. He held me close against him, his hand wrapped around my waist. Even under water, his thumb danced up and down my bare skin. His left arm and legs were in repeating motions that kept us afloat.

"Why are you mad at me, my queen?" He purred into my ear.

Ephraim

Chapter 39

S he was upset with me by the way she refused to completely lean against my chest. Not a word slipped her precious lips.

Was she upset because I had been busy all day?

Did she want to be with me as much as I did?

I knew I always messed up. I guess it came with the nature of being myself but I couldn't stand it when she was upset with me. When she stayed quiet when I wanted to talk, killed me on the inside. When I wanted to hold her and she pushed me away made me taste death again.

When she didn't respond after I waited for what felt like an eternity, I spun her around and made her face me. I was surprised that I was keeping her and myself afloat, I guess working out when I am angry, which is all the time, was worth it. I didn't really work out, I mostly punched people.

"Why did you go quiet?" I whispered the question. I knew she couldn't resist me when I talked like that.

"Maybe because you invited me on this trip and on the first

day you already left me to the side to resolve who knows what."
She huffed. Her bronzed arms crossed over her chest.

"You don't need to worry about it. I resolved it and now I
am back." I offered her a small grin, her frown remained.

"Well that's your response to everything, isn't it? Your
answer is always that," She looked behind me for a few seconds
and then refocused her chestnut eyes on me. "You weren't
normal at breakfast. You had an outburst with me and you
were troubled since we got here until now. So don't pretend or
lie because I have noticed everything."

I knew there was no way around her. She noticed the way I
had avoided her eye contact and the way I was pulled to the
side multiple times.

"Something happened at the kingdom that I needed to
start resolving now and then I'll finish once we get there." I was
beginning to think that she wasn't going to let this go until she
was satisfied with my answer.

Between dealing with political problems or her upset face, I
was weaker for her. Her pout was my deepest weakness.

"How about this," I brushed a strand of wet hair from her
face, her lips slightly parted in an *oh* shape.

So I have an effect on her. That brought me more satisfaction than it should. "We put this on the backburner for now
and once we get home, you will be right by my side as I resolve
that issue. Deal?"

Now it was my turn to hold my breath. In hopes that she
was going to agree with me and decided to leave this situation
in the back of our minds for now.

"And how are you going to make up for today? I was all
alone, may I remind you." She uncrossed her arms and instead
wrapped them around my neck. I don't know how I was still
withstanding both our weight but I didn't care if my arms were
going to burn, all I wanted was to keep her close to me.

I leaned closer to her, my lips brushed against her wet skin. She leaned her head slightly back which gave me space to kiss over and over again.

I will never get tired of kissing her.

She shivered slightly and that brought a deeper sense of satisfaction. I knew deep down, even if she was mildly upset, she wanted me like I wanted her.

I don't know how over a short amount of time, she has been able to break through my walls and have such a deep effect on me. After years, building up the walls around my heart and mind, she tore through them like they were nothing and that worried me slightly.

She could do anything to me and I would be her slave in it all. She could break my heart and I would accept it. She could trade me for another and I would let her, if it all meant to make her happy but how could I. How can I leave my heart to be so exposed and so fragile. I am king and I have the power of death and darkness inside me, yet with her I am nobody and I don't like that.

I became vulnerable and weak and I couldn't let that happen because everytime I used to let someone in, they would betray me and break me in the end.

"Oh don't worry, my jewel, I will make it up to you tonight-" I whispered softly in her ear. My words came to a halt when I pressed another kiss on her cheek.

She giggled and gripped onto me a bit tighter. "I saw the most beautiful jellyfish under water."

I pulled away slightly. "Only you would find beauty in an animal most hate. Describe it to me."

For several moments, she described the group of jellyfish she saw under water. How they glowed beautiful colors in unison. Her eyes glowed the longer she talked about them. Her hands flew everywhere as she explained every detail.

She had passion in her eyes and fire in her soul and every time that she got like this it just proved to me once again that she shouldn't be with me. The voice in my mind said that I wasn't good enough and I shouldn't be with something that was too good for me.

I have convinced myself that I deserved the worst in life and I don't think anyone has ever changed my mind about that but Soraya. Soraya has challenged me in every way that I used to believe. The path I am walking on is the only way. The truth about myself and others, everything. Over time I have convinced myself that everyone hated me and was only around me because they wanted something.

Soraya has never asked me for anything or shown me otherwise but if she ever betrayed me for something or someone, I wouldn't be surprised. I would be heartbroken and betrayed but it's what I accept out of everyone. I accept everyone at one point or another to stab me in the back and walk away, I just don't know when and sometimes that kills me.

"Why are you looking at me like that?" She looked at me with the biggest smile on her face. Her cheeks were a bright pink color and she looked beautiful under the almost dark sky.

"Convincing myself once again that I don't deserve you because I know I don't." I admitted out loud.

She will backstab you at some point. Kill her first, a voice spoke loudly.

I whipped my head around to see if it was someone but there was no one. Soraya slightly titled her head to why I was startled out of the blue. I gave her another kiss to silence any questions that might come.

"And once again I say that you deserve love like anyone else. You have to stop allowing yourself to be robbed of that." She spoke softly, her gaze dropped to my lips.

I wanted that kiss more than anything. I wanted it more

than the breath in my lungs because she had become my oxygen. She kept leaning closer and closer and when our lips almost brushed together, when I could almost forget about the torment in my head, a loud *bang* pulled us apart.

I whipped my head around and looked back to land and something was happening that I couldn't tell from this distance. Soraya gripped onto me even tighter, her heart pounded rapidly from the loud sound.

"Hold onto my shoulders." I spun around, waited for her to grip onto my shoulders and started to swim to shore.

As we got closer, I noticed a few people from our kingdom and a few more guards. I cursed underneath my breath because I don't think people get the hint when I say that I don't want to be bothered. It was like my *no* was their *yes*. I kept swimming as fast as I could, using the rest of the strength inside of me.

Once we got to land, I used my body to cover Soraya as I guided her inside the tent. I whispered for her to take a bath, get ready and prepare herself for a dinner together.

Her face looked worried and I assured her that nothing was going to happen and that I was going to be okay. After much convincing and a few stolen kisses, I turned around and headed to the group of people and guards.

"Do you not get the definition that I don't want to be bothered. I left the kingdom to be left alone yet you come after me" My hair dripped against my bare chest.

I could feel my back start to tense up and the darkness start to rage. My gaze darkened as I looked at each and every person that had the courage to not listen to my orders.

I was about to kill each and every single one of them. Make them wish that they had never bothered me. The darkness started to radiate off me and when they saw, they took a step farther from me.

"It better be important because if it's not, it will be worth your life." I hissed at them.

One of the men took a step forward from the rest of the group and automatically I recognized his face. He was the boy that I sent to find out who the queen was. It had been weeks since I had last seen him. He better have not come here to tell me that he found more information but still didn't know where she was.

"We don't know who the queen is." He explained.

Before he could get far, I took a big step closer to him and wrapped my hand around his neck.

Did I give him a chance to explain himself? No.

Was he already annoying me by being here? Absolutely.

I began to tighten my grip around his neck that was slowly turning black but before he lost all ability to talk, he gasped out: "But I know where she is."

Ephraim

Chapter 40

I slowly took my hand away from his neck and looked at him with confusion on my face. He had a sly grin on his face and for a moment, I regretted not slapping that look off his face.

"Where is she?" I could feel my hands slowly tightening around themselves.

Whoever this woman is, she deserved to die because she has wasted my time and riches more than I wanted to. Above all that, she was giving me a big headache and I wanted to get rid of it.

"She is somewhere within the borders of your kingdom."

Those words dropped into my stomach like a chunk of ice and I hated how it was making me feel. I yelled out a long line of cuss words and threw the cup that was in my hands.

"How could you idiots not have noticed this earlier?"

I spun around to look at each one of them, shaming them with the look of my eye.

"We didn't know but the last piece we used to figure out

that she was here was that someone from her kingdom snuck inside yours."

I took a step away, rubbing my hands over my face and running it through my hair. It was as if when I decided to get away from all this, it got worse someway, then I remembered.

Mavros told me that someone had snuck inside the kingdom and they weren't from here. Maybe the queen and this man were connected somehow. Maybe he was bringing her important information that would be the end of me.

"Go back and tell Mavros to hold him prisoner until I get there tomorrow night. I will question him as soon as I get there."

The man nodded and turned around to set up camp for themselves at the far end of the small island. I signed the guards for them to go back to their posts and to leave us alone once again.

This woman was starting to get on my nerves and I wanted to end not only her but everything that belonged to her. My father was never able to keep them under control and reign them with power but I will. I will prove him wrong and show him that I am more powerful than he ever will be.

That whatever he wasn't able to do, I will. I will make him turn in his grave with jealousy.

Once I had walked back to the tent, I sighed loudly and threw myself face forward onto the bed. I heard Soraya walk back and forth in the room but not a single word came out of her mouth. My hands were cupped behind my neck as I laid there in silence.

When I became king, I hadn't expected all this to be thrown into my hands. I thought it was an easy thing where I didn't have to think much about anything or anyone. This was causing a big headache because instead of it going away in the blink of an eye, it was lingering. I couldn't get rid of them no matter how much I tried but I was getting close. Victory was near, once I finished with them then I only had Apiritah to end, but I knew they were going to be easy.

"What's wrong?" Soraya's sweet voice spoke from somewhere nearby.

"Kingdom problems that seem to follow me wherever I go." I moaned loudly into the pillow in front of me.

She sighed. "Well I was going to see if you wanted to dance with me underneath the stars but I don't want to bother you."

That perked my interests. I slowly sat up right and turned around to look at her.

Breathtaking wouldn't even begin to describe how she looked in that moment. She was the definition of beauty.

Flashbacks of the first time I saw her inside the kingdom came back to memory and I couldn't help but smile at the thought. If you would have told me that I was going to marry her then I would have called you crazy. I didn't see her face that day but only someone as beautiful as her could have eyes like that.

I stood up and slowly walked closer to her, her eyes growing wider and wider but I wasn't focused on them. I was taking each part of her in, breathing her in. The way her long green dress covered her. It was simple, almost no details but she seemed to make the dress worth so much more.

The way she barely had any jewelry on. The only ones she had were on her barefoot feet. I smiled because for once she wasn't trying to hide them from me.

Then I looked at her face that was covered in the most beautiful green fabric. It cascaded down her long loose hair and wrapped around her face, leaving only her big brown eyes visible to be seen. She was practically clothed and covered from head to toe and never once in my life did I think that was beautiful.

Never once did I think that having a woman covered would draw me in and make me desire a taste of her. I had been led to believe that beauty was measured by the amount of skin shown but that theory was destroyed in only moments.

Soraya didn't follow those guidelines I had formed inside my head. She wasn't like any other woman I'd been with in the past. She glowed not from the outside but within. The power that was inside of her, was stronger than any wine I have ever drank. She made me drunk with only a look from her. She made me high with only a touch.

How could a man not be obsessed with that, with her. Sometimes I didn't even feel like a king beside her. I felt like a servant and she was my master. She could tell me to die and I would in a heartbeat. Her command was my reason for living.

"You're," The words of my mouth couldn't even come out. Everything I was thinking in those moments, it wouldn't come out even though I wanted them too.

I planted a kiss on her hand, our eyes locked with one another. I let my lips linger on her glowing soft skin for a moment longer. Giving her the same effect I knew she had over me.

"Beautiful." I took a small step closer to her. She had to force her head up to keep looking at me. Our height difference made it all the better. My hands slipped down to her waist as I pressed a gently soft kiss to her forehead.

"And you're mine." I whispered into her ear. I could feel her tremble and shiver slightly as I said it.

"I am happy that I have an effect on you like you do to me. Oh my jewel." I wrapped my arms around her and kept her close to my heart. Her head was pressed gently against my heart and I hoped that she could only hear the heartbeats and not the threatening darkness inside me. That the heartbeats she heard pound inside my chest was only for her, that they began to beat again because of her but I still wanted to keep every dark and crippeled part of me away.

"What are you doing to me?" I whispered quietly. I didn't know if she had heard me because she didn't even answer or move.

She took a step back and even though I couldn't see her sweet lips, I knew she was grinning underneath. She took a slow turn around, letting me drink her in.

I was hypnotized by her beauty.

I was a lost man at sea and I don't think I want to be found.

Soraya

Chapter 41

We were already heading back home after three crazy yet peaceful days. We danced under the stars, swam in the ocean and slept late every night. I got to know Ephraim on levels that I never imagined and I loved every moment of it.

The boat ride was quiet because Ephraim was talking to one of the guards. His facial expressions would go unreadable to visibly irritated. Once in a while he would steal glances at me with a small smile on his face and then turn back his attention to the conversation he was in the middle of.

Once we arrived on land, the guards and servants transferred our items onto the carriage. One of the guards extended his hand out to help me get off the boat. I looked for Ephraim but he was still busy talking, so I decided to take it.

I would have never thought that in a million years I would desire him. I didn't think that I would want his touch or his soft words being spoken to me but my world was being challenged. Everything I thought he was, he wasn't. He was a man that was dealing with the weight of many on his shoulders while trying to keep himself sane and I couldn't judge him for that because I don't think I would do any better.

I have been trying to reign a country and keep myself sane while living in a place that I don't know anyone. Where I can't speak freely and have to examine every word to make sure I wasn't exposing myself in any way. Even with all my small problems, I panicked and I feared.

I feared that I wasn't making my parents proud and that I wasn't ruling our country to the best it could be. With the countless pieces of advice I have had over the years, I still felt inferior.

How was I going to rule a country that I was queen of and I was married to the man that was secretly wanting to kill me and my people?

I was living a double life that he didn't know about and my heart was starting to be torn in two. The part of me that was starting to fall for him, couldn't say anything about where I was from or who I was without revealing my secret. Every time he would ask me, I would have to make it so broad that he wouldn't be able to put the pieces together.

The queen side of me didn't know when it would be the right time to tell him, to ask him to have mercy over myself and my people. That if he truly loved me and if all those words he spoke to me at the dead of night were true, that he would spare me from the blade that was prepared for my death.

I sighed because a part of me has given up trying to find those answers because I have begun to learn that only time was going to reveal it to me and I hated to wait.

Then something inside of my stomach made my yelp in pain. It was like a shake went through me and I was left in agony. I wrapped my arms around my stomach as if it was going to do something and closed my eyes, praying that it was going to go away.

A few moments later, the carriage shook slightly like someone was coming in. I didn't open my eyes but my heart seemed to come out of my chest when I felt a large hand gently touch my knee.

I looked up, my vision correcting itself to notice a concerned Ephraim in front of me. His eyebrows were scrunched together and his hands gripping my knees.

"What's wrong?" he asked softly.

I shook my head, signaling it was nothing and that I was going to be fine but when he wouldn't move and was not convinced I answered him, "I just have a stomach bug but it's probably from the boat."

He looked at me trying to find anything that could signal a lie but when he found that I was telling the truth he simply nodded and then without me saying anything, he grabbed me and brought me to sit beside him. His arms gently pushed my head to lie down on his lap.

I didn't go against him or say anything but allowed myself to lie down beside him as he kept brushing my hair with his fingers. He rarely had a gentle touch, it seemed to be only with me he did. His fingers kept going through my hair and massaging my scalp.

A wave of relaxation and comfort came over me as he did that. My eyes began to get heavy and my body started to relax. When I was about to fall asleep I heard him say something underneath his voice. It was so quiet and soft that I would have missed it, if I hadn't paid slight attention. So I went to sleep not only in peace but with my heart warmed by the small actions of affection that my husband showed me.

"Are you the answer my heart has been longing to have?"

"Soraya, wake up." Ephraim's voice muttered from a distance.

I grumbled. "Five more minutes."

All I could hear was him chuckling. It hadn't even been five minutes and I felt a strong arm wrap around my legs, and another behind my back.

To get out of the carriage it was a bumpy ride but once we were out, I was being swayed back to sleep by his footsteps. Ephraim was talking to guards, greeting them with a simple nod.

I blacked out for several moments, nothing was awakening me but then I heard a voice. A voice that I have grown used to know and it belonged to a person that I deeply admired. I gently shook my head, maybe I had been dreaming.

It can't be him. He wouldn't dream of coming here unless it was something important.

I opened my eyes and Ephraim didn't even notice that I had woken up. He was so busy talking to Mavros that both of them didn't notice me.

When Mavros noticed that I had my eyes open, he smiled, "Hello, my queen. How was your nap?"

Ephraim turned to me, his eyes meeting mine and like if it was an instant reaction, I blushed. I could feel my face become hot and red so I hid my face against his chest. Both of them laughed and continued to talk.

I didn't pay attention to anything he said, my mind trying to figure out if the voice I heard was in a dream or it was real.

For reasons that you do not need to know. I do not have to explain myself to anyone beside the leader of this kingdom, It was undeniable that it was him.

I knew his voice from the back of my mind but what is he doing here? Ephraim told Mavros to go away and then let me carefully on the ground.

He brushed his clothes back to the way they were, untouched.

"I have to go resolve that intruder." You could already tell that he was annoyed.

"You said that I could go with you" I reminded him of his words that he told me.

He grinned for a moment and then went back to his unreadable face, "You were asleep in my arms just moments ago."

I raised my eyebrow and challenged him with just a glance. He looked at me with the same amount of challenge and his arms crossed. We stayed there for several moments, looking at one another, waiting for the other to give in but neither of us did.

Then I remembered what he told me and smirked. I took a step closer to him, my hands gently brushed against his arms and chest. He squinted his eyes, not expecting my next move.

"I remember you telling me that I have an effect on you." I beamed for a second before reaching on my tiptoes and placing a soft kiss on his cheek.

He closed his eyes for a second before fluttering them back open and I knew that he was starting to give in. "I also remember you saying that you were hypnotized by me."

His eyes opened wide. The edges of his eye crinkled with humor. "You weren't supposed to hear that."

I played with the button of his shirt. "Oh but I did."

He gave me one last look before taking a step back. "You're going to pay because of that. You're not allowed to torture me." He hissed and took my hand. I knew he wasn't mad by the way his thumb kept brushing against my skin. The way the skin underneath his touch felt alive with every stroke.

We stood in front of the gate for several moments, waiting for the guards to open the door. I held my breath like it was going to be the last one that I was going to have because this moment was going to either keep me together or be my undoing.

When the guards finally opened the door, the creaking sound signaling that they were opening, I closed my eyes for several moments, hoping that whatever I was about to see was going to be a dream but then my heart plummeted to the ground.

It wasn't a dream because what I saw broke my heart slowly. Ephraim gripped my hand a bit tighter letting me know that we had to start walking inside the throne room. I looked at him several times, praying that he wasn't actually here.

Once we sat down on the thrones, I looked at him, tears threatening to overflow but they couldn't. I couldn't allow them to run down my face because Ephraim would think I had gone crazy.

The guard by the intruder's side gripped onto his arm so tight that I almost yelled for him to let go but I bit back my tongue.

The guard looked at him with disgust and then focused his eyes back at the king. "This man is an intruder. He is not from here and has insisted in saying that he doesn't need to say anything to anyone except your highness."

I examined Ephraim as he examined the man. Ephraim looked him up and down before he spoke. "Who are you?"

Ephraim's voice was booming off the walls. The man he was when it was just us two was long gone and now stood in his place was a hard, dark unreadable king.

My emotions were riled up and I no longer knew how to feel or what to think but my emotions were truly a mess once the man said something.

My voice broke with every single word that he said, "My name is Zion and I am from Uosulia."

That moment made my heart break in a million pieces because those words confirmed what I was afraid of. I was okay with putting myself in the middle of danger but I didn't want him to be here as well.

I wanted Zion to be far away from here. My heart could take everything that was happening. My mind started to think about a thousand possibilities.

What if Zion came to tell me something important about home?

What if Ephraim found him guilty for no reason?

What if he died before my very eyes?

I didn't like the answer to any of those questions and my heart began to pound harder and harder. My stomach grew cold and uneasy. I didn't know what to feel or what to think. My mouth went dry and the ground underneath me started to move.

I gripped the arm rest of the throne and closed my eyes.

Maybe if I close my eyes this nightmare will pass and I will wake up.

I wanted to convince myself that I was going to wake up from this.

"The queen and I will judge this cause." Ephraim spoke loudly beside me and with that, the world went black.

Ephraim

Chapter 42

One moment, Soraya was well and the other she passed out beside me. I don't know what was happening and why I was feeling like someone was ripping a part of my heart out as well.

I dismissed the questioning for now and sent Zion into the dungeon. The thought of losing Soraya to something I didn't know how to fight against would be the death of me.

The moment Soraya fainted, I rushed to her side as her weak body fell into my extended arms. I gripped onto her and began yelling orders. With her small body pressed against mine, I ran like my life depended on it.

I placed her in bed and paced back and forth in the room. The fear gripped my heart and it left my heart in complete anguish. Flashbacks from when my mother laid in bed sick or out of the blue would fall ill, I remember every single feeling those nights. Now it was like it was being repaid and the only thing that has changed was that I got older. The one thing that never changed was that things like this happened to the people I most loved.

I couldn't allow myself to care for people because this was inevitable. Things like this would happen and I felt like this is my fault, I have convinced myself it has to be my fault.

I looked at Soraya again, slowly walking up to her and checking if she was still breathing but I stayed there and continued to look at her.

What if I want to feel hope?

What if I want to be different?

After all these months, Soraya has been teaching me and changing me. I never asked her and she never forced me to but she simply did. She changed me without having to speak something but her actions have been speaking more than words will.

And for the first time in my entire life, maybe I was feeling hope. Maybe I was starting to feel the change and didn't want to go back to the way I was.

The darkness inside me slowly haunted me less and the thoughts didn't keep me up at night. She was the reason because of all that, I didn't do anything.

I didn't keep on smiling when someone threatened me. I didn't care about the names of those who lived with me for so long but she did. She did that all and more.

That was the moment I realized that Soraya was my escape from all this; my hope.

So no, she couldn't die because I needed her in my life. If I had to step between her and death I would but nothing or no one was going to take her away from me.

I kneeled beside the bed, holding her hand inside of mine, "Don't leave me Soraya. I have been a fool" the words started to get stuck in my throat, "I haven't realized until now. I didn't realize until now that I needed you this much but I do."

Maybe that was the first time in my life that a single tear

rolled down my face. I haven't cried since the death of my mother, that was the moment since I boxed up my emotions.

"Don't leave me." Those words were so small but they were what my heart was screaming at that moment.

I couldn't lose her, especially not when I began to realize the difference she was making in my life.

Not now, not ever.

I opened my eyes like those words would be a miracle to wake her up from whatever struck her but she still laid there, looking close to lifeless. It was killing me and my emotions were being stirred inside me.

Every moment she wasn't with me, or when she was just a dream away was another moment that I couldn't breath. Another moment where I was struggling to keep myself from going insane.

I decided to get up and away from her before I did something that I would regret or the answer and confusion inside me would get too crazy and before I knew it there was already a cup of wine in my hand. I was drinking it, demanding another cup after another. When I started to sway side to side was when I finally knew that the effect I needed was starting to happen but it didn't settle right with me like it usually did.

I slowly swayed side to side as I walked down the hall, not knowing where I was going to go. Concubines threw themselves at me but I quickly strolled away.

Never did I think that staying with multiple women was wrong but lately I am repulsed at the idea. The idea of having another woman's hand touch my body beside Soraya left my stomach in agony.

Soraya, I wanted to run back to her to see if she was awake but I needed to hold myself back. I couldn't be so dependent on her, I needed to give her space.

Don't show weakness. Don't allow her to be your downfall, a voice spoke to me.

I shook my head, trying to shake those words away but failed when I tried again.

You are unworthy of love, it spoke again.

I gripped my head, *No. Soraya told me that I am worthy of love. That I need to allow myself to know it before I can determine I am unworthy of it.*

It was like I could hear a laugh, like the darkness was laughing at me for having hope and for dreaming of being loved.

I might have spoken too soon. You have already fallen into her trap.

I hissed outloud, heads turning in my direction and before they could even say anything, I waved them away. Crouched onto the floor, my hands trying to cover my face and head.

You're worse than your father ever was, the voices spoke again.

"Can't you just leave me alone?" I spoke out loud in suffering.

The voice stopped for a moment but then continued to torment me. They spoke of possibilities that made my heart scream with fear.

Memories of the past flooded into my mind as I remembered my father when he died drunk. That night was the greatest nightmare that turned into my reality. I didn't want to become like him, I didn't want my life to be lived in such a void.

Yet until now, that's what my life has been; dark void. All I wanted was wine, power, and woman and nothing else but that all seemed to make the hole inside me bigger.

Then I remembered the rose all the way down the hall. Picture frames blurred past as I ran with everything that I had left. The door swung furiously as I shoved myself into the room.

When I reached it, I swore it was a brighter shade of red and even if it was unnoticeable to most, I knew it was. I touched the glass once more and the words *hope* appeared. I touched it again and the same word appeared once more.

Hope. It was something that I was starting to experience because I never realized that hope was even available until I met Soraya. She has brought hope into my life and a new point of view, what was I going to do without her?

She wasn't becoming my reason to live, she was my reason and motivation. I would repeat it to myself until every doubt in my mind went away.

She was my wife which I had been treating so poorly all this time and yet she always treated me with honor.

Memories flashed in my mind of all the times she was there for me, bringing me comfort when a nightmare tortured me in the dead of night. When she would put my mind at ease when I was confused.

It all made sense. Every piece connected. The old lady that came here all those years ago had said that I was going to only have one chance. And the dots were finally connecting. Ever since Soraya entered my life, everything changed and my perspective shifted. Soraya was my hope and my saving grace. And I had a chance to accept it or not. I had a chance to change my story and be better than those who came before me.

That moment I decided that I was going to take that hope, that chance. It wasn't going to be easy and there were going to be times I wanted to turn back to my old ways but I wasn't going to give up. She was my last saving grace and I was going to pour everything I had and was.

As I walked out of the room, I heard something and that left my stomach in small knots.

Was this all a test?

Maybe this was all a test to see if I was going to change and be different. Maybe these small mishaps had a purpose and meaning.

There were a thousand unanswered questions I had. There were many that I knew I might not like the answer too but I needed to face them all. I needed to become a better man.

Ephraim

Chapter 43

W hen I woke up, I turned around to see if Soraya had awakened but she was still in the same spot from where I placed her yesterday. Her hair was tied in a loose braid and her face was still the color of snow.

I blew out a breath and used my pointer finger to brush away a piece of hair that covered her face. Even pale and ill she was beautiful.

Mavros had already told me that I needed to finish judging Zion's cause but I told him that it was going to have to wait. I wasn't in the right head space to tell someone he was going to die while my wife was laying in bed fighting against death.

The pieces didn't fit right in my head. She was fine when we got there and we had a good time. Yes, we disagreed when I was swept away with work but after talking for several moments she finally gave in. When we came back, she started to feel stomach pain and when she entered the court room, she fainted.

Nothing about that sounded right. Maybe it was some-

343

thing that she ate or the rocking of the boat that made her sick. Even if it was either of those, it wouldn't make her ill to the point of not waking up for more than an entire day.

I rubbed my hands over a beard that was starting to grow which reminded me that I needed to shave it off. I never let it grow because it made me feel out of place and unable to focus.

Slowly, I shaved off my beard, making my jaw visible once again. It felt like a deep relief that I could see myself again. I turned around to see if Soraya had moved an inch but she was still pale and still. My heart started to pound a bit faster because what if I wouldn't get her back or what if she came down with something that her days were numbered.

I shook my head to try to keep those deadly thoughts away because I couldn't bear to keep feeding them. Maybe I could go into my studies and try to find the answer to what she was going through. There might be a food that she could eat that would heal her, I was desperate at this point.

I looked myself back in the mirror and fixed the dark waves on my head that had gone deranged. I brushed my fingers constantly through them yesterday and had no willpower to fix it but I needed to keep going. I needed to keep my kingdom going even if half my heart was in bed.

Before I walked past her, I kissed her head and whispered words that she would only hear from me. That no other human that has ever walked on this earth or would walk would hear those words from me.

How much I desired her and that I was waiting here for her.

Then I walked out that door and through the curtains with a determined goal; I was going to keep going. Even if I wanted to stay in bed and beside her all day, I couldn't. I needed to keep being a king and reigning, not letting my emotions get the best of me but I was going to find an answer. I was going to help her in any way possible because until now, I never found a reason to help anyone except myself.

The day seemed to slow down, everything lacked color. I dreaded every time a person would come up to me, telling me something else I needed to do like I didn't have enough on my plate. Surprisingly, I didn't kill anyone today but a part of me couldn't bring myself to do it. The thought would make my head hurt and my stomach turn like I was going to puke.

Mavros told me endless things that happened when I was gone and that they were close to finding who their queen was. I kept nodding, pretending like I was understanding or caring for what he was saying.

"My king, the palace is on fire." Mavros said and I hummed like I was agreeing.

Several moments passed before I realized what he said and when I turned to him, he had the biggest smile on his face. His arms crossed and papers at the crock of his arm.

"I am sorry Mavros, I am not in the headspace for any of this." I sighed because even though I was trying my hardest to keep my mind busy, my thoughts kept going back to her.

Mavros placed a hand on my elbow to try to comfort me, in reality, it did very little. He continued to say, "Fine, I will leave right after you sign these documents."

He placed the folder that was in his hand on my lap and extended a pen. I didn't even bother to read what it was for and I would probably regret it later but the faster I could get him out of my hair the better.

When I finished signing all the documents, I extended the folder and pen back to him. He had the smirkest grin on his face, "Thank you, my king. The world will be a better place, long live the king." With a deep curtsey, he walked away and left me alone.

I looked at the walls around me and it was like they were history books. I remembered countless of banquets and feasts that were held here. The times where I would witness criminals being punished and the poor being restored what was stolen from them. Everything was in detail to me and I could remember everything from beginning to end and in all of that, my life was voidless.

I was judging causes not to bring peace but because I judged them simply by if they annoyed me or didn't get on my nerves. I killed someone if they even breathed wrongly in my direction. Hundreds, maybe even thousands of deaths happened in these palace walls and I started to feel the weight of every single one of them, the burden they had within me.

Out of nowhere, my vision began to turn black. Smoke started to swirl around me and cover everything in sight. I couldn't see the ground underneath my feet or the throne I was sitting on. Everything was gone and it all was replaced by a cloud of dark heavy smoke.

I turned my head side to side, fear crept into me slowly. I could feel its claws start to dig inside of me and leave me in suffering pain. My hands immediately went to my chest, gripping the shirt I was wearing.

I hissed loudly. "What do you want?"

This wasn't something new because I felt it before. I never could tell when this would happen but I always hated it when it did.

The dark voice spoke to me like an old friend. The darkest days of my life, the darkness used to be a comforting whisper in my ears. Now, it had become a voice that tortured me and left me gasping for air.

"You are not doing what we agreed on." Till this day I didn't know exactly what it was but I knew that it was angry and there was nothing I could do about it. It could and would kill me piece by piece until there was nothing of me left.

"Well I don't want any part in that anymore." I rumbled back to it.

As if it were nails inside my soul, the screeching pain that I was feeling before turned into nothing compared to what I was feeling that moment. My heart skipped beats it wasn't supposed to and everytime I took a breath in, it was like another knife was being pressed into my chest.

"Your soul is mine. Your father was a failure to me, didn't do what I wanted. That's what you get for demanding something out of a prideful man."

I used my hands to try to move the smoke but it was like a stone wall. There was nowhere to go and nothing I could do but allow myself to be slowly tortured.

"She has been weakening you."

My body, soul, and everything inside me stopped. My heart and lungs stopped for a moment and for a second I wondered if I died.

"What did you say?" I threatened the voice but he didn't speak back. He stayed in silence for several moments like he didn't owe me an explanation.

"And whoever gets in the way of my plans will perish." Those were his last haunting words before the smoke began to clear and my vision turned back to normal.

No. No. No, No, No.

He couldn't have said that, I must have simply heard it. If I heard him right, which I was trying to trick myself that I hadn't, then Soraya was going to be crossed in the crossfire.

That's what I least wanted in this. I wanted her to be long

gone from this but it was too late and I don't know if there was something I could do about it.

I didn't know if the devil's voice could still hear me but I threatened it like it just did to me, "You touch my wife, and you will perish because of it."

No one touches my wife, not even my haunting demons.

Soraya

Chapter 44

My mind couldn't replay what happened the past few hours. And after only being awake for a few hours, I realized I had been asleep for way more than a few hours.

It was already nighttime, the stars were the only source of light in the room, I kept looking around for something that was going to tell me what day it was and how long I had been sleeping for.

When I reached out my arm, it hit a hard chest and a faint smile was on my lips. I knew it was Ephraim and I was so glad that it wasn't anyone else, he was the only one with me.

"Ephraim" I whispered barely, my voice was mostly gone.

Nothing, I lifted myself slightly to see if I could see his face but his shoulders were covering my view. I softly placed a hand on his arm and whispered his name again.

How much did he have to drink, I questioned.

I leaned closer, my chest brushed against his arm and I noticed that he was dead asleep. His snores were low and constant but you could tell that he was passed out. There was nothing that was going to wake this man up.

I smiled and leaned in to press a gentle kiss on his cheek which made him move slightly. Calling his name didn't make him move a muscle but a simple kiss did, which gave me an idea.

He moved so he was laying down on his back. An arm hanging off the bed and the other one on top of my pillow, I gave him another gentle kiss on the other cheek, he moved again. Then I moved a little bit to the left and placed a sweet kiss on his lips.

I don't remember anything while I was knocked out, all I saw was endless void and black but something I missed was his kisses while I was gone. It's like my soul could feel the lack of sweetness on my lips.

He hummed in his sleep and quietly whispered. "Soraya come back to me."

My heart warmed instantly, he was dreaming of me. He was thinking of me in his slumber and that did something to me. He used his hand to rub his face and then went back to snoring.

I couldn't help but giggle because a big man like this, who took up more than half the bed, was just a gentle giant. People saw the demons and the darkness that followed him everywhere he went but I saw him in a different light. A light I was beginning to fall for.

My lips brushed against his ears as I spoke softly. "Wake up, my king."

His eyes shot wide open, his memorizing eyes visible again. He blinked several times, trying to wake himself up. He looked around himself to make sure he wasn't dreaming.

"Soraya?" His voice was husky and deep.

His hand came up to my face and lightly brushed against

my cheek. He let his fingers run down my hair. A wave of tingles followed his trace until he let his hands fall on my hands.

"Is this a dream?" He questioned.

I shook my head once again as I intertwined my fingers with his. He smiled and sighed. "It's been three tortuous days without you."

His arms wrapped around my waist as he came in for a hug. His head leaned right against my stomach, but as each second passed he gripped a bit more tighter like he couldn't believe that I was awake. He gripped onto me like I was his only chance of surviving.

"What happened?" My mind still couldn't process what had happened. The last thing I could recall was when I entered into the throne room and saw-oh that's what it was.

I passed out shortly after seeing Zion in chains and his clothes a mess. My heart ached at the sight of him like that.

Why did I pass out?

He lifted his head but did not let go of me for one second. "You passed out in the throne room. Then I grabbed you in my arms and ran to put you in bed. Since then you have been sleeping and haven't woken up."

I nodded slowly because I couldn't remember anything in detail but I trusted him to tell me exactly what happened.

He leaned back against my lap and yawned loudly. "What have you been doing since then?"

He huffed. "I have been trying not to lose my mind and not go insane."

"But why would you go insane? It's only me, it's not like I make much difference around here."

Was I more important to him than I thought I was?

It was one thing to care about someone because you were bound by law and marriage but it was a whole other thing to love them, to die for them. I was falling for Ephraim; something I swore to myself not to do. I was in love with a man that might just be my undoing.

He sighed as if I didn't understand what he was trying to say. "When I finally felt hope and love for the first time in my life, almost losing that made me feel like I was going to die."

He moved to lay back on the pillow and patted the spot beside him. I crawled over and let my head lean on his arm as he continued to speak, "When you are married to someone who has been changing you without you knowing and they are between life and death and there is nothing you can do about it, you feel like you're dying too. You feel like there is no other reason to keep living, like you were supposed to be in their place." He pressed a gentle kiss on my forehead and slowly closed his eyes.

I couldn't believe that he admitted to that, it wasn't the exact words of *I love you* but it was a process in getting there.

A part of me was overjoyed but I couldn't take it completely seriously because he was mostly asleep, people talked while they were sleeping but I also felt hope.

I felt hope because this meant I was breaking down the walls of his heart and that he was becoming another man entirely. That I was starting to be cared for and loved.

But that's not the reason you came, you came to save your people, not fall in love.

That thought was an anchor in my stomach, plummeting the hope because I don't know if I tricked him into thinking he cared about me. He still didn't know who I was and how I truly ended up here.

He was in denial, you tricked him, thought ran through my mind like a race.

"Sh- go to sleep." I was about to move away but he held me by my wrist. It wasn't hard or hurtful but it was like he was asking me gently to stay with him.

"Stay, I know you need to eat and freshen up but stay with me just until I fall asleep, please?"

I nodded once more because I didn't have the words to speak. I couldn't think of anything to respond to him and if I had the chance, I would say something wrong.

"And where was the prisoner sent to? What did you do afterwards?"

He yawned once again, "I just threw him into the prison. My focus was on you at that moment, I didn't care about him."

With that, he pulled me close, kissed me gently on the cheek and fell back to sleep but I couldn't. I was wide awake, my soul and heart troubled because everything was starting to sit in.

I had lied to him, I haven't told him the truth about anything yet he tells me I am the most honest person he has ever met. He told me he wanted to kill me without knowing it was me and what then, what will happen that it was me he has been looking for this whole time?

That the person he said was a constant headache, that troubled his kingdom was my people. I was being looked for and now one of the people I most care for was locked up on the floors below me.

In the midst of all that, I let my heart be mixed into it. I let myself start to fall in love with a man that I didn't want to even marry. I healed him and calmed him in ways that I never did with anyone else.

He said I was changing him but what about me? My heart was changed and fell for a man that against my better judgment knew I wasn't supposed to love.

What will be of me now?

When I could tell that he was deep asleep, his snoring giving him away, I slipped myself out of his embrace and started to get myself ready.

I looked down at myself and saw that my dress was taken off and all I was wearing was a very thin silk dress. I hope that it was Ephraim who dressed me because the thought of another man doing that repulsed me.

Quickly grabbing the robe that was hung on the door, I tied it around my waist and quietly walked out the room. The palace was dead quiet, there wasn't anyone awake except a few guards who were stationed.

Their eyes widened as they saw me but when I placed a finger on my lips so they wouldn't wake the others, they understood. They bowed deeply with an understanding smile.

I continued to walk down the stairs, looking for the secret kitchen entrance, my stomach was dying to eat something. When I finally found the door, I entered it and was greeted with maids who were still frozen. They looked at me horrified that I was inside the kitchen probably because they have probably never seen a royal here before.

"It's okay, I have just come to get a quick snack and I will be out of here. Don't tell anyone you saw me, let's keep this between us." I pleaded with my eyes that they would keep this secret and after several long moments, one by one nodded their heads.

I grabbed two apples and a few pastries that were out before slipping myself back out. I didn't know where the dungeon was but I was going to find out where it was.

Turn after turn, hall after hall, I keep ending up at a dead end. Nothing was indicating where the door was. When I saw a guard, I asked him where the dungeon was and after much convincing he gave me the directions.

Many spiders seemed to have found their home in the

corners of the stairs. Faint fire illuminating the way as you walked. When I looked up, my stomach seemed to twist at the sight. Left and right there were dried bones, dead bones. There was nothing alive in sight, rats running everywhere.

I kept walking down the dark hall and at the very end, there was a small light. I hoped it was what I was looking for. When I was finally close enough to see, my heart seemed to finally be able to beat again when I saw a body laying down on the floor sleeping.

There was a piece of fabric that covered only his feet and a rock as a pillow. There wasn't a source of light or even a decent bed in sight. My stomach twisted once again but I had to keep myself composed.

If it was really him, he couldn't see me all broken and unwell.

"Zion," I whispered.

He couldn't hear me even if the whole dungeon was quiet. You could hear the crickets and the rats scurrying across the walls.

"Zion, it's me." I tried once again to catch his attention.

Instantly, he got up and sat upright, when he finally saw me, he came crawling near the iron bars. This was probably the hardest thing I have ever faced. His face was covered with dirt and grim. His clothes were worse than before and he looked like he was bruised on his legs and arms.

"Soraya, is that you my dear?" Zion's voice was filled with deep slumber.

I couldn't help but not cry because it was a mix of emotions. I missed him so much that it hurt and to see him like this made it even harder but I was happy to see him. I was happy to see that he was still alive.

"What happened? What are you doing here?" For him to be here and risk his life then he must have a very good reason.

Zion wasn't a person to put his life on the edge of death for no reason.

"Our land is in danger. Everything is slowly dying because you're not there, the people are starting to go hungry and the decree-"

I instantly froze. The ticking of a distant clock was the only thing I heard and everything else faded away. "What decree?"

He stopped and went quiet. I repeated my question several times before a single word came out his mouth.

"A decree has been set forth for our annihilation. We will all perish. The decree has also said that because they haven't found you yet, they will torture us like never before" he paused for a moment, I could tell the struggle he was having because this meant more than we thought.

A decree couldn't be taken away, once something was said it became law. A decree could be from something small like taxes to the death of an entire nation, it all had to be done.

I could feel the weakness start to increase and the power inside me start to fade away. My breath started to go faster and faster. My heart felt like it was being squeezed under pressure.

"Soraya, my dear child, you must keep yourself contained. Your emotions must be bottled, you can't let your emotions get the best of you. Stay with me."

I have failed. I was supposed to save my people and I have failed.

A single tear rolled down my face and before I could even say anything, Zion reached through the metal bars and cried with the pad of his finger.

"Don't cry, sweet child. You haven't failed, there is still hope." He spoke with such positivity and like there was still something that could be done, but there wasn't.

"It's been signed into law, there is nothing I can do now." I felt even more tears roll down my face, a river of water.

Zion looked at me with that fatherly gaze and I knew he was reading me without having to explain anything because I was scared to admit everything that I was thinking and have gone through.

"And you fell in love with him." He didn't ask, he stated it like a fact. That was his ability, he knew what your heart was feeling just by the look on your face.

Zion was a father, I don't know if he ever had children but he had become the father I needed in my life and there was never a moment that I needed him more than I needed him now.

"I have failed. Not only have I failed to protect my kingdom but I have given my heart to a man that doesn't know it's his and have fallen deeply in love with him."

I can't believe that I admitted that outloud. That those words actually came out of my mouth. I didn't want to believe it and I didn't know how but it was true.

I was falling in love with Ephraim. A king who is desperately trying to kill me.

"Oh, he loves you." Zion said that with the biggest smile on his face. There wasn't a flicker of doubt in that statement.

It came to me more than a shock. It felt like those words stopped my heart.

"But how do you know?" My voice was shaky and uncertain.

He gave me another one of his fatherly smiles. One of those smiles that I know are true and honest, "Well my dear, when you were unwell, he rushed to you in the blink of an eye. He didn't care about me or anyone for that matter,"

He reached out his hand through the bars and gave my hand a small squeeze, "He grabbed you in his hands like you were the last breath he had. When the guards came down to give me food, they kept talking about how the king did not rest at all while you were asleep. He read hundreds of books and kept going into your room multiple times, to see if there was something that he could do."

My eyes slowly welled with tears. There weren't sad tears, they were tears of realization. Even if I couldn't see everything he saw, I started to feel it in my heart.

"What about the decree? Would he do that if he truly loved me?" my voice was barely there, thick with tears.

"Does he know our secret?" He asked.

I shook my head and he continued, "Then that's the reason why. He might have been blackmailed or tricked into doing it but now,"

He shifted closer to me, his expression instantly changed. "You must reveal to him who you are and what this means for not only you but your entire family."

I shook my head rapidly. I couldn't believe that Zion was asking me to do that. In other words, I was going to risk my life right after a decree of my death had already been signed. This was a game of death and life.

How was I supposed to tell him that? To confess to something that could get my head chopped off? Say a thing this big right after I came to the realization that I care about him.

"You just told me that he loves me and you said I care about him. How do you expect me to tell him that I have been lying to him this whole time? That's just a petition to have my head chopped off."

Another single tear rolled down his face as looked at me with sorrow. I never once judged him for what he told me to do, for what advice he gave me but this crossed every boundary. This was another thing entirely, this was literally between life and death.

"Do you think that just because you're within these walls that you will be safe? No my dear, you will perish one way or another. If you decide to be quiet and let the decree go forward, help will come from another place"

He stood up and began pacing around the room, "but you will perish. Who knows, what if you came to this palace for such a time as this. To save your people from a death sentence."

I began pacing around the room, unable to sit still. Until I thought of a question to ask him, "And you came all the way here to simply tell me to risk my life while risking your own?"

He placed his hands behind his back and stopped midway in his tracks, "Yes, I did because it's worth more to risk my life and tell you the truth. To let you know that your people are dying and we need you. Don't forget where you have come from and what it took to get you here."

I put my hand on my heart because the pain I have been feeling started once again. An indescribable feeling, like I had to choose between death and life, happiness and sorrow.

"I fell in love with a man that I knew I couldn't. He fell in love with me and we have lived together for months together. Then comes a decree that he wants to kill me without knowing it's me. This seems to be planned, well planned."

He mouthed an agreement because nothing, not even if a king tried their hardest could plan something so well thought.

"You choose my dear. Either way I risked my life to come and tell you this. We need you and now it's your time to choose what you're going to do about it."

I came here to try to feel lighter but after we said our good-byes, the heaviness I felt was beyond comparison. It was like my mind didn't want to think about anything or how everything made sense.

My feelings about everything seemed to be the size of a spec of dust compared to everything that has been thrown on top of me. If I do this, I risk my life and all of my people and if I don't, I still risk it.

Either way I was going to lose something or someone. I was either going to have to lose my kingdom or lose the man that I have a growing affection towards. It wasn't a win-win situation for me, I was going to have sacrificed something for the greater good and I knew which one I had to choose.

Once I reached the room and laid back in bed with Ephraim by my side, that's when I lost it. I let myself cry about everything that I have endured in the last few months. The heaviness that I feel on my shoulders, the weight of secrets on my heart, the love I knew I had for the man lying beside me.

At moments it felt like it was too much to bear, I didn't know what to think or how to think for myself. All I knew I had to do was make the best decision I saw.

I let my hand brush against Ephraim's freshly shaved jaw. I cried a bit more as I felt his touch and reminded myself of all the moments we have had with one another.

I don't think I was ever going to be ready to lose him because it has taken me this much to realize that I had fallen in love with him.

When I think about what passes in my mind everyday, it is consumed by him. The way his eyes shine and sparkle when he is himself, when he asks to be loved and cared for and shows me a side of himself that he has never shown anyone.

How was I supposed to let him go?

I kissed him, letting myself say goodbye. He moved slightly but his arms gripped onto me a bit tighter. I was leaning on top of him, letting me feel his embrace once more.

Maybe I was making this a bit more than it had to be but people who don't experience love wouldn't know what it feels like.

They don't know how it consumes your body and mind. People who aren't in love don't know how when you have to let go, it's like a part of you is going along with them because it is.

You have learned each other on levels that no one understands. You know each other like the back of your hand. They comprehend you with just a glance across the room. You have become one with them.

We have become one.

I placed another kiss on his lips, savoring the few moments I have. I wasn't worried that I was going to wake him up because he was in deep slumber, but I wish he would so I could tell him how I feel. To jump into the water like there was no looking back.

"I have fallen for you Ephraim, can't you see that. I have fallen for you when I cannot."

I continued to cry, letting my head rest gently on his chest. My head was rising and falling at his steady breathing. The way I gripped onto him like there was no other place that I rather be.

My heart ached in ways that no word could describe, the weight that rulers had on their shoulders was beyond compare. There was always something you had to give up at one point and my time has now come.

I didn't know how I was going to tell him but I needed to find out soon because my death sentence is soon and there was no way around it.

"Please forgive me, I didn't mean to hurt either of us but I don't know what to do."

Then I let myself sleep against his steady chest and the slow stream of tears running down my face. I fell asleep with his scent and touch all over me.

What will happen to me?

I don't think I would ever have the answer to that question because only time would reveal the plan for your life.

Soraya

Chapter 45

I woke up with a hand brushing up and down my back. I didn't want to wake up or face another day. I knew what had to be done either if I liked it or not but I had decided one thing. I was going to tell him what I felt about him and everything that my heart was aching to let him know.

He deserved that at least, more than anything he should know the truth and deserved every single detail.

"My jewel, wake up." His deep voice whispered against my skin like a sweet song.

I fluttered my eyes open and was greeted with a pair of dark eyes. There were days where you could see the different shades of black and brown swirl around.. I savored them for a moment, not saying anything. I didn't want words to destroy these last few moments we had with one another.

"What are you looking at? Do I have something on my face?" He began to touch his face, looking for something on it.

I pulled away his hands and intertwined our fingers together. Our hands fit perfectly together like they were made for one another.

I simply smiled at him. "I am just admiring you for a moment."

I needed to memorize his touch and feel in case this was going to be the last time.

He smiled one of those beautiful smiles of his, where he showed all of his pearly white teeth. He pulled me closer and gave me the sweetest kiss.

It wasn't something hard or demanding but it was something soft and sweet. It was one of the sweetest kisses he has ever given me and it was one that I never was going to forget.

"You complete me." he whispered in between his kisses.

I was hanging by a thread, so the moment he said that, I began bursting out in tears. Tears streamed down my face as he continued to kiss me and hold me tight.

When he noticed that I was crying, he pulled away and cradled my face with both of his hands. He looked at me with the same amount of worry like he had so many times.

"What's wrong?" he asked, he looked like he would murder anyone in a split second if I would just ask.

"Nothing. I just miss you, that's all." My voice was shaky and barely even audible. I wouldn't be surprised if he hadn't heard those few words.

He examined me for several minutes. He checked my face and my whole body, seeing if there was anything wrong with me on the outside but in reality it was my heart which was in agony.

When he decided that he saw nothing wrong, he pulled me against him, as tight as he could. Where there wasn't a single spot that we weren't touching. Our bodies were pressed against one another as he simply held me close.

I didn't say anything and I didn't feel the need to because there was a certain comfort you only found in silence. He didn't say anything but instead played with my hair with his fingers.

Then I finally got the courage to tell him what I have been needing to say, "Ephraim-"

"King, we need you urgently." Someone yelled above me.

His head whipped to the entrance to the door and then back to me. Too much noise all at once, he was trying to decide which to answer first.

When he was about to open his mouth, the guard at the door spoke. "There is blood spilled." The man spoke with urgency and demand.

He looked at me with pity in his eyes like there wasn't even much of an option anymore. His eyes went from the door and back to me several times.

Ephraim then held my face between his hands. "I hate having to leave right when you need me but I need to resolve whatever happened quickly. Can you give me a few minutes?"

I nodded. A single tear rolled down my face. You could see in his face that he was curious as to why I was crying but instead of asking, he brushed it away with the pad of his finger and rushed away.

I continued to sit in bed, looking at him putting on his royal attire and before he walked out the door he took one long glance at me.

Our eyes told things that words could never explain. With a small smile and a quick kiss he went off and I have never felt so alone like I did in that moment.

One minute, one hour, five hours, the time flew by fast and he still wasn't finished. I could hear the urgency in the guards footsteps as they walked down the hall.

I splashed cold water on my pale face, there was no color on my lips and no strength in my bones. Water drips down my face and into the sink.

My fingers gripped around the bowl of water as it began to dig into my skin.

When I walked out I didn't know I was about to face a greater fear. From afar, I could see a small piece of paper on my bed. It wasn't there from the beginning and I didn't hear anyone coming in.

I walked slowly up to the note, looking all around me to make sure no one was hiding. My heart is pounding uncontrollably and my stomach is feeling unwell. My eyes gazed over the words several times before they actually made sense.

Hello my queen or are you?

I have you all figured out and there is nothing you can hide from me. I see all and am all. Your husband is even petrified of me but let's not waste time, talking about him, his time will come soon enough.

Let's just say you should spend as much time as you can with him while you have the time.

Sincerely, Your worst nightmare.

I couldn't help but yell at the top of my lungs when I dropped the note onto the floor. No guards came in because they were probably busy with whatever was going on. A few seconds later, I hear footsteps running and coming at a lighting speed into my room.

Mavros arrived, gasping for air. "What is it, my queen?"

I stuttered for a few seconds, unable to speak. Fear silenced my tongue and voice. When I noticed that Mavros only kept looking at me with his arms crossed, I fixed my position and facial expression.

"I thought I saw a snake, that's all. You can go now." I

didn't like lying but how was I going to tell him about this letter?

He nodded. "Yes, they have a tendency to sneak in when no one is paying attention. Be careful, they could be your worst nightmare."

I shook my head in agreement and continued to stay there in complete silence. I could feel the power inside me begin to fade from the stress and amount of worry that I was in.

I fell onto the floor with the note in front of me. It slightly crumbled in front of me. I kept reading it over and over again to see if I was actually understanding it.

Someone was watching me and simply at that thought, I felt uncomfortable. The paper didn't say who it was from, so there was no way that I could know who it was. The uncertainty petrified me.

I don't know how long I sat there but Ephraim came in without noticing me at first. He was talking to someone behind him and when his eyes finally landed on me, he stopped.

"What's wrong?" he asked. Ephraim took slow steps closer to me.

I knew that he saw the note in front of me so there was no point in trying to hide it. "Read it."

My trembling voice responded. It was like my biggest fear had become a reality. The overwhelming dose of feelings in that moment was close to what I felt the day my parents were murdered.

Was I going to end up the same way they did?

Did someone figure out my secret?

Ephraim bent down and held the note in both of his hands. His eyes skimmed quickly over the neatly written words. When he finished reading, his hands crumpled the paper until it was the size of a grape.

"He has taken this too far." He whispered and began pacing back and forth in the room again.

After all this time, I noticed that everytime that he got nervous and stressed, he would pace around and drink too much. Ephraim would run his fingers through his hair until there were no more defined waves.

I stood up on my shaky legs and before I could even walk correctly, I tripped over my own feet but didn't hit the ground. A pair of strong arms wrapped around my waist and held me close.

"Soraya, I am getting worried about you. You are more tired than normal, more clumsy and very sensitive." I could tell that he wasn't trying to make fun of me but that he actually cared about my health. His eyes were filled with constant fear and worry.

"It must just be the stress that I am feeling right now." I couldn't expect him to understand what those words actually entailed.

"I came back to see what you needed." He backed away from me and sat on the stool in front of the bed.

How was I going to tell him now? I don't know how I was going to have the courage to tell him that my heart flutters every time he is near when I just received a death note. There was no way that I was going to tell him my feelings after he spent an entire day resolving problems.

"How did it go?" I asked to avoid his question. After that note, I don't know if I was ready to talk about my secrets.

He covered his forehead with the palm of his hand. "There was a murder inside the palace. A note was found on top of the body."

My voice is thick with fright. "What did you say?"

He got up and began to undress himself to go to sleep.

Taking off his belt, his cape, and shirt. With only his pants on and his hair all messed up, he laid in bed.

Ephraim used his tatted arm to hold his head upright. Our eyes focused on one another. "I am not going to let you worry about that." I knew that he was trying to protect me but that wasn't going to stop me from asking again.

"How many notes have you received?" I questioned.

Maybe he has received several death threats?

He shook his head, and told me once again that he wasn't going to let me know. He said it wasn't my problem and I didn't need to worry about things like that.

"I will not lie down with you until you tell me how many death notes you have received and how long you haven't told me."

He mumbled underneath his breath and stood up. Both of his hands were placed on either side of his hips. "You don't need to worry about that. I am handling it and all you need to do is leave all the worrying to me."

He doesn't understand.

"How much and how long? That's the final time I am asking." I crossed my arms and tried to keep my breathing in control. I was not about to lose it and tell him everything that will risk both of our lives right now. There wasn't an ounce of bravery in my lungs to admit everything I wanted and needed to say.

"I don't know how many but probably a week or two after you and I got married."

My voice screeched louder than I wanted it too. "You have been keeping this secret from me for that long. What else have you been hiding from me?" I barely have any self control in me to not burst out in anger.

I could tell that he was beginning to get angry as well. The way his hands turned into fists and his body stiffened signaled that if he wasn't careful, he would lose himself.

"It's not like you have been doing much better than me. You haven't told me a single thing about yourself. Where you're from, your parents, your history, nothing."

"Well none of that matters. My parents are dead, I have no family and it's not like you actually care about my feelings."

I breathed out a long breath and let my hands fall to my side. "How do you expect me to rip my heart open to you when I don't know for sure your intentions."

Instead of talking, his voice turned into a loud shout. His voice boomed off the walls. "Don't tell me what I am allowed to feel and not feel. I have never opened myself to anyone so it's odd and out of the normal for me," He took a step closer. "Why haven't you opened up? Are you scared I won't want you anymore?"

Tears were going to be spilled and that was inevitable.

"I tried to tell you today but you didn't listen. You wanted to solve kingdom problems rather than hear your own wife talk about what she feels and knows."

He continued to yell back after everything I said. Ephraim didn't even notice that there was no more strength inside me and I was holding onto a chair for my dear life.

"Were you going to tell me that you don't have enough jewelry?" I couldn't believe that was his first assumption. After everything I have worn over all this time, I would think he knew at least one thing about me. *Maybe he only said that because he's mad.* "Or maybe you were going to tell me that you regret marrying me? What were you going to tell me that is more important than my kingly duties?"

"I was going to tell you I loved you!" I yelled back and instantly the room went completely silent.

We didn't say anything as we allowed the silence to say everything. Never in a million years did I plan to say this.

"I was going to tell you that I have fallen in love with you. That your smile and voice consume my thoughts day and night. That your embrace and touch have become my wine. And if I need to die because of my love for you then so be it. I just thought maybe you loved me too but I clearly guessed wrong."

I picked up the skirt of my dress and speedwalked away from him. What broke my heart in that moment was that he didn't even go after me. His hand didn't hold me back. He didn't beg me to come back, Ephraim simply let me go.

Zion was wrong because when someone loves you, they wouldn't let you go because of an argument. They would fight for you even if you're fighting against them.

Maybe I was wrong. Maybe he did love me but his love for me apparently wasn't important enough to him.

Soraya

Chapter 46

I t's been 3 days since Ephraim last called me, since I last saw him. I was beyond petrified that I ruined everything between us when I admitted my feelings.

I kept waking up with an empty space beside me. My room felt cold and dark all day even when the lights were on. I kept looking at the fireplace to see if he would walk in any moment, but it never was him. My mind wondered if he was able to sleep because I wasn't.

I haven't rested correctly in the last three days. The only people who were giving me company were my maids and sometimes Mavros would come in to visit.

Today, he decided to come visit me and have a cup of tea with me and never have I been grateful for his company.

"How is he?" I awaited his response as I took a sip of the tea.

"He is doing fine but I know him better. He isn't concentrated and wants to be left alone all the time but that isn't a surprise to anyone.

I nodded in agreement, "We had an argument and he hasn't called for me in several days."

I didn't want to admit how much that ached inside me. I ached to know that he might be with another woman and drinking more than he was supposed to.

"He has a lot on his plate. He is trying to solve many problems all at once." Mavros added. His gaze focused on the spook he was stirring in his tea.

I set down my cup and played with the edge of the sleeve of my dress.

"Can I ask you something?" He responded yes and then let me continue. "Why does he want to kill the people of Uosulia so much? What have they ever done wrong with him?"

Whatever he says I will know if it's the truth or a lie. In reality, we never did anything with them. We never caused a war, a famine or stopped providing resources. I know my people are those that sacrifice and want to see their brothers satisfied.

He took a long sip of tea, holding the cup in his hand as he kept glancing out the window, "They simply aggravate him and he hates anything and everything that gets in his way," He cleared his throat and gave a nervous smile. "He also kills anyone and anything that gives him a headache."

To end a person's life because they annoyed you was foolish. Who would ever kill someone for simply not doing what he wanted all the time.

I have always reminded my people that we weren't going to start a war. I wasn't going to start a war but if one did happen, I was willing to stop it. And in our silent cry, I have had to watch people invade our land and take all our resources.

The times were they would burn our gardens to the floor and I would spend hours and hours building it back up. My powers were spent like it was nothing, every day I could barely keep myself upright, my strength sucked away from me.

"And why do people send him threats?"

Mavros shifted in his chair and placed a hand on his chin, rubbing back and forth. Several moments of silence passed before he ever even spoke a word. "They see him as cruel and evil. People see him as a road block, a stone in the midst of their way. They think that if they get rid of him then they will have freedom and all the power they could ever desire."

Out of the three kingdoms, Aales was the richest. It had the biggest population and resources. They had the longest history and the most riches. No one knew how they got all that. Their history was locked away from any and all prying eyes.

"And what would happen if someone overtook his throne?" I could tell that with each question I asked, he began to move and fiddle around a bit more but no one has ever asked such questions. There was never a single soul who decided to find the dark secrets that made up these walls.

"That person would have power and riches beyond their comprehension. People would fear that person beyond anyone else." Mavros finished explaining.

We continued to chat back and forth, part of me glad that he was giving me the company that I needed. When a guard entered the room and told Mavros that the king needed him, he stood up and left gracefully.

My eyes focused on the horizon and the sun all the way in the distance. I took a few more steps to the balcony to see the people. Even if I was a bit far, I could still see the children running all over the place. Their happiness seemed to be returned and that filled my heart. When I was about to leave, a small child spotted me and began waving.

People turned to look in the same direction and started to

wave to me, calling me to come. I smiled and nodded, the people erupted in cheers.

I quickly covered my hair with the closest covering and added a cape to cover me from the slight cold weather. The skirt of my dress in my hands, I ran as fast as I could, not stopping when a guard asked me where I was going.

When I finally snuck out one of the back doors, I smiled when all the children ran to hug me once again. Never once did they not do this and it made me feel loved and cared for.

A part of me desired to have children of my own. Bear my own child and be able to hold the child in my own hands. That dream has been pushed aside multiple times. Politics, the world, and endless problems have always gotten in the way of it. I never wanted to be a mother who had other priorities than her own children.

"We missed you." The children yelled in unison and that's when the tears rolled down my face.

I bent down and let myself be hugged by children. Letting them whisper to me that they love me and that everything was going to be all right.

When I finally composed myself, they let go but their bright smiles never once dimmed. I took a look over each and every one of them. My heart bursted in gratitude as I looked at their new clothes and their stuffed bellies. The little girls had their hair washed and put into braids.

"You look so beautiful." I looked at a little girl who had a pastel pink dress and her hair was tied into two braids.

She smiled and showed her two missing front teeth, "Thanks to the king we were able to buy a bunch of new things for our family. We even bought bread, clothes, and toys."

She jumped up and down, clapping her hands together. The other kids began to say what they received and how they could never be more grateful.

"You said the king did this?" They all nodded and that left me speechless. Unable to stand up or pay attention to what they continued to rattle about.

The kids finally decided that they wanted to go play and run after one another. Mothers came and gave me the kindest hugs, thanking me for making a difference.

"The king is better with you by his side" one of them said.

My heart was unable to detect how it felt about that comment so I just smiled and nodded. If I was making a difference in his life, wouldn't he tell me how he truly felt.

Then like out of the blue, out of nowhere, my stomach felt nauseous. I gripped my stomach and closed my mouth to prevent me from throwing up. My body swayed side to side but I didn't fall to the floor. Instead my body hit against a elderly woman who was right beside me.

She gripped me, to keep me upright and kept asking if I was okay but I didn't answer. Her voice was so far away and everything started to become a haze. A woman started to circle around me, leading me to the nearest chair in the shade where I wouldn't pass out.

A woman said she was going to find a doctor and some food for me to eat. It felt like someone was ripping out my guts and it was turning around and around.

"Here, eat this" a woman crouched beside me and offered me a piece of fruit dipped in honey.

I ate it, not even paying attention to what it was or how it tasted. I had enough faith in them that they wouldn't want to kill me in the middle of the street.

A few moments later, the doctor came rushing in. The woman replayed to him everything that happened which I was grateful for because I did not have the energy to speak at that moment.

My strength seemed to have been soaked away from me in an instant. The doctor asked what I was feeling and if it had just started now, in reality it hadn't, it has been on and off for a few weeks.

Ever since me and Ephraim came back from our trip. That can't be. I don't think that could even be possible. But after the doctor made sure I was okay, and took notes of everything that had been said to him, he came with one conclusion. The one thing that I didn't think it was.

"You are with child, my queen." he affirmed. He gave me a positive smile before collecting his things.

The woman whispered amongst themselves, overjoyed and happy with the news. I couldn't grasp the idea that I was with a child. The dots hadn't connected in my mind; *Someone must be pranking me.*

"How long has it been since your last menstrual cycle?" The doctor questioned.

I didn't want to say such private information in front of so many people but I didn't have a choice. All the voices quieted so that I could answer.

It took me a few moments to remember when it last was but then it clicked, "Just a few days before the trip."

He pointed out all the symptoms and calculated how far I was along. He gave me congratulations and then walked to his next client.

The women around me started gushing and telling me how happy they were for me. One said that they remembered being pregnant with their first child and the other one said that I would birth the heir to the kingdom.

It all sounded perfect and it seemed to be a dream. A dream that felt amazing yet horrifying at the same time. Hundreds of emotions and thoughts flooded my mind. I was petrified at the thought of bearing a child.

Was I going to be a good mother?

How was the delivery going to be?

How was Ephraim going to react?

How was I going to bear a child when I was still trying to figure out my own emotions?

Hundreds of unanswered questions left an uneasiness over my soul. My heart kept beating faster and faster, the anxiety creeping in between the broken cracks. That's when I cried. Every single pent up tear that I have been holding back was finally let go. I didn't care about what everyone was thinking about me, all I wanted was to get my emotions out.

Not a single lady judged me, they just looked at me for several moments and enveloped me in their arms. They whispered kind words and statements to me.

Every single tear was every time that I felt back stabbed by someone. Those moments were when I felt unloved and not cared for. When I felt alone in this battle and that there was no one around me. No one to support me and know me. I wanted to be truly seen and not have to hide myself behind a mask.

I haven't figured out who I am. My purpose was unfathomable to me. Pain and trauma were deeply rooted with me. Unsolved mysteries and questions constantly filled my mind.

I was more broken than I thought.

I was so broken that bearing a child made me feel unworthy. To take care of a soul when mine wasn't restored yet felt unwise.

I looked to the sky, the sun shining without a flaw. It didn't depend on the things around. It continued to shine and even if clouds covered its light or rain covered the shine, it never stopped shining.

"Everything will work out for the best, my queen" a sweet

mother softly spoke. Wisdom and authority were intertwined with her words and voice. Each line on her face told a story.

"Don't call me your queen. Just call me Soraya." She smiled and nodded.

I laughed nervously, "I am such a child. Look at me crying non-stop in the middle of the market."

The same mother looked at me and grabbed my hand in hers. "No, you're not. When you cry, it's simply telling you that you have pent up your emotions for way too long and they finally need to come out."

I took those words to heart because it didn't need further explanation to make sense. No one cried the first time they got hurt. A person would cry when their soul has withstood against too much.

When it was finally night time, I began to settle into bed. Mehra had already prepared the bath and my clothes for the night. She brushed my hair with long strokes, gentleness in each stroke. My mind debated if I was going to tell her that I was with child but I didn't know if I was supposed to. I didn't want Ephraim to find out just yet, we weren't in a good place right now. The ladies and guards would spill the news in the matter of seconds but I trusted her.

She hasn't just become a friend but a sister. A source of comfort in the midst of all of this. She didn't know about my secrets yet and I didn't know if I should tell her that as well but I wanted to. I wanted at least someone to understand me and help me with my overflowing emotions.

"I have something to tell you, Mehra." I whispered. I glanced at her with a heavy heart.

I turned my head around to see if the door was closed and

when I saw that it was, I breathed in deeply and began to tell her everything that I have been hiding.

"I am with child." My heart lifted at admitting that to someone.

Her eyes went wide and instantly filled with tears. She was very emotional but always controlled herself from going overboard.

"Oh that is wonderful news. How did the king react?" Her voice radiated happiness and I could tell that the smile on her face was genuine and that she meant it.

"No, he doesn't know and no one else is supposed to." I warned her. She nodded and I knew I could count on her silence.

"I have something else I need to tell you. It's very important that no one else knows or figures out. This is between life and death." My voice already trembled because I couldn't believe that I was going to admit this.

She set the brush down and sat in the nearest chair. Her leg kept trembling up and down, anxiety replaced all the happiness that she was feeling just moments ago.

"I am not from here" there was barely any confidence in my voice.

She smiled. "I would understand. The king called all the woman from his providences to-"

"I am from Uosulia"

Her eyes opened wide like she saw a demon. Her leg went still and the color of her skin was whiter than snow. She was frozen still and I couldn't read a single emotion on her face.

"And I am the queen" a single tear rolled down my face as I saw the rest of the color of her face fade away.

"Ephraim isn't trying to kill a hidden queen. He is trying to kill me."

Ephraim

Chapter 47

———— ✦ ————

She said that she loved me.

After four days, my mind couldn't wrap around that. It's been four days since I last called Soraya, and not for reasons that she probably thought. I had no reaction when she admitted her love.

You're such a fool, I reminded myself. She was going to think that I was mad and irritated with her. I wasn't; I just didn't know how to respond to someone when I heard those words for the first time in so many years.

I hate I forced it out of her, that I made her say it that way. Maybe she didn't mean it and only said it because I forced her.

What if she wanted to tell me when we were in bed and I had stopped her?

I didn't know how I was going to make this up to her. How was I going to tell her how I felt? This was something new and life-moving. Those words stirred the dead man inside me. This was going to make it or destroy it.

I haven't seen her or talked to her in days. Every time I walked down the halls, I wished I would run into her, but I

385

never did. Every time I would ask someone where she was and how she was doing, they said she was in her room.

Maybe I should simply let go of my pride and go talk to her. Apologize for how I talked and for not letting her speak in her own time. For putting the kingdom and everyone before her.

It was finally dawning on me that I had been hurting her more than I thought I was. I have been switching my priorities and it has been setting me back.

I am going to make it up to her. I will restore anything that I have might hurt her.

Mavros kept me occupied for the majority of the day. Giving me details about things that didn't matter to me anymore.

Maybe not only did I need hope but needed to change my perspective. Knowing what was important in life and what I wanted was true.

Each second that passed without her by my side was another moment for me to realize that I needed her more than I thought. That I was more than in love with her. I cared about her well being and feelings. Her life was worth more than any jewel and diamond that I could ever have.

Her worth was more than gold and riches and it had taken me all this time to realize that. People realized it faster than I did. People who I reigned over, gave her more credit and honour than they ever had with me. Deep down inside me, I knew she deserved all that and more.

I woke up already knowing what I was going to do. The plans formed inside my head before I fell asleep and once I woke up, the plans continued. Every detail was planned out to the last dote. What I would say and how I would say it was written down on paper so that I wouldn't forget what I was going to tell her.

I was going to remind her of her worth. That she was worth so much to me and I would be a fool to let her go. What type of man would I be to let go of a person that has made such a difference in my life.

Then I was going to tell her that I loved her. That her love changed me from the inside out. It changed my thoughts, my feelings, and the way I acted. She found a worth inside me that I thought I didn't have.

The worth of my life was brought back to life and my eyes were open. There was no way that I was going back to the torment that was within me.

The darkness, the voices, and the lies faded a bit more everyday because I had the strength too. I had the will power and drive to fight against what was over powering me and never have I ever felt stronger because of that.

Getting out of bed was easy because there was a lady that was worth all the hours of my life.

Mavros entered with a serious gaze but even that wasn't going to change my plans, "Whatever you have to say, keep it to yourself Mavros. I don't want anything to damper my mood."

I started buttoning my shirt, combing back my hair and putting on my shoes. My clothes never changed but I would consider that. If Soraya said she couldn't stand the color black then I would throw it all away. If she said she wanted to choose my clothes for the rest of my life then so be it. I wanted to do anything to make her happy, to make her smile.

"There is a rebellion happening and we need you to resolve

it." He talked about it like it was the end of the world and that I needed to drop everything and anything because of it.

"When was the last time that I took a vacation?" I looked at him as I continued to button my shirt.

He looked at me like it was an obvious answer, "A few weeks ago sir."

I shook my head, "Wrong. When I wanted to take a vacation and I specifically told you to not let anyone bother me, a boat filled with guards followed me."

He opened his mouth several times to protest and make an excuse but I knew that there was no excuse that was convincing and important enough.

"When was the last time I had a day to myself?"

The silence was his answer. "Tell me when was the last time I didn't have someone running to me every few minutes telling me that they needed me. Death, wars, rebellion, and unsolved situations were the constant things that filled my ears."

He lowered his head. Mavros' hands gripped onto the stack of paper.

"But I guess I don't have an option to live like anyone else." I pointed to the paper in his hands. "Leave that there and I will get to it when I can."

He nodded, placed the stack of paper on the table and rushed out the room. I couldn't help but sigh because it was always like this but tried to not let it change my mood.

Today I had a goal, a mission. Nothing was more important than for me to get it done. I was going to make a special romantic banquet for her. In one of our secret gardens that she didn't know about. It was my mothers and I didn't let anyone except the gardener go in there.

It was sacred and a separate place. I should have shown it to her a long time ago but I didn't even think about it but now it is the time. I was going to tell the servants to hand the lights that there once were.

I was to set a table just for us, there wasn't going to be anyone else. I was going to use her favorite flowers to decorate the table. Every detail even down to the music was planned.

At the end of the night, I was going to dance with her underneath the stars that she loved so much. I would give her several kisses until we both forgot our names and when I least expected it, I would tell her.

Then tonight, we were going to stay together and I never was going to let her go again. She was going to be with me until the end, death had no power between us.

Maybe my mother was right all along. She was right when she said that I would find love one day. That true love did exist because if this wasn't true love then I didn't know what was.

If love was the ocean then I would choose to drown in it everyday.

Soraya

Chapter 48

The night was still young but I had no desire to sleep. My body kept tossing and turning, trying to find a comfortable spot for me to sleep but nothing worked. A part of me thought that it could be because it was cold or maybe because I was alone.

I wasn't with Ephraim but I wasn't alone anymore. Mehra surprised me and broke down the fear that I had. I thought she would leave me and go straight to tell the king but after I explained that I came to beg for mercy she smiled.

I told her everything. The reason I came and my entire plan that I was going to fulfill but instead of doing that, I ended up falling in love. I told her how difficult it has been to keep my powers a secret. The conversation ended quickly because Mavros entered and decided to alert us about some things but I knew Mehra was going to keep it a secret. I trusted her not only with the secrets but with my life.

The child would remind me everyday of what we had between us. It kept reminding me that I didn't keep my distance like I thought but I still wouldn't want my life any other way. The child would remind me how all this began and how much we have grown. The first encounter me and Ephraim had we were almost trying to kill one another.

I rubbed my hand over my small stomach. It wasn't big enough to be noticed but the dress would cover the bump for the most of the pregnancy. The dresses weren't going to be able to be so tight. Heels were the first thing I had to give up because my feet couldn't carry my weight in them anymore. I was barely able to walk in them and now my feet wouldn't even slip in the shoe.

I was going to be one month in a few days and the time flew by so fast. Even if I didn't know that I was pregnant for most of the time.

Mehra came rushing into the room with two scrolls in her hand. She finally stopped bowing to me every time she saw me, so she came rushing to my side and started speaking at a million miles per hour.

"The king told me to give this to you" she handed me the first one.

It was sealed with a red wax seal. It had the official stamp of the king. I carefully opened it, making sure to not rip the paper in the process.

> *Dear Queen Soraya,*
> *Your presence is required tonight. The king will pick you up from your quarters at sunset. Be ready and do your best.*
> *Please come, I promise you won't regret it.*
> *Sincerely, King Ephraim.*

I read it multiple times, my heart jumping for joy because I would see him again. I think even the child danced in my womb because he could sense that this was something important.

I set it on the bed beside me and then turned my eyes back to Mehra who was waiting patiently to continue.

"This one doesn't have a name or where it came from. It just appeared beside your door with a note to give it to you."

I nodded and took the note in my hand. There was no seal, signature or any indication of where it was from.

Your presence is required immediately. It is the matter of life and death and you're the only one that can help us. Come right before sunset and don't let anyone see you.

Sincerely, your friend

I didn't recognize this handwriting. I asked everyone to stop sending me letters so that information wouldn't be leaked.

It better not be anyone from Uosulia because I don't think I can bear another person that I love in prison.

There was a smaller piece of paper with the directions to get there. It wasn't far from the palace and it was in a secluded spot. I have been there before but not many people did.

I nodded and rolled the letter once again and placed it beside the other. If I planned everything correctly, then I would be able to go to both.

"What did it say?" Mehra asked, she was curious

I told her exactly what was written on the paper and then she fell silent. I already knew she was going to say no to the second invite and only attend the dinner the king had prepared but something pushed me to go.

"I would have enough time to come back and attend the banquet and what if it is something very important like it said it is." She shrugged her shoulders and reminded me that it was my decision.

I decided that I was going because nothing bad was going to happen. Someone needed my help and I was going to do everything in my willpower to be there.

I told Mehra to get me ready with the best jewelry and clothes that I had so that I would be ready for the encounter with the king. Before I go, I would cover myself with a black cloak to hide myself when creeping down the streets of the city.

We had only a few hours until the beginning of sunset which meant I had little time to get ready and I didn't do very well under pressure.

The bath I took was the quickest one and I had even washed my hair. Mehra helped me with everything she could possibly do. Her hands worked their magic as she began to do my hair which she decided to let loose and let the curls and waves do their magic.

Her exact words in that moment was, *The king loves your hair more than you think he does. Let it be on display.*

When I was finally ready, the sun had already begun to go down. I quickly grabbed a black cloak and covered myself so that I wouldn't draw attention.

After living in this palace for so long, I had already figured out when and how to get out of the palace unseen. Their moves were predictable, so sneaking out wasn't as hard as some people might think.

Mehra insisted on coming with me but I reminded her that she couldn't. If the king or someone else came looking for me earlier than supposed to, she would have to be there to give an excuse.

She hesitated for several moments but then gave in after I made my point. She wished me all the best and said that if I didn't return by nightfall, she would alert the king.

Barely anyone was walking on the streets, which I thought was odd. During this time, there would be parties, dances, and kids running around everywhere but there was something going on and I didn't know about it. Maybe there was a national event that I hadn't learned about.

I was almost there and I could already hear voices. They were whispering among themselves, I could barely make out what they were saying.

I started to go slower and slower, proceeding with caution. Everything my mother taught me about not going to strange places alone had gone out the window. I was walking somewhere with people I didn't know and I was all alone.

When I arrived, I was encountered by the backs of men. There were three men that were facing away from me and the fourth was looking directly at me. His eyes were dark and evil, his grin gave me a slight shiver.

When the men noticed that he was looking at me, they all started slowly turning around. Each of them had a worse expression than the last and that moment I decided this wasn't going to be something good.

When I looked around me to see if there was anyone else, two guards appeared and blocked the entrance. I looked down at their clothes and noticed that they weren't any guards, but guards from the palace. I was in complete shock but I needed to keep my feelings a secret.

What seemed to be the leader started walking towards me. I hesitated and took a few steps back but to my surprise, he simply bowed and the others followed.

Now I don't know what to think or how to act, I told myself.

The leader stood back and up and looked at me with stern expressions. My eyes quickly gave him a glance over, my first thought was: *He has nothing on Ephraim.*

His arms weren't a fraction of his. This man would have to

look up to even be able to see Ephraim's eyes. I could imagine, Ephraim crushing this man like he was a twig.

My thoughts were interrupted when he began speaking, "Queen Soraya, I have awaited this moment for quite a while."

His voice was everything but calming. It sounded rough and disgusting. His hair was distressed and he looked like he had fought a bear to get there.

"What do you need?" I finally had the courage to ask.

He smiled like my question was funny to him. He shook his head and continued, "Oh I don't need anything but he will."

He stepped to the side and in that moment I have never felt so scared. I stood a bit taller, despite everything that I was thinking and feeling.

Then a man stepped out of the shadows. His legs were long and bulky. His footsteps seemed to shake the ground slightly. The shadows began to let go and reveal small details about him.

First his legs, then his chest, his arms, and then his face. His eyes were focused on mine, he didn't even look around him, he was looking at me. They made me uncomfortable in a way and I didn't know how to feel about it.

"Hello Soraya" He spoke slowly, his voice made me hold my breath. Everything about him warned that he wasn't a man to play with or to be trusted.

His clothes were all black, just like Ephraim's but they didn't look anything alike. He had light brown hair. His skin was darker than Ephraim's. His fingers were covered with rings and his arms with tattoos.

I bobbed my head up and down, unable to trust myself if I opened my mouth.

"I have been keeping an eye on you for a while now. And I have come to learn that" He took several steps closer until we barely had any space between one another.

I took a small breath in and was intoxicated by his smell. It was strong and powerful but not in a good way, it could make anyone pass out in seconds.

"You aren't new to this thing of being queen. After all, your parents were a king and queen, correct?"

No.

He couldn't have found out.

I stayed quiet because it was the best thing I could have done at that moment but the man in front of me had no problem in filling the silence.

"Yes I have been keeping a very close eye on you and so I know everywhere you have been and who you are closest to since you stepped foot in the palace."

His smirk made me want to vomit. My hands automatically clutched my stomach. His eyes fell down to my womb and a small grin appeared on his face.

He couldn't know about that.

He then took another step closer and then leaned in. His mouth brushed against my ear and I wanted to cry at the feeling. This is something between me and my husband and with anyone else it felt like betrayal.

"I know he doesn't know about the child yet"

He grabbed me by the hand and even though I slightly fought against it, he gripped it even tighter and pulled me to sit beside him at a table.

He sat across from me, his arms crossed and his dark eyes on me.

"If you worry that you will die, I don't plan on killing you. If you give me trouble, then maybe I recommend you to work with me." He raised his eyebrows to see if I had understood.

I spoke a small yes and that was enough to bring him satisfaction.

"I will not reveal my plan to you because I don't owe you an explanation. However, I will introduce everyone."

As he pointed to each man, he announced their names and purposes. One was his bodyguard, the other was his right-hand man, and the other took care of people who didn't want to listen.

"Oh, and I almost forgot to introduce myself-" he laughed loudly.

"I am the king of the Apiritah kingdom. I am the very man your husband is trying to kill."

Oh no.

The king, whom my husband despised, was sitting right in front of me. The man Ephraim tried desperately to annihilate, had found me.

Pieces slowly started to fit together. For him to have found me, there were snakes and rats inside the palace. There were people who kept tabs on everything I did and said. The two guards had already given themselves away, but it couldn't just be them.

Only someone close to the king could find all this out. My mind mentally checked every single person who was always beside the king.

"Oh, you don't need to figure out who told me everything. He is here with us and about to make his grand appearance. Come out, my friend."

I couldn't believe it was him, and I didn't want to believe it either. I trusted him more than anything, and I felt like he had become a friend, but I guess that was only me, from me, and he didn't feel the same way I did.

When he arrived, and stood right beside the king and looked down on me like I was nothing to him. The faint strength in my bones faded, and the comprehension in my mind went away. My fingers gripped onto the metal chair, the pieces of metal dug into my skin which made me hiss under the pain.

I didn't take my eyes off him because this had to be a bad dream, this had to be a nightmare. If this was a fraction of what Ephraim went through then I felt even more compassion because I wouldn't wish this on my worst enemy.

I guess someone doesn't have to be your worst enemy to turn their back on you.

I fumbled with my words, unable to think or say anything straight and when that man spoke, all my worst fears came true.

"Hello, Queen Soraya," Mavros spoke deeply. His voice was as haunting as the darkness that haunted Ephraim.

Ephraim

Chapter 49

L ighter shades of the rainbow replaced the baby blue sky. Clouds framing the beautiful blended sky, leaving a magical feeling over my soul.

My body and mind ached from all the preparation. Never had I done this type of manual labor and it wasn't something I was planning to get used to. Planning a whole dinner wasn't for the weak which made me slightly wince at the thought of what I have done to everyone else.

Everything was like I envisioned it. My heart beat faster and faster and for several seconds I thought it was going to leave my chest. My slippery hands couldn't stop fiddling with the buttons of my shirt. Hundreds of possibilities of what could happen made my mind race. The amount of adrenaline in my blood was beyond comprehension.

Mavros had decided to take the night off and I finally let him after all these years. The servants were baffled by the things that I dared never to do.

Their cautious faces every time they would pass me in the halls, worried every second. Whispers and questions were the constant sound in the palace. They were all suspicious but maybe they were blind to the reason for the change.

I found a woman who loved me despite my flaws and imperfections and after all my stubborn moments, I knew my heart was hers. She could break and smash it into pieces or run away and never come back but I was never going to be the same man I once was.

These days, there is more joy in my body. A heart and mind that wanted to live more. Everything was working in my favor and it just felt right. It felt right with her. I knew I chose her in the beginning only for her beauty but now she was more than that. She was worth more than asking for death day in and day out.

This last week I needed to keep to myself, to let myself feel emotions I never had before. She wasn't the reason for the change but she made me want it. Whatever my father had, didn't have to be mine. I could regret it if I wanted to and I knew that without her, I was never going to come to this revelation. A world shattering revelation that shook my mind, body, and soul.

When I turned the corner, I almost slammed myself against someone. My feet automatically took a few steps back before I hurt someone. When I looked it was Mehra. Her head was hung low yet I could see her eyes which glistened with unshed tears. Mehra's face was slightly swollen and red, her body trembled without ceasing.

I smiled and when she didn't return the small act, my smile slowly died.

Her hands fiddled with a strand of hair, then the edge of her clothing and then her fingertips. Repeated tapping of her feet left me slightly annoyed. Her hair wasn't combed back, instead it was free and in knots all over.

I never asked what her name was and I have never used it

until now. The only reason I knew her name was because of Soraya. She implemented in my mind that they were as much human as I was and deserved to at least be called by the name.

I cleared my throat trying to bring her attention to me instead of the shiny floor, "Mehra."

Her eyes widened, she looked paralyzed for a second, "I am so sorry, my king. I didn't mean to run into you. Please don't kill me." Her voice trembled in fear. I wasn't worried about her almost killing me but at the fact that she was nervous.

Something is wrong, that thought passed through my mind at the speed of light.

"It was an accident, don't worry. How is Soraya, is she ready?" Just the mention of her name, my heart skipped beat after beat.

Her head bobbed up and down rapidly like she wanted to leave as soon as she could. She told me that Soraya was almost ready.

I looked behind me and saw her little legs carrying her at a surprising speed. Then I remembered something that I had forgotten to get Soraya: *flowers.*

How could you forget that?

It wasn't going to be just any flowers but the best and most unique ones I could find in the gardens. I had never picked flowers like this since the passing of my mother. A flower brought many bad and good memories.

Soraya was worth facing every bad thought, she was worth it all.

Guards were a few steps behind me, they whispered between one another like I couldn't hear. When I stood again, I turned around and looked them both in the eyes. With a simple glance, their chatter was silenced.

My ears were automatically drawn to the sound of the people not too far away. The dancing and music made me want to go there, see everything in its full glory but I had to hold back. If I ever was going there, I wanted it to be with my angel by my side.

Queen Soraya really made a difference in all our lives, the older people would tell me.

I don't think I would be here right now if it wasn't for her taking a chance on me. Sometimes people can't and won't change if they are not first given a chance. People needed to know that hope isn't all gone.

I fiddled with the flowers in my hand, rearranged to perfection. Mix of different colored roses which only she and I knew the meaning behind. Green things that I didn't even know the name of and other flowers that I picked simply because they were beautiful.

Each flower was a different color, shape, and size yet they looked better with one another. Soraya was the same because she had so many sides of herself but they were all beautiful.

The way she angers when someone is mistreated or the way she will shut everyone away when she feels overwhelmed. She pleases other people but hides her own intentions. I knew she had imperfections but they weren't anything. Never did they have more value then who she was to me.

Today I was going to prove to her that I was changing and that she could believe in me. Her secrets and thoughts would be kept within me until my last breath.

I wanted to be there for her like she was for me.

I strolled back to the palace but something caught my eye. In the far distance there was a man who was wearing all black, just like me. His arms were covered with tattoos and his dark hair was cut short. A part of me knew who he was but he was too far away from me to be sure.

He stepped away from the shadows and into the faint light source in front of him. When I finally saw his features, it felt like an anchor in my stomach. A sly grin on his face as he bowed down before me. I knew that he didn't mean it, it was just for appearances.

Right before he blended back into the shadows, he tapped on his wrist and mouthed *tick tock tick tock.*

I didn't know what Deimos was doing here but I was not going to get hotheaded because of it. Nothing was going to take away my focus and my plans tonight. My heart was settled on the night ahead of me.

The petals and leaves of the flowers kept swaying side to side as I paced to her room. Everytime I tried to knock, my sweaty hand would stop mid air.

A deep shaky breath within my lungs, my hand finally touched the door.

No one answered.

I waited a few seconds and knocked again but yet again no one answered. *I'm coming in,* but her sweet voice didn't respond back to me.

My pacing slowed, unaware of what I was about to walk into. The only source that illuminated her room was a dying fireplace. The wood continued to burn with little fire on it.

My hands gripped onto the bouquet a bit tighter, the thorns of the stems dug into my skin. My throat thick and tight, barely allowing air to pass through.

I walked into the bathroom and deep inside I knew that something was off. I dipped a finger in the bath water and it was frigid cold.

She must have taken a bath earlier, way before we were supposed to be meeting, I tried to convince myself.

I looked at her bed table to see if there was anything that could show me where to find her. The bed was made to perfection, pillows placed exactly how she liked it. Sheets were stretched out to excellence, not a single wrinkle in sight.

My eyes slowly drifted over the entire room, desperate to find an answer. When I was about to give up, I noticed something on her table. My feet were dragging against the cold floor, my heart feeling tighter the closer I got.

Despite my size, the small stool was the only chair in sight. It released a small creak when my entire body weight rested on it.

My fingers were frigid cold, trembling with the envelope in hand. This wasn't her hand writing, I had remembered it. The way she wrote in cursive and dotted her sentences with small hearts. Each letter she has ever written to me, was stashed away secretly.

My eyes quickly read the words on the page, a part of me convinced I was reading it all wrong. Maybe I was hallucinating and I just needed a pair of glasses.

> Dear King Ephraim,
> It's been long, too long since I have written to you personally. You probably will hate me more than you already do but then again, I never cared much for your opinion.
> First things first, let me tell you that it was nice to see you again today, even if it was for a brief moment. Always a pleasure to remind myself that I strive to kill and destroy you.
> Second and most importantly, you picked up this letter because you want to know where Soraya is. She's well and very feisty if I must add. Can't believe a single woman broke down your walls...
> I know how you hate to beat around the bush so let me get straight to the point. I have her, she's

mine and I don't think I need to tell you that I won't give her up so easily. I will keep her under chains and torture until I get what I want.

Fun thing about all this; I am not telling you anything. Not telling you where she is, the secrets that I know about her, or how to get her back.

So let the war begin. I know you way more than you think I do but I feel compassionate. I'll give you at least a bread crumb to get you started.

Here is what I'll say; Not everyone you trust is faithful. And not everyone you think is a liar, is an enemy.

So let this begin. If you give me what I want then maybe I will give Soraya back without killing her. I can't promise she won't have a few bruises, but at least she will give my men good company.

Oh! Even if it's not important anymore, it's been me all along. All those letters were sent but not written by me. Everything planned to perfection just to show you how inferior you are.

Sincerely your worst nightmare,
Deimos

The words on the page made me paralyzed. All my mind could think about was that he had *my woman*. That means she was taken from me, bribed and forced out of my safe place.

There was more than one rat in this palace.

What was I going to do?

The flowers fell from my hand and dropped onto the floor. Petals falling in slow motion.

This wasn't happening and I didn't know what I was going to do. I couldn't just grab my army and go, I didn't know who was who anymore.

Deimos had crossed every line and the anger I had for that man made my blood boil. The things that I would do to him would make his kingdom ashamed of him. And if he laid as much as one finger on Soraya, even death would be grace to what I would do.

If he touched her or even looked at her in the wrong direction, he would die. Even if I had promised myself that I wouldn't kill anyone anymore, it would be the only exception. I read the letter once again before the brass doors of the room slabbed open. Half of the court, the inner court, rushed in. Panic in their eyes and fear radiating off them.

Every word that I wanted to say wouldn't leave my lips. My mind felt like it was in a horrific dream, a dream that I wasn't waking up from. Each man looked at me, horrified to ask or say a single thing.

Until one of them took a stride closer. He was tall but not as strong as me. His shriveled hair and clothes showed me he was undercover. Nothing in me was ready for what he was about to say.

"My King, I have figured out the secret queen." His voice was flat, not a single emotion showing through.

I stood up, meeting him almost eye to eye. My head tipped downward slightly to see his face. There wasn't a nerve in my body that was ready for this. Never in my life did I think I would prefer my wife by my side than the head of my enemy in my hands. Yet every cell in my body wanted her beside me, I wanted her touch against me.

My voice was sour and strangled, "And who is it?"

He closed his eyes, eyebrows furrowed together. Even in

the darkness I could sense his tense body. Every single man that stood before me was worried about what was going to ensue.

His eyes widened as big as the vast sea. They were filled with fear and despair. "The queen is-" The young man looked around him to make sure he was doing the right thing. He bit the inside of his mouth for several seconds, completely petrified. "The queen of the Uosulian people is Soraya."

All time, space, and understanding froze. The voices that tormented me were instantly silenced. The darkness around me completely silenced. Even they were petrified to what had ensued.

Comprehension crumbled like old bricks. Fatigue replaced the strength inside my bones. My heart broke under this new truth.

Our love was a forbidden fruit. A forbidden fire. Now my soul was entangled with a person I swore to kill.

THIS IS THE END... FOR NOW

Leave a Review

I hope you enjoyed His Hidden Jewel!

If you loved the book, please leave a review for my book on any platform.

Thank you!

Author's Note

This is a story that has been in the works for multiple years. An idea that went through multiple drafts and late nights. And when I was about to give up, God did a download and I wrote until 3am that day.

This story is beyond special to me and I love it so much. I love Ephraim, Soraya, Zion and all the characters (except the ones that get on my last nerve.... We all know who that is). Each character has a reason for being in the book. Each scene and detail has a reason why I wrote it. Even the unanswered questions have a purpose.

So the idea, the inspiration, the book, the words... None of it is mine. Everything came from God and all the glory goes to him. So may I decrease so that he will increase.

And may this book reach those people who feel lost. Those people who need hope, love, and peace. The people that feel like they have no purpose on this earth.

Well... this story was for you. You might not see what God is doing but know for sure that he is working behind the scenes. All the pieces of his puzzle will fall into place at the right time.

Acknowledgements

First of all I wanted to say thank you to my Lord & Savior, Jesus Christ. I wanted to thank God the father, Christ the son, and the Holy Spirit. This book wouldn't be possible without you. You gave me the inspiration, the strength, and the creativity. All honor goes to you and not me. I love you more than life or anything this world could ever offer me.

Next, I want to say thank you to my family. Thank you to my mom for giving me endless hours to edit this book. Thank you for being my best friend and always being supportive and a shoulder to lean on.

Thank you to my dad for being supportive and buying me multiple energy drinks to get through the whole writing & editing process. Also, thank you for bringing me food when I forgot to eat. Thank you for helping me throughout the entire process.

Thank you to my siblings for being my emotional support. Thank you to my cats for allowing me to squeeze and kiss them when I needed a mental break.

Thank you to Estheticah, for making this stunning cover! Thank you for getting it done in such a short amount of time and doing such a fantastic job!

Thank you to Jessica Spruill for being my mentor and always being supportive. Thank you for taking a chance on my book. Thank you for responding to my messages and having the patience to teach me. Thank you for the endless texts and phone calls. You are such an inspiration and I am eternally grateful to have had the pleasure of knowing you.

Thank you to my Beta readers, Rebekah, Elizabeth, and Sara. Thank you for reading His Hidden Jewel in its raw form. For giving me feedback and sending me messages about how swoony Ephraim is. We all agree he is very, very swoon worthy.

Thank you to my amazing church. Thank you to my pastors for asking how my book was going and always giving me encouragement. Thank you for believing in the mission God sent me on and all the prayers you prayed in my favor.

Thank you to my Family in Christ. Thank you for always being there for me. Thank you for the countless prayers you all prayed for me.

Thank you to M.H. Woodscourt, who formatted my book. You are so sweet and kind and I appreciate the time and dedication you put into formatting my book. May God bless you and prosper you as you walk in his ways.

Thank you to Erica, Rosie, the author bestie chat, Mary W, and all my book besties on bookstagram.... You are the best. Thank you for sharing my posts & reels, being supportive and always celebrating another milestone with me.

I love each and every single one of you. I don't think I would be here without you. By the grace of God this book is out. It is by the mercy of God this book finally came out.

Now onto writing Book #2...

Also by Sarah Da Silva

Once Upon a Cowboy's Heart

(Available: December 5, 2025)

About the Author

Sarah Da Silva writes Closed Door and fade-to-black love stories that will make you laugh, cry, swoon, and kick your feet at 1am.

Her books have sizzling chemistry with heart and a meaningful message while keeping the bedroom door closed. Her mission is to write love stories that bring Love, Joy, and Peace to those who think there is none left. She hopes that these stories shine a light in the midst of the darkness and that you should never lose hope.

Jesus loves you. You don't have to be perfect to come to him. Come as you are, and he will do the transformation.

instagram.com/authorsarahdsilva